KISS ME LIKE THIS

~ The Morrisons, Book 1 ~
Sean & Serena

Kiss Me Like This
© 2014 Bella Andre

Visit Bella's website at: www.BellaAndre.com
Follow Bella on twitter at: http://www.twitter.com/bellaandre
Join Bella on Facebook at:
http://www.facebook.com/bellaandrefans
Sign up for Bella's newsletter at: http://eepurl.com/eXj22

Sean Morrison, one of six siblings and the top college baseball player in the country, is reeling from a heartbreakingly painful loss. Nothing seems to matter anymore...until the night Serena Britten unexpectedly ends up in his arms.

Serena is a world-famous model who has only ever wanted to be normal, even though her mother has always pushed her to become a superstar. Though it isn't easy to try to leave everyone and everything she knows behind, Serena is determined to enroll in college. More than anything, she wants to turn her love for books into a new career that she actually loves. Only, she never expected to meet someone like Sean on campus—or to be instantly consumed by their incredible chemistry and connection.

But when the pressures of her high-profile modeling career only get bigger and more demanding, will it make living a normal life as a college student—and falling in love with the hottest guy on campus—impossible?

CHAPTER ONE

Serena Britten had dreamed of this forever.

Not bright lights and designer dresses and fame and meeting rock stars...but an enormous library with more books than she could possibly get through even if she stayed right here for an entire lifetime and just read and read and read. In the past two weeks, Green Library had become her absolute favorite place on earth, with its endless shelves of books.

Oh yes, she thought as she smiled and ran her fingertips over the spines of the books nearest to her, it really was just *wonderful.*

At 9:45 on a Friday night on the Stanford University campus, there weren't many other students in the library. In fact, as she emerged from between the stacks, it didn't actually look like there were *any* other students here. Just Serena and the woman behind the privileges desk who was looking at her watch, obviously waiting for her to leave so that she could close everything up and start her weekend.

Serena checked out the three great new books she'd found, then took a baseball cap out of her bag and put it on, tucking her long hair up into it. Due to the Indian summer in Northern California over the past couple of weeks, it was still fairly warm, but since it was too dark out to wear sunglasses, putting on a hat and a shapeless Cardinals sweatshirt helped increase the odds that she could walk past people unnoticed, particularly any paparazzi who might be lurking in the shadows. She was used to strangers wanting to take pictures with her, and most of the time they were really nice. It was just that sometimes guys made her feel uncomfortable by standing a little too close or by making borderline dirty comments about pictures they'd seen of her.

If only she could wear a disguise in her *History and Theory of the Novel* class. Her professor, Dr. Julian Fairworth, had actually made her skin crawl today when he'd looked at her like he was trying to see through her jeans to what lay beneath. Despite the warmth of the evening, she shivered at the memory of the way he'd walked by her seat just a little too close and had bent over the book in front of her just a little too far when she'd asked him a question.

Serena had met plenty of lecherous men in Hollywood and on photo shoots over the years, but her mother had always been there to scare them away. This was the first time Serena had to deal with them all on her own.

Which was exactly what you wanted, she reminded herself as she breathed deeply to take in the sweet-smelling night air. The freedom to make her own decisions about school. Career. Clothes. Men.

Life.

Serena's mother, Genevieve, had taken her to her first modeling open call when she was three years old, and for the past sixteen years, she'd worked nonstop all over the world. Her mother was the quintessential "momager"...or rather, she had been until two weeks ago, when Serena had left it all behind.

* * *

Two weeks ago...

"Mom, I need to talk to you."

Genevieve Britten was carefully studying a layout Serena had been in for a French fashion magazine, taking detailed notes of every brilliant nuance the other models displayed in the photos and where Serena needed to make improvements to stay competitive.

"You've looked better," her mother said without looking up from her intent study of the pages, "but, fortunately, you still outshine the other girls." Her upper lip curled slightly as she pointed at a sixteen-year-old model who Serena remembered had been extremely nervous about her first big job. "I still can't believe they let this one do the shoot without losing ten pounds first."

The girl was gorgeous and not at all in need of losing any weight. But Serena knew better than to try to debate this with her mother. Especially not when she'd finally reached the make-or-break point where she needed to tell her the big news.

"I'm going to Stanford."

Genevieve didn't even raise her eyes from the magazine. "Did Damien book a college shoot that he forgot to tell me about?"

"What I mean is that I'm going to be attending Stanford University. As a freshman." When her mother finally lifted her gaze from the pictures, Serena added, "In two weeks."

Every time Serena brought up the possibility of

college during the past few years, Genevieve had laughed and asked what she could possibly want with college when, as a model, the world was already her oyster? It wasn't that her mother didn't have a point. Most people probably *would* think she was totally nuts for walking away from her career for college. But even if what she was doing didn't make sense to anyone else, it made sense to *her.*

All her life, she'd loved books. Loved the smell of them and the feel of them in her hands. To read across genres and subjects in every spare moment, and dream up stories of her own. She didn't yet know if she wanted to write books or study books or edit books or publish books or sell books, but that was what college was for, wasn't it? To throw herself into new experiences, some that would hopefully turn out great, others that might not be quite as good...but to know through it all that she'd never regret really, truly—*finally*—getting to live her life.

"Is this a joke?"

Serena shook her head. "No, it isn't." She'd steeled herself for months to be brave and stand up for what she wanted. "You know attending college has always been my dream." Whereas modeling and Hollywood had always been her mother's dream. Twenty years ago, Genevieve Britten had been the hottest thing on the catwalk...until she'd gotten pregnant with Serena. All her life, Serena had felt like she was making it up to her mother for being born. But she couldn't do that forever. She just couldn't.

"Are you crazy?" Her mother's tone left no question that Serena had absolutely lost her mind. "Why would you even think of giving up your career, especially when you're not only one of the top supermodels in the world, but you are also poised to become a serious actor?"

"Smith Sullivan's movie has been shelved," Serena reminded her, "so it's not like I'm walking out on a commitment to him."

Being in a movie would have been a new challenge, but it wasn't one she'd chosen for herself and Serena was beyond glad that the film was no longer on the calendar. It was one thing to walk away from future modeling jobs, but if she'd actually been cast in a major motion picture, she could never have walked away from it in good conscience...and then she would have had to postpone her plans for college another year. Or longer, probably, if the movie did well.

"Smith's film will happen, even if it takes a little longer than he originally planned," her mother insisted, her voice rising in pitch with each word, as if she'd just begun to realize that Serena was actually *serious* this time. "Even without it, you have runway commitments, print bookings."

"I've already spoken with Damien. We haven't yet signed any new contracts with makeup and fashion houses, and he told me there are plenty of other models who can step in to the shoots or runway shows that I'm booked for during the next few months."

Serena could have sworn everything in the room went still, even the tiny molecules of dust floating in the air. Completely, perfectly still, as if time had frozen.

"You went behind my back and talked to your agent about this?" Every word Genevieve spoke was pure, seething fury. "How dare you?"

Serena had so badly wanted to be honest with her mother and show her the college applications, rather than secretly filling them out online. She wished she could have shared her excitement when the acceptance email had come. *Probationary* acceptance. Since she hadn't ever been to any regular school, but had tested really high and written several long essays specifically for placement in the English Department, Stanford had agreed to admit her for the fall quarter with "Special Registration" status. Which meant they had given her one quarter to impress the heck out of the admissions committee with phenomenal grades and recommendations from her professors. If she did that, she'd be accepted as a permanent student.

Serena wasn't proud that she'd kept the news from her mother for so long, but she'd been so afraid that it would all come crashing down otherwise. All her life, it had only been the two of them. She'd never known her father—when he'd found out her mother was pregnant, he'd immediately split, and had passed away a few years later. Even as a little girl, Serena had realized that her mother's smiles, her praise, her hugs only came when she was pleased with a job Serena had done well, or when good news came that she'd booked an important shoot or runway show. She'd done everything she could to make Genevieve happy.

And maybe she could have continued like that were it not for the fact that Serena's own dreams had begun to diverge more and more from her mother's. Books, not fashion shows. Libraries, not movies. Quiet nights devouring a story by one of her favorite authors, not splashy Hollywood parties.

Serena wanted, more than anything, to live a life that she was passionately excited about.

She wanted to wake up each morning feeling exhilarated.

She wanted to laugh and love and *feel*.

"I'm sorry, I never meant to hurt—"

"When?" Her mother had risen from her seat and

stalked toward Serena, standing four inches taller in her heels. "When did you do this?"

"February is when I learned that I was accepted, but I applied in the fall."

"I can't believe you would do this to me." Genevieve raked Serena from head to toe with a harsh look. "Secretly applying to college. Secretly accepting a spot there. Secretly making all of the arrangements to leave me behind completely. And after everything I've *sacrificed* to help you become a star."

Genevieve's hand rose as if to slap her, and Serena was already flinching when her mother lowered it. But something raw and icky had her wondering if the reason the slap hadn't come was less because her mother had an issue with hitting her...and more that she didn't want to risk marring Serena's money-making face before tomorrow's shoot.

"I remember what it was like to be a teenager wanting to rebel against my mother," Genevieve said in a voice that was suddenly too calm. Too dismissive. "I suppose I should have seen this coming."

It was almost worse to have her mother dismiss her dreams so thoroughly that she was no longer even fighting with her about it.

"You'll soon realize how crazy you're being." Genevieve's eyes were cold. Certain. "I have no doubt that you'll be back. Soon. Especially when you realize that you will never, ever fit in with the other students. Do you really believe that you will be able to walk around on campus like a normal student would?"

It was as if she had pointed a laser straight at the heart of Serena's biggest fear. Not just that she wouldn't be able to hack a full load of classes and difficult tests, but that she wouldn't fit in with the other freshmen. She hadn't ever had a group of girlfriends, not when she'd constantly been on planes with only her mother as a companion. Serena was utterly terrified that she would always be a freak and that she'd never be able to live a normal life outside of the cameras and the spotlight.

But Serena's dreams had become even bigger than her terror, so big that she was finally willing to risk everything to take a chance on them.

Genevieve was almost out of the room when she turned back to Serena, eyes narrowed as if some horrible new thought had just occurred to her. "Is this about a boy?"

"No. Of course not. When would I even have met anyone?" *How could I when you keep me under lock and key?*

Her mother had that look in her eyes, the one that always glittered when she talked about how all men were scum, that they could only be trusted to take and use and hurt.

"If I find out that you're tossing away everything I've given you for some boy who only wants to fuck you and forget you," her mother said in a low, menacing voice, "it will be the ultimate betrayal. And I will never, *ever* forgive you."

But there had never been any boy, or any man, who had stirred Serena up inside. She'd heard other models giggle about their boyfriends, their lovers, but the truth was she'd not only never been kissed, she'd never longed for a kiss from any of the boys she'd known, either.

"There's no one," Serena promised. "I'm going to college for me."

For the first time in her life, she was doing something entirely for herself. And even when her mother slammed the bedroom door of their hotel suite in her face, Serena vowed to keep boldly sticking to her guns. No matter what obstacles might pop up along the way.

And all the while, Serena would also never give up hope that her mother would forgive her...so that they could finally have a loving relationship that didn't have anything to do with business.

* * *

The music streaming out of the open dorm windows drew Serena out of her memories of the conversation with her mother and back to campus. When Serena had first moved in to the three-story building, she had expected everyone else at Stanford to be a bookworm like she was. Only to find that most other students' bookshelves held everything but books—makeup, magazines, and a surprising number of already empty bottles of alcohol.

Thus far, she hadn't seen too many of her fellow students crack open a book, either. How, she wondered, did they all manage to be so carefree about their classes when she felt like she was drowning already? Were they all *that* much smarter than she was that they didn't even have to try? Good thing she loved the library so much, because it was clearly where she was going to be spending most of her time trying to squeeze everything she was being taught into her brain.

But as she headed for the second floor and saw groups of students chatting and laughing as they got ready to go out, she had to ask herself—had she come to college just to spend all of her time in the library? Hadn't she also dreamed of living a "normal" life for once? Of taking risks and trying new exciting things that she never would have been able to experience in her old life? Of finally being *free*?

And yet, she hadn't been to one single campus party.

She'd always had a paper to write or a test to study for. But those were just excuses. And regardless of how much she loved books and the library and her classes, she knew there had to be more to living life than just studying and reading. Besides, she'd been to dozens of terrifying Hollywood parties over the years, so a campus party should be a piece of cake, shouldn't it?

Unlocking her door, she saw that her roommate wasn't around, but there were several girls at the end of the hall who were clearly getting ready to go out. Serena made herself smile through her nerves as she headed over to them.

"Hi," she said as the girls turned toward her. She started to give an awkward little wave before pulling her hand back a moment too late for them not to see. "Are you guys going to a party on campus tonight?"

Jen, a pretty blonde, nodded. "Delta Tau Delta."

When Jen didn't say anything more, and neither did Larissa or Holly as they focused on pouring each other tequila shots, every cell in Serena's body screamed at her to go back to her room for another quiet night of studying before she made a complete fool of herself.

No. She needed to go for it, not hide out someplace safe like she had for the past two weeks she'd been at school.

"I'd love to join you guys, if that would be okay?"

Jen made a sad face. "Actually, the three of us are already late. We are just about to head out the door." She looked pointedly at Serena's clothes before adding, "And you'll probably need a while to get ready. So maybe we'll see you there."

Serena had momentarily forgotten about the baggy jeans, sweatshirt, and baseball cap she was wearing. Her disguise, as she liked to think of it, to throw off any photographers who might be lurking around wanting to get a picture of her to sell to the gossip sites.

"Sure," she said, in what she hoped was an easy voice that didn't betray how lame she felt for asking them if she could tag along, only to have the answer be no. She tried not to let her smile slip either. "I'll see you there."

While the girls continued to drink and laugh as if they had all the time in the world before they needed to leave, Serena headed down the hall to the bathroom. At this time of night, the showers were blessedly empty. She hung up her towel on a hook in the tiled enclosure, then stood under the warm spray and tried to let it wash away her doubts about actually going to the party.

Soon it would be show time. Only, instead of playing the supermodel role she'd somehow managed to pull off for so many years, she'd be trying to act like she was a perfectly normal college student who knew how to have a good time at a frat party on a Friday night. In the wake of the rejection from the girls down the hall, she felt like she needed to pull it off now more than ever.

But even as she thought it, she knew tonight wasn't about proving anything to those girls. It was about proving something to *herself*. That she could go to her first-ever campus party and have fun just like everyone else. That she could make good on her vow to make going to college work despite how badly her mother believed it would go for someone like Serena. And, even if it wasn't always easy, that she would never let herself forget how magical it was just to be here, on a college campus full of so many new opportunities. Opportunities she simply needed to be brave enough to reach for.

Forty-five minutes later, however, when Serena got to the Delta Tau Delta house, her feet froze on the front steps as she stared wide-eyed at the party already in full swing. A rap song was cranked up so high her ears were already starting to ring. Students were dancing and making out and drinking in pretty much every corner of the big main room that she could see into, including Jen, Larissa, and Holly, who were hanging all over some frat boys, giggling at whatever it was they were saying.

It didn't take long for people to start doing double takes in Serena's direction, pointing and whispering as they recognized her, despite the fact that she'd pulled her hair back into a ponytail and wasn't wearing any makeup. All thoughts of having fun, of throwing caution to the wind and really living her life, fell away as she silently asked herself how she could have chosen the short denim skirt and form-fitting white top to wear tonight. She felt totally exposed…

It's okay, she told herself silently as she worked to come unfrozen, *you can do this. Just get out there and start dancing like everyone else.*

Thank God, that was when Abi spotted her. "Hey, roomie, I'm so glad you're here!" A few seconds later, Abi was sliding her arm through Serena's and pulling her onto the dance floor. "Ready to work it?"

No, she was definitely not ready to work it. But, thankfully, her roommate's friendly smile and the funny antics of the DJ spinning the tunes helped Serena finally relax into the music. Closing her eyes a little while later as she lifted her arms and swayed her hips, she could almost pretend that she was just the same as any other freshman girl at this party.

Perfectly normal.

CHAPTER TWO

Sean Morrison refilled his red plastic cup from one of the kegs in the corner and downed half of it in one long swallow, even though beer wasn't doing it for him tonight. He'd been drinking steadily for the past couple of hours and barely felt buzzed.

The frat kept the good stuff in a locked cabinet in the back of the dining room. Heading through the crowd, he found Kurt and Zane, two of his frat brothers and baseball teammates, making their way through a bottle of tequila. Kurt held out a full shot glass by way of greeting Sean.

"We were wondering when we were going to see your sorry ass in here." Both guys were already drunk enough to be sprawled on two beat-up leather couches.

"If I knew you were waiting on me for a tea party," Sean said as he took the glass from Kurt, "I would have at least worn a tie."

Used to be, a couple of shots of tequila would make his throat burn and his eyes water. But lately, he'd been drinking so much that downing it in one gulp was no sweat. He didn't bother to wait for the buzz to hit him before he refilled the glass, and a couple more shots in, he finally got to where he was trying to go.

Numb.

Totally numb.

For the past three months, everything inside his chest had felt raw. Splintered. Broken. Hell, he thought as he reached for the bottle and splashed more booze into the glass, it had been longer than that.

One year ago, his family had gotten the news that his mother, Lisa, had cancer. She'd been supposed to beat it, only forty-seven and in great shape. She'd always eaten right and worked out, and taught her kids to do the same.

But none of that had mattered. Not how healthy she was supposed to be. Not how hard she fought with medicine and meditation and positive thoughts. Not even the fact that she had six kids and a husband who all needed her to live.

Sean had missed his finals last year, had been at her bedside along with the rest of his family when she'd finally slipped completely away. They'd known for a few weeks that it was coming, as she drifted in and out of consciousness depending on how much pain she was in and how high they'd cranked up the medicine. But knowing it was coming hadn't meant Sean had been able to prepare for it at all.

Every moment he wasn't with her, he'd been taking the pictures he knew she loved so much , and that had been her connection to the world outside her fifteen-by-fifteen-foot hospital room. Pictures of his brothers and sisters and dad. Pictures of the bayside path by their house where she'd always walked their dog. Pictures of the magnolia tree in their yard as its large pink flowers bloomed. Whenever she woke up, he'd made sure there were at least a couple of new pictures hanging from the lines he'd rigged up on the ceiling.

Each of his brothers and sisters had helped with something. His oldest brother, Grant, who'd founded one of the most successful social networking businesses in Silicon Valley, had taken over the day-to-day of running the household finances and managing their parents' portfolio. Drew, his second oldest brother who had become a pretty big rock star in the past year, had wanted to cancel his European tour to sit in her hospital room with her, but his mother had made him promise not to do that, a promise he had made himself keep until those last few weeks. Olivia, his middle sister, who was a year ahead of him at Stanford, had appointed herself the one in charge of making sure their littlest sister, Madison, stayed on track for her senior year at high school and got all of her college applications in. Justin, Sean's twin brother, who was also a junior at Stanford, had put his science brain to work on researching the best possible doctors and treatment plans. Maddie, who loved to cook, must have made her mother every single recipe in every single diet book that promised to cure cancer with nutrition. And all of them had taken care of their father, Michael, who had barely left his wife's side.

Since her passing, Sean hadn't taken a picture. And three months later, even with buckets of beer and tequila pumping through his veins, he could still hear his father and Maddie sobbing, Grant and Drew cursing, and the scary silence from Olivia in his mother's hospital room.

Sean had had to get out, get away from it all. When he'd finally gotten outside into the sunshine, before he even realized what he was doing, he'd lifted the classic 35mm Canon film camera his mother had given him for his thirteenth birthday over his head and smashed it down onto the concrete. He was strong enough from years of playing baseball and weight lifting that it had shattered immediately.

He couldn't imagine wanting to take pictures again. Not when they hadn't helped one damned thing.

For tonight, at least, he'd managed to get to the point where nothing could touch him. Where he could pretend to be the carefree jock that everyone thought he was. Stanford had begged his brother Justin to come here based on his grades and science trophies. Sean's grades weren't quite as good, but when combined with his baseball skills, they were enough for a scholarship. Everyone looked at the Morrison twins and saw one as the brain, the other as the jock. Only when they were at home did those labels fall away, and they were just brothers.

For a moment, Sean wished Justin had come to the party tonight. The two of them could have hung out and turned their minds to mush playing video games upstairs. But Justin had never been into frat parties, especially not when he could be hanging out in some science lab with one of his fellow brains. Especially Taylor, the girl he was too much of a wuss to make a move on. Just think what egg-headed kids those two would have if they ever managed to get it on.

Zane finally pushed himself up off the couch and wobbled for a second before saying, "Time to go see what gifts the freshman class is offering up tonight. Give me a ten-minute head start, Morrison," his friend said, "so that I don't have to get second-best."

"Third best," Kurt said to Zane as he got up in just as wobbly a manner. "You're going to have to get in line behind me."

School had been back in session for two weeks, and every night so far there had been a party during rush. The main room was already overheated as everyone danced and drank. The loud music, the laughter, the sour smell of beer that never left the frat house no matter how hard the cleaning crew worked to eradicate it—all of it felt like a vise tightening around Sean's chest. Just as he'd needed to get out of his mother's hospital room, he needed to get out of here, too.

Sean was pushing through the crowd, hell-bent on reaching the door, when he suddenly stopped dead in his tracks.

Because he was looking at the most beautiful girl in the world.

* * *

See, Serena told herself as she kept moving to the music, *this isn't so hard.* In fact, she was having a really good time dancing with Abi. Serena hadn't gotten to know her roommate too well yet, as they both always seemed to be running in different directions, but it was definitely awesome of Abi to stick with her like this. Especially considering Serena wasn't exactly sure what she would have done if some guy had come up to her instead and wanted to dance with—

Just then, a large, warm hand curled around Serena's waist. Her breath whooshed out in surprise as she was spun around, but when she looked up at the guy who was holding on to her, she momentarily forgot about the need to breathe at all.

Because he had the most striking green eyes she'd ever seen.

She knew she probably should have told the stranger to take his hands off her. And she should already have been pushing out of his arms, too. But when he smiled down at her and said, "Hi," she was so drawn by his incredible magnetism that she simply echoed him.

"Hi."

"Damn," he said in a low voice that rippled up her spine, then down to her toes, "you're beautiful."

For all the times that Serena had been told she was beautiful during the course of her modeling career, it had never meant as much to her as it did right then, from the lips of a gorgeous stranger holding her in his arms.

Maybe that was why her reply made its way past her brain to her lips. "So are you."

Again, his smile flashed, but a moment later it was gone. That was when she belatedly realized that neither smile had reached his eyes. And when she looked more closely into the green depths, the twisted-up torment she saw in them had her instinctively raising her hand to his cheek.

"Whatever happened," she said softly, so close to his lips that she could almost taste them, "I'm sorry."

Pain flashed through his eyes before a brutal sound tore from his throat, pain so intense that she swore she could feel it herself. The next thing she knew, his mouth was on hers, claiming her lips in a way no one ever had as he pulled her closer against him.

Time and again, she'd read books about passion so deep that the characters would throw away everything in their lives for it. Only, no matter how skilled the author, she'd never really understood it. So even though her mother had warned her over and over, all the way back to when she was a very little girl, that she should never, *ever* let herself be seduced and enthralled by a man's pretty words or caresses, Serena hadn't worried about it. Not when it had always felt like any passion, any heat, she gave off for the cameras was all for show. Inside, she'd worried that she'd always feel frozen.

But this—the thrill bumps rising across the surface of her skin, the way her tongue instinctively licked out to stroke his, the perfect fit of her curves and softness against his muscles and strength—*this* was the kind of passion people threw away perfectly good lives for. And it was no wonder, when just kissing him could make her feel this way.

Like she was thawing from the inside out.

Serena couldn't believe how good it felt to be in his arms and how quickly his kiss was heating up her body. And as he showed her the passion, the wild heat, and the wonder that she'd been seeking for so long, instead of stopping him or pushing him away, she moved even closer between his strong thighs and twined her fingers into his soft, dark hair to keep his mouth against hers.

On a groan, he captured her mouth more deeply. For a few perfect moments, they were equal partners in passion. He wasn't leading and she wasn't following. They were both simply taking and giving to each other exactly what they needed.

A break from the cold.

A reminder of what it was to feel alive, completely alive.

And a chance to forget what they each needed to forget.

For herself, all she wanted was to forget that her life had never been hers, not until she'd set foot on this campus. And for him? Well, it was obvious that whatever it was that he needed to forget had wounded him deeply. Very deeply.

"My room."

The air brushing against her lips as he spoke startled her for a moment. Why, she wondered, had he stopped kissing her?

There was no forethought on her part as she pulled his mouth back down to hers. All she knew was that when he kissed her, everything felt right and she didn't want the feeling to go away. Not when she'd finally found something—someone—to make her feel this good.

Thank God, he immediately lowered his mouth back to hers. This time she was the one running her tongue along his lower lip, then nipping it lightly with her front teeth. When he groaned against her lips, she had to do it again, loving that she was affecting him just as much as he was affecting her.

"My room," he said again, only this time he punctuated each word with another sizzling-hot kiss.

With his kisses intertwining with his words, she could almost just let them wash over her like the music. But when he pulled away enough to take her hand and lead her through the crowd, without his mouth on hers to lull her, the cautious voice inside her head that she'd tried so hard to stuff away earlier that evening popped back up, front and center so that she couldn't ignore it.

What are you doing? You don't even know this guy! He's planning to take you to his room...and you can't be such a naïve, dense virgin that you don't know why, can you?

The voice, the words, all sounded like her mother's. But it was true, she realized as ice-cold reality suddenly splashed over her, that if anyone had taken a picture of them making out—or, God forbid, a video—it could already be up on Twitter or Facebook right now.

It was a horribly sobering thought to think about the way the gossip sites and magazines would eat this up...but it was far worse to think that her mother would see them. Especially after Genevieve had made it perfectly clear that she'd never forgive Serena if she tossed everything away for a boy.

What had she been thinking?

But that was just the problem. She *hadn't* been thinking, hadn't been able to form a coherent thought from the moment the stranger's lips met hers.

Just then, he moved close again, close enough that her body betrayed her by leaning into his heat rather than away from it. "I've never wanted anyone as much as I want you," he said in a low voice that rippled through all the parts of her that he'd just brought to life with his kisses.

And the truth was that she was nearly as lulled by his sensual words as she'd been by his kisses. But that was just the problem: When she was in his arms, she wanted so badly to never let go of the wonderful feelings he sent rushing through her, that she was afraid she'd do something stupid. Like giving up her virginity, two weeks into college, to a beautiful stranger at a frat party. All because she wanted to *feel* something real and big and true.

"I—" She faltered as he kissed her again because it really did feel so good, so perfect. She couldn't believe how hard it was to make herself tug her hand from his and start to take a step back. "I should go now."

But instead of moving away from her, instead of letting her go, he slid one hand around the nape of her neck. "Stay." He stroked her skin as if to coax her to change her mind. "Come upstairs with me and I promise we won't do anything you don't want to do."

He lowered his mouth as if he was going to kiss her again, but the more he tried to convince her to come upstairs to sleep with him, the colder every part of her grew.

Too late, she realized that she'd been so stupid and needy that she'd mistaken the heat of his drunken kisses for something more, for something bigger. For something she'd been waiting her whole life to feel.

Suddenly she could see that all he wanted was to take her up to his room to have sex with her, even though he couldn't possibly know anything at all about her apart from the fact that she was famous...and that she obviously loved kissing him.

Angry with him—but also with herself for being stupid enough to think it could *ever* have been a good idea to go to a frat party—she put both of her hands on his chest and shoved him away. So hard that, for the first time since he'd spun her into his arms out on the dance floor, he didn't try to kiss her again.

"What's wrong?"

"I know you've probably seen my pictures in magazines and think I'm easy—"

God, she couldn't believe her voice was starting to break. She needed to get out of here before she made an even bigger fool of herself. But she couldn't leave without letting him know that whatever he'd assumed about her just because she was famous was wrong. Completely wrong.

"I shouldn't have come here tonight and I *definitely* shouldn't have kissed you back," she told him. "But I still can't believe you would actually think that I'd want to sleep with you when I only just met you five minutes ago. I would *never* do that." She made sure to look him straight in the eye. *"Never."*

Then she reached deep for the poise she'd used on hundreds of runways, and walked away.

* * *

What the hell had just happened?

Sean stood frozen in the spot where the girl had shoved him away and then called him out for acting like a total jerk. One second he'd been buzzing from the alcohol, the next he'd been kissing the prettiest girl in the world. And then, just minutes later, everything had gone horribly wrong.

What the hell had he just done?

The girl was gone, but he could still see the expressions that had raced across her face right before she left. First, she'd been stunned. Then, she'd been angry. But by the end, she'd simply looked hurt. And so incredibly disappointed, as if she couldn't believe he would treat her the way he had, like nothing more than a piece of meat.

What the hell was wrong with him lately?

Any buzz the alcohol had given him, any numbness he'd managed to attain, immediately disappeared in the wake of her disappointment in him. When she'd shoved him away, when she'd looked at him like he was scum and then laid out the really good reasons why he actually *was* scum, it had been like having a huge bucket of ice water dumped over him.

Sean felt like he was finally waking up from a long, bad dream.

Especially given what she'd said to him when they were on the dance floor: *"Whatever happened, I'm sorry."* It was as though she'd seen straight through to his heart, everything he'd been trying to hold back, to hold inside, to ignore and forget. And when she'd reached up to touch his cheek, it had been the first time he'd felt alive, truly alive, in months.

When Sean was a little kid and got into his first fight on the playground at school, his mother and father had taught him how to apologize. Tonight, though, he didn't need his mother's voice in his head telling him the right thing to do. He *knew* it already. Because he'd been a dirtbag.

An epic dirtbag.

Sean pushed through the crowd and out the door in hopes that she'd still be outside talking to friends, telling them what a total ass he was. But she wasn't out there and he hated the thought of her heading back to her dorm alone at night, even though the campus was usually safe.

Plus, since he didn't even know her name, how was he going to let her know how sorry he was?

"Damn," Kurt said, shaking his head as he walked up. "I never thought the day would come when you'd strike out. Big time, too. I guess that's what happens when you try to put the moves on a supermodel; they're not that easily impressed."

"What did you just say? You know who she is?"

"Seriously?" Kurt looked at Sean over the rim of his beer cup. "You didn't know you were putting the moves on one of the hottest supermodels in the world? Everyone has been talking about Serena Britten being a freshman this year. People have been trying to spot her, but she's been pretty elusive until tonight. I couldn't believe it when I saw that she was here dancing. Of course, that was right when you swooped in to make your move."

When she'd been dancing with her eyes closed, her hands raised as she moved to the beat, her long hair falling in waves over her shoulders and her legs going on forever, she hadn't looked as young as the other girls. Sean had wondered if she could be a sophomore or junior, and had thought there was something familiar about her. But he hadn't been able to put his finger on it. Now, though, he could totally picture Serena's face on the cover of the magazines his sister Maddie pored over.

Suddenly, what she'd said right after she'd shoved him away made perfect sense: *"I know you've probably seen my pictures in magazines and think I'm easy."*

Damn it, no. He didn't think that. He hadn't even known she was famous. And if he wasn't absolutely sure that showing up at her dorm room tonight to apologize would only freak her out more, Sean would already have been halfway across campus to tell her all this.

When he headed back inside, it wasn't to party or to drink any more, but to change into his shorts and running shoes. Already he knew that the only chance he'd have of getting any sleep tonight would be through pure exhaustion.

Especially when the disappointment in Serena's eyes wouldn't stop haunting him.

CHAPTER THREE

After baseball practice early Saturday morning, Sean headed on foot to the freshman dorms. Now that he knew who Serena was, he must have heard her name at least a dozen times since last night. Clearly, the only reason he'd missed the news of her being on campus was because he'd been so deep in his numbed-out haze of drinking every night and then trying to keep his shit together out on the field and in class during the day that he hadn't paid attention to anything else.

As he pushed through the front doors of her dorm, though he hadn't been nervous around a girl since his early teens, his heart was pounding hard. He had just jogged up the stairs to the second floor when one of the doors opened and someone stepped into the hall.

The girl had on baggy jeans and an even baggier sweatshirt. Her hair was tucked up into a Stanford ball cap, and she had a loaded messenger bag slung across one shoulder. But even if most people would have looked right past her, he recognized her immediately. What, he wondered, was Serena doing wearing that disguise? Because that was clearly what it was.

She kept her head down as if she was thinking really hard about something, so it wasn't until she was nearly at the stairs that she saw him.

He didn't wait, couldn't wait another second to tell her, "I need to apologize to you for the way I acted last night."

For a moment surprise lit her features, but then her expression closed up so that he couldn't figure out what she was thinking—or feeling—at all. "It doesn't matter," she said in a flat voice as she moved past him and down the stairs to head outside. "Just forget about it."

But it *did* matter, and he couldn't just forget about it. Or about *her*.

He'd been up all night trying to figure out a way to make things up to her, but now that he was with her again, the words he'd planned to say got muddled together in his head. "Last night, I was drunk and—"

She spun around on the grass to face him, her previously restrained expression now blazing with anger. "Do you really think that saying you were drunk and didn't know what you were doing is how you apologize to a girl for grabbing her out of the blue and trying to convince her to sleep with you two minutes later?"

Damn it, he thought as she turned and started walking away even faster, he hadn't meant to screw things up again. Or to make things worse. Especially when beneath her anger he could still see her disappointment.

"You're completely right that it doesn't matter how much I had to drink or what state of mind I was in. I shouldn't have come on to you the way I did, and I *definitely* shouldn't have tried to convince you to come upstairs to my bedroom. There's no excuse for it, and I really am sorry for the way I behaved. You should be able to kiss a guy at a party without him dragging you off to bed by your hair." He wished more than anything that he could just hit rewind and go back a day. A year, actually. So that he could have his mother back in time to save her from cancer *and* not screw things up with Serena. "I have two sisters, and if any guy tried to do to them what I did to you, I'd tear him apart."

In her obvious shock at everything he'd just said, she stumbled over a thick tuft of grass. Her bag was so heavy that she would have fallen if he hadn't grabbed her arm. He heard her gasp softly at his touch before she pulled her arm away, but her face remained flushed...and she looked even more beautiful than she had the night before when she'd been in his arms.

He had come here today to tell her how sorry he was, not to hit on her again, but Sean still couldn't stop his reaction to her. It was natural. Primal. Chemical. And so powerful that just being near her made him feel better—and clearer—than he had in months.

She took a deep breath, then blew it out, pulling her hat off and shaking out her hair as if she didn't quite know what she should do next. Maybe, he hoped, it was because she could still feel their connection, too, despite what an idiot he'd been?

"I also want you to know that I didn't have any idea who you were last night." When she looked at him in disbelief, he raised two fingers on his right hand. "Scout's honor. I thought you looked a little familiar, but it wasn't until after you left that my friend Kurt told me who you were."

The way she tensed at that told him more than she likely intended to reveal about how she felt about her fame. Clearly, she wasn't big on it. The thing was, Sean wasn't too surprised by this because his rock-star brother was like that, too. Drew hated when his ever-increasing fame got in the way of his music. Then again, Sean thought, modeling wasn't exactly the same as writing and performing songs, was it? So if she hadn't done it for the fame, why had she done it? And why was she here at Stanford when she could have been in Paris making thousands of dollars an hour in front of the cameras?

"If you didn't recognize me, then why did you come up to me like that?"

Was she joking? Did she truly think that the only reason a guy would approach her was because she was famous and he wanted to say he'd made out with a celebrity?

Wanting to be as honest with her this morning as he'd been scuzzy the night before, he said, "You are the most beautiful girl I've ever seen, but it was more than just your beauty that drew me, Serena." When she looked back up at him, he felt as though he was falling into her deep blue eyes. "You *saw* me." He swallowed hard before adding, "And when we kissed, it was the most explosive, most intense thing I've ever felt in my life—" He reached for her cheek in the exact same way she had reached for his the night before. "—and everything bad just disappeared."

* * *

The very last thing Serena had expected to see this morning was the guy from the frat party.

But he'd just surprised her even more with his heartfelt apology.

She didn't have much experience with the opposite sex—*much* actually meaning *none* given the way her mother had hovered over her for her entire life at photo shoots and at industry parties and even in their hotel rooms—but she was still almost certain that most guys wouldn't have apologized. No, they'd have told their friends that she was a frigid bitch, and they'd have been happy to let her think she'd brought it on herself by responding to his kisses the way she had. But they definitely wouldn't have said that there was no excuse for what they'd done.

And everything he'd just said about the explosive sparks set off between them when they kissed? Well, the truth was that she was already feeling those sparks again.

Simply by being near him and looking into his eyes.

Last night, she'd been so intent on trying to experience new things that when he'd kissed her and it had been *incredible,* she'd temporarily forgotten everything but him. And that's what had gotten her into trouble. She couldn't let herself forget again just how hard she'd fought to leave her life as a model behind to come to Stanford and figure out who and what she actually wanted to be. Not just a hanger for designer clothes, not just a blank slate for makeup artists to paint on, but a teacher or a researcher or a writer. Or maybe something else entirely that she would discover during the next four years. The point was that she needed to give herself the chance to find out.

So even if he was one of the most beautiful boys on campus, and he made her heart flutter like crazy—along with other parts of her body that had only come to life with his kiss—Serena would never forgive herself if she let a guy derail her focus. One bad experience at a frat party didn't change the fact that her new life was still full of so many opportunities. She just needed to be smarter about the ones she went for from now on.

Still, even knowing all of that, it wasn't easy to take a step back from him and the delicious warmth of his hand on her skin. "Look—" she began, before she realized she still didn't know his name.

"I'm Sean. Sean Morrison. And I know we got off to a rough start, but if you'll give me another chance, if you let me start over, I promise I won't blow it this time."

"Sean," she made herself begin again even though she was *so* incredibly tempted by what he'd just said, "I can tell that you do feel bad about what happened, and I appreciate that. A lot, actually. But—"

"Hey, aren't you that famous model?" Another student had been riding past on his bike when he'd slammed on the brakes and skidded around to closely scan her hair and face. "You *are* her! Serena Britten live and in the flesh."

She belatedly realized she was holding her baseball cap rather than wearing it. She hadn't meant to take it off, not when her long, wavy hair tended to be a dead giveaway. But she'd been so flustered by how earnest Sean's apology had been—and how incredibly *alive* she felt around him despite everything—that she'd forgotten to stay in disguise.

"Can I get a picture with you?"

Knowing from previous experience that the easiest thing to do was just say yes and smile for the picture— even if the way the guy had said *flesh* gave her the creeps—she nodded. "Sure. No problem."

"Hey, man, can you take it?" The guy shoved his phone into Sean's hand without waiting for him to respond. "And Serena," the stranger said as he turned back to her and stared straight at her chest, "why don't you take off that big sweatshirt for the pic? You know, since I'm not sure my friends back home will believe it's really you unless they can see your smoking hot body."

Serena knew better than to be shocked. She'd heard plenty of things like that before—it was just the way things went when you modeled bikinis and lingerie for a living. Nonetheless, for a few moments she could only stand there speechless, staring at the jerk who had just told her to put her breasts on display for his friends.

"Here's your phone back, asshole," Sean growled, snapping her out of her stunned state as he took aim with the phone.

It bounced off the guy's forehead and he barely caught it before it crashed onto the ground. "Dude! What the hell was that for?"

"Apologize to Serena."

"For what?"

Sean growled the words, "For talking to her like that."

"What the hell are you, her bodyguard?"

She hadn't realized quite how tall or how muscular Sean was until he took a very menacing step toward the stranger. "No. But I'm happy to be one if she needs it. And she's still waiting for you to apologize."

The guy shoved his phone into his pocket. "I don't need the picture that bad." But it was clear that he was more than a little scared of Sean coming after him as he added, "Sorry," before quickly riding away.

"Jesus," Sean said as he scowled at the stranger's retreating back, "no wonder you don't want anything to do with any of us. We're all a bunch of assholes."

No question, she'd dealt with her fair share of assholes over the years. Only, Sean Morrison no longer seemed like one of them. Because even though he *had* screwed up last night, she could see how genuinely, truly sorry he was about it. Something told her he'd never, ever do anything like that again. And, she thought with a little inward sigh of longing, if she said good-bye to him for what would surely be the very last time, she was *really* going to miss the way his kisses had made her feel. As though her heart were whirling and twirling around inside her chest at the sinfully sweet thrill of being in his arms.

And yet...

She still couldn't lose sight of why she was really at Stanford, of all the dreams she hoped to follow. Plus, from the quick Internet search she'd done this morning, it didn't look like anyone had posted a picture of her making out with Sean. Hopefully her luck would continue to hold on that front, because she hadn't gotten nearly enough sleep to be able to deal with a call from her mother—or worse, if she'd really meant what she'd said about never forgiving Serena. Because after all the lessons Genevieve had taught her since she was a little girl about how men couldn't be trusted, Serena shuddered to think how she would react to a picture of her daughter with her tongue down some guy's throat in the middle of a drunken frat party.

No question about it, even the possibility that a picture might leak from last night was a *really* good reminder not to take that kind of stupid risk again. Which meant she couldn't keep standing here wishing Sean would kiss her. She needed to say good-bye, instead.

"Thank you for coming to say you were sorry. But even if there is some kind of connection between us—" And there was really no point in pretending there wasn't when she knew they both could feel the sparks shooting off between them when they weren't even touching. "—I really need to make sure I stay focused on my classes." Serena was almost positive she was doing the right thing by walking away from him...only why did it have to be so hard? "So if you'll excuse me, I've got a paper to write."

With that, she made herself head into the library to

get started on her paper for her *Poetry and Poetics* class. But all the while, she had to work really, really hard at pushing the thought of Sean Morrison—and his kisses—away.

CHAPTER FOUR

The following Friday, Serena tried not to flinch as her *History and Theory of the Novel* professor came too close and leaned over her to point out something in her book.

"Do you see the lyrical way the author uses metaphor to express emotion?" Professor Fairworth read aloud a passage from the classic text, but she could have sworn he was looking down her shirt rather than at the book on the table in front of her.

As several students chimed in, Serena worked to concentrate on the book they were studying. She'd had to fill out a special application for this class, where only fifteen students were lucky enough to study with the Newbery Medal-winning professor. But as the weeks went by, she sometimes found herself wishing for the anonymity of being one of four hundred students in a huge lecture hall, instead. A class where a professor couldn't "accidentally" brush up against her, or stare at her boobs.

Vowing to wear her big, shapeless sweatshirt in class from now on, regardless of the heat in the room, she shifted slightly away from her professor and held her breath as she waited for him to dismiss them for the weekend.

Finally, he stepped away from her. "Good work, everyone."

Serena immediately put on her sweatshirt and was quickly shoving her books and laptop into her bag when he added, "I'd appreciate it if I could have a few more minutes of your time, Serena."

The sound of the door closing behind the rest of the students in her class felt like the locking of a prison door. Telling herself she was being overly melodramatic, she forced herself to relax her tense muscles. "What would you like to speak with me about, Professor Fairworth?"

He was smiling at her, but his pale blue eyes didn't seem nearly as friendly as his smile should have suggested. *Predatory.* That was how it felt. As if he was imagining her without her clothes on...

"You're a bright young woman, Serena."

Trying not to betray her nerves, she said, "Thank you. I'm very passionate about literature."

"Passionate," he repeated in a low voice.

The word hung between them, and she inwardly cursed herself for saying exactly the wrong thing. For all she knew, he'd think *she* was trying to lead *him* on.

"What I mean," she said, fumbling over her words now, "is that I really enjoy reading. Everything from classics to genre fiction to literary novels."

"When I first received the class list and saw your name on the roster, I'll admit I had my doubts. But your analysis is spot-on, your use of language is far beyond your years, and you have a knack for explaining your reasoning in a way that often helps the others better understand the material."

Again, she thanked him, but where pleasure at his compliment should have been was only wariness about what he might be leading up to.

"As this is the first year I've taught such a select group of students, I have come to realize that I should make some changes, and quickly, so that everyone will get the most out of the course. How would you like to be my teaching assistant for the quarter?"

"I thought teaching assistants have already taken the classes they're helping with?"

"Actually, it's far better that you haven't yet taken my class. What I'm proposing is that you and I work together a week or two ahead of the rest of the class. I will run my weekly plans by you and then you can let me know where I need to clarify or highlight certain aspects of my lectures and assignments."

She should have jumped at the opportunity. It was all of her dreams come true to work with an academic of Julian Fairworth's stature. But...he made her so uncomfortable.

Rationally, though, Serena knew that every guy in the world didn't want to get in her pants, no matter how much her mother had raised her to believe that they did. And she'd be crazy to give up this opportunity when she needed his recommendation to the admissions department so that they would make her a permanent student after this quarter.

"I'd love to help you out in any way that I can."

He returned her smile with another one of his own that she couldn't quite bring herself to buy into, even though she really, really wanted to. "Wonderful. I will email you several things tonight and if you're able to get through them quickly, we could meet Monday afternoon a couple of hours before class begins."

"Okay," she said, belatedly adding, "Great!" just in case it sounded like she wasn't as excited as she should be about helping him. And, really, with all the windows in this room looking out on the main Quad, it would be pretty difficult for him to actually try anything inappropriate with her. No doubt, she was worrying for nothing, letting her mother's endless and crazy warnings poison her.

"I'm so pleased you're amenable to my plan, Serena. I know we're both going to get a great deal out of it. As there is another class in this room before ours, I'd like for you to come to my office for our meetings. In any case, given that all of my materials are already there, it makes the most sense to meet there."

He hadn't said or done anything inappropriate. Despite that, she could still barely stop a shiver at the thought of being alone with him in his office next Monday.

"Sure," she made herself say, "that will work."

Serena was just reaching for her bag to sling it over her shoulder when he held out his hand to shake on the deal. She willed hers not to tremble as she put it in his, but when he closed his fingers around hers and somehow managed to tug her closer, she froze as renewed panic skittered up her spine. Unlike what she'd imagined most English professors would look like, he was fairly tall and muscular. And all she could think in the few moments that he held on to her hand was that if he wanted to overpower her, he could easily do it. Very easily.

During the course of her modeling career, she'd been in many high-pressure situations. But standing here alone with her professor on campus felt more stressful than all of them combined. Her mother's hovering had often frustrated Serena—but at least Genevieve Britten knew precisely how to scare men away from her daughter.

No longer able to pretend to be comfortable, she said, "I need to get going." She slipped her hand out of his and quickly grabbed her bag to hold it between them like a shield. "The dining hall closes soon and I've got to get all the way across campus before it does. I'll look for your email and see you on Monday in your office. Thanks, 'bye."

She didn't manage a full breath until she'd made it down the long pathway to the corner of the Quad and onto the bike- and footpath between the buildings.

What had she just gotten herself into?

Because no matter how much she tried to tell herself that she was making something out of nothing—would Professor Fairworth really jeopardize his career at one of the most prestigious universities in the world just to try to get into her pants?—she couldn't stop freaking out about it. Especially now that their private Monday meeting in his office was looming over her like a dark shadow.

When she blinked, she could feel wetness on her lashes and was afraid she was going to start full-on crying any second now. But she couldn't. Not here in the middle of campus, not when she'd seen so many students take pictures of her on their phones during the past few weeks and there was a good chance someone might catch this moment on film, too.

Needing to get some place where no one could see her, Serena ducked off the main footpath and walked quickly through the doors of a random building.

Straight into a guy's broad chest.

"Whoa," he said as his size and her speed nearly sent her toppling backward. He had to put his hands around her waist to keep her from falling. "Steady now, I've got you."

His voice sizzled through her system a beat before his touch sent a rush of scorching heat through her...and she looked up, stunned, into Sean Morrison's green eyes.

CHAPTER FIVE

He'd been smiling at her, but the moment he saw her face—and the fact that she'd obviously been about to lose it—his smile fell away. "Serena, what's wrong? Did I hurt you?"

She shook her head, but before she could manage to get any words out, his hands were already moving over her. Not in a deliberately sexy way, but with concern.

"No," she finally said, although given how his touch was making her feel, the word sounded like it had at least two syllables. "You didn't hurt me."

His hands finally stopped at her waist again, and he was still frowning at her. "But you're upset." His frown deepened as he asked, "Did another jerk bother you for a picture?"

"No." Although in many ways, her professor seemed *way* worse than any of those guys who hadn't even bothered to hide their dirty thoughts about her.

"Then what happened?"

"It's nothing," she said automatically.

"I doubt that," he said softly, and from the way he was looking into her eyes, she knew he could see he was right.

Sisters, she reminded herself. He'd told her last week during his apology that he had sisters. She could guess that he'd probably spent plenty of time soothing them when they'd skinned their knees or had their feelings hurt.

Still…she didn't know him, so it felt risky to trust him. Besides, how would it sound if she told him how much her professor creeped her out? Or how lonely she felt in her crowded dorm even though she was surrounded by a hundred other people? Or how she wished she could just be normal for one day of her life?

"Sorry about barreling into you like that." She made herself step out of his arms. Arms that were, amazingly, just as comforting as they were arousing. "The dining hall will be closing soon and since I missed lunch I should get go—"

"Come grab some pizza with me."

He didn't reach for her again or try to keep her from fleeing, but his abrupt suggestion had the same effect. "You want to go get pizza with me?"

She could still see the concern in his eyes, but he was doing his best to mask it with a grin. "Have you eaten at Pizza My Heart on University yet?"

"No." She hadn't ventured too far off campus yet. Barely beyond the library, in fact.

"Then someone's got to introduce you to the best pizza place on the West Coast."

She'd made herself walk away from him so many times already. But right now, she just didn't have it in her to do it again. "Okay. I'd like that."

He reached for her bag and had it off her shoulder and onto his before she could think to protest. "I know why you looked so upset," he said as he shifted her bag over his back.

She'd been walking beside him as they headed down from the path to Palm Drive and into downtown Palo Alto, but now she stopped cold. "How could you possibly know?"

His brows lowered as he stopped and faced her. "I was making a joke about how the load of bricks you're carrying around in this bag is practically making *me* cry." He reached out for her again, put his hand on her arm. "Serena, what the hell happened today?"

Sympathy was the worst thing of all, she realized, because it brought up all the emotions again. "I don't want to talk about it." Belatedly, realizing how cold her response must have sounded when he'd been nothing but awesome today, she added, "I mean, you've been so nice about it, but—"

"You don't know me."

She blinked up at him, surprised that he'd understood. *Sisters,* she thought again. Something told her he'd been a good brother to them.

"Given what I do—" She stopped to correct herself. "I mean, what I used to do—"

Ugh, she didn't want to sound like a prima donna, or as if she thought she was such a big star that she couldn't say anything to anyone for fear that it would end up in *People* magazine. But the problem was, sometimes it did. It was the same reason why she hadn't really hung around her dorm room much since the frat party the week before. Of course Abi would want to know what had ended up happening with the guy Serena had been making out with. On the one hand, Serena desperately wanted a girlfriend to confide in. But on the other, what if it turned out that Abi wasn't trustworthy?

"I get it," Sean said easily as he walked beside her. "My brother Drew has a band that's getting pretty big.

He's into it for the music, not the fame, but there doesn't seem to be an easy way for him to escape the spotlight."

"Wait a minute," she said as she suddenly put two and two together, "Drew Morrison is your brother?" When he nodded, she said, "I love his music."

"It's pretty good," Sean agreed with another heart-stoppingly gorgeous grin. "We're all proud of him."

From the way Sean talked about his brother, she could see that he really was. There was no jealousy over Drew being one of the biggest up-and-coming rock stars on the planet. Only good-natured ribbing from one sibling to another.

"You mentioned sisters before. How many of you are there?"

"Six."

"Wow. I've always thought it would be cool to have siblings, but I always imagined one or two. Not growing up with five other people always around. Do you like having such a big family?"

"I do. Most of the time, anyway. Everyone's got their weird quirks, but you learn pretty quickly how to avoid the rough spots...or use them to your advantage if you need to."

She laughed, realizing with no little surprise just how easy he was to talk to. *And to kiss,* a little voice inside her head reminded her. But she shouldn't be thinking about kissing Sean right now. Not when she was enjoying their conversation so much that it no longer seemed completely impossible that she might actually be making a friend.

A really hot friend.

"I'd love to hear about the rest of them."

"Grant is twenty-five, and never lets any of us forget he's the oldest. His office is actually not far from where we're having pizza, near a bunch of other high-tech companies."

"That must be nice that he's still in the area."

"It is, though we haven't seen much of him since he founded Collide."

"He started Collide? The social networking company with the tagline *When Worlds Collide?*"

"Yup, that's Grant's company."

She knew she was sounding like a dork, first with how she'd goggled over his rock-star brother, and now how stunned she was to learn that Sean's oldest brother had founded one of the fastest-rising social networking companies in the world.

"That's amazing."

"It is. But," he said with another grin, "if you tell him I said that, he'd probably have shirts printed up with the word *amazing* and his face on them. So let's just keep that between us, okay?"

Since she seriously doubted she'd ever get the chance to meet Grant Morrison, she wasn't particularly worried about breaking Sean's confidence.

"Drew is the next oldest, and then my sister Olivia. She's a senior here, majoring in Education."

"Are you all geniuses?"

"Olivia definitely is," he said with a fondness that told Serena just how much he admired his older sister. "Although my brother Justin's brains pretty much put all of us in the dust. He's also on campus, doing a double major in Biology and Robotic Engineering. He got all the brains in our twin cave, but I'm okay with that."

"Twins?" Her mind reeled trying to imagine a second guy who looked as good as Sean walking around campus. No doubt just seeing them together in one place would make a girl's brain melt out her ears. "Are you two close the way they say twins are?"

"Yup, we get along pretty well, probably because we're so different and rarely compete for the same stuff. Although, he's one hell of a baseball player."

In the week since she'd met—and kissed—Sean at the frat party, Serena had learned that Sean was a junior and the star first baseman and hitter on the Stanford baseball team. Funny, she thought as they crossed at a traffic light, he spoke so easily about his family but hadn't yet mentioned anything about his own achievements. Wouldn't most guys have bragged about themselves by now?

"Does Justin also play on the Stanford team?"

Sean raised an eyebrow at her *also,* as if to say, *So you do know something about me, huh?*

She blushed in confirmation as he told her, "Nope. He'd rather spend hours geeking out in a lab than standing in the outfield waiting for someone to hit a fly ball in his direction."

"Do you guys have that twin sense you hear about in movies? You know, where one of you cuts himself and the other feels it?"

Sean laughed. "No, thank God. Although, sometimes I do feel like I can read his mind. Especially when it comes to this girl, Taylor, that he's been friends with forever and is secretly in love with. He's so frustrated, it's sad."

"If he's in love with her, why doesn't he let her know how he feels?" She was surprised to find herself asking such a personal question, but Sean made it so easy. "Is it because he's afraid to ruin their friendship just in case it doesn't work out?"

"Maybe. Or maybe she's made it clear that she's just not interested."

"Do *you* think she's not interested?"

He thought about it for a second. "Taylor is a cute girl, but all up in her head like Justin. She's pretty nervous around guys." He shrugged again. "Heck, who knows if she's even been on a date before."

Serena tucked her head down just in case Sean might guess from just looking at her reaction that *she'd* never been on a date before, either. Maybe she'd have to go look this Taylor up and the two of them could bond over their utter cluelessness around men.

Especially the Morrison twins.

"And then there's my sister, Maddie. She's still in high school, graduating this year." He shook his head. "She's a little spitfire. Not to mention too smart, too talented, and too pretty for her own good. We all try to watch out for her to make sure she doesn't get into trouble, but it's hard now that we're not at home with her anymore."

Sean opened the door to the small pizza place and they stepped into what had to be the best smelling restaurant on the planet. "What do you like on your pizza?"

Pizza was one of the many menu items at the top of her mother's *Do Not Ever Eat* list. But, what the heck? If Serena was going to eat pizza, she might as well do it right. "Everything."

He looked momentarily surprised and then pleased as he said, "Two slices with everything. And two Cokes."

The restaurant was small, with only a handful of scratched-up Formica tables. A couple of minutes later when they were sitting down with the biggest pieces of pizza she could have imagined in front of them, she said, "Your brothers and sisters all sound amazing. I'll bet your parents are great, too, aren't they?"

Suddenly, that same pain she'd seen in his eyes on

the dance floor at the party flashed through them again.

She instinctively reached out to him. "Sean?" His arm was warm beneath her hand. "What happened?"

His expression had already shuttered, but he told her, "You're right, my parents are great." He swallowed before amending it to, "Were great. My dad is still around," he clarified. "He works in real estate, gives out loans to people. It's my mom." He inhaled a breath that she could see shook him. "She passed away three months ago from breast cancer."

"Oh Sean, I'm so sorry."

"I am, too. She was great. A schoolteacher. Third grade. Everyone misses her."

Serena had never come face-to-face with such grief. "She sounds like she was an amazing mother."

"She was." But it was obvious that he didn't want to talk about it anymore. "What about your family? You said you're an only child, right?"

"It's always been just me and my mom." She wasn't telling him anything he couldn't have read online if he wanted to look her up, but it still wasn't easy to admit, "I never met my father."

"That sucks."

She looked up at Sean, surprised by his bluntness. But somehow, it helped settle her down a bit. "Yeah, it does. But I've never known anything else."

"Must have been hard for your mom to let her only kid go away to school."

"You have no idea." Her mouth felt so dry that she picked up her Coke and gulped down half the bottle.

Soda was another thing she'd very rarely had due to the empty calories and potential bloating from the sodium and carbonation. But as she licked her lips to savor every last drop…wow, all those bubbles and sugar and caffeine tasted so good. No wonder people got addicted to it.

Sean had already eaten half his slice by the time she took her first bite. And when the mingling tastes of the pepperoni and mushrooms and onions and peppers and sauce and cheese all hit her tongue at once, she couldn't keep her eyes from closing or a low moan of pleasure from leaving her throat.

"Good?"

Sean was clearly amused, but she didn't have it in her to be embarrassed, not when this pizza was the very best thing she'd eaten in her whole life. *Ever.*

"So good," she managed to get out between bites as she concentrated her entire being on her meal for a few minutes. Each new taste was as big a revelation as the one that came before it, and washing it down with Coke felt so deliciously sinful. In fact, it took several minutes for her to resurface and remember that she was sitting in a pizza joint with a gorgeous guy from school. Who just happened to be grinning at her.

"I take it you agree that it's the best pizza on the West Coast?"

"I've never eaten pizza anywhere else, but it's so amazing I'm sure you're right."

His eyebrows went up. "You're joking, aren't you?"

She was momentarily confused. "About what?"

"You've never eaten pizza before?"

Ugh, her and her stupid mouth. Between feeling increasingly comfortable talking with Sean and the food coma she was quickly slipping into, she'd said more than she should have.

Knowing there was no point in trying to laugh off her comment, she simply said, "My life has been pretty weird up until now. I haven't done a lot of normal stuff. Especially," she added, "when it comes to junk food. It's not exactly true that I've never eaten pizza before, just that I was really little the last time I did. My mom would freak out if she saw this."

"You mean because of your modeling career?"

Serena nodded, hoping he would drop it. She didn't want to talk about her mom or the career she'd left behind. Not when, for a few precious moments, she'd actually managed to forget all about them.

"So," he said as he toed her bag on the floor and it didn't budge, "what's in all the books you've got crammed into this bag?"

Relieved that he'd decided to change subjects, she said, "Nearly everything ever written about the Brontë sisters and their books. I'm in love with the way they use language, with how their books can make people feel so much, from hope to despair, laughter and tears." On a roll, she told him, "I love that I can learn almost anything from a book—how to build a boat, or speak a new language, or probably even fly a plane. I even love the way books smell. If I were locked inside a library or a bookstore for weeks on end, I'm certain that I would never run out of interesting things to discover."

She finally realized she was rambling, but fortunately he didn't look like he minded and his eyes weren't glazing over.

"Do you want to write?"

"Maybe. Or teach. Or study the origins of language. Or work in a library. Or—" She cut herself off before she went zooming again. "That's why I'm so excited to be at Stanford. Everything seems possible."

"Most people would have thought you already had everything."

She didn't want to sound ungrateful for her success. And since she still didn't know him well enough to know if she could totally trust him, she simply said, "My career was great. I worked with a lot of wonderful people."

"But you didn't get to live in a library all day."

Again, he surprised her with how quickly he boiled everything down to the heart of the matter. And how well he understood what she was feeling without her having to say much at all.

"No, I didn't get to spend nearly enough time in libraries. But now I do." Which reminded her... "I should actually be heading back to campus. I have a lot of reading to get through tonight."

"On a Friday night?"

"I've agreed to help one of my professors with some new class material he's working on, so my load has gotten a little heavier." As they stood up and he slung both their bags over his broad shoulders, she said, "Thank you for the pizza. It was great."

"You're not done with me yet," he said with a grin. "We've still got to make the walk back to your dorm."

"Actually, I think I'll head to the library to work there until it closes." Just as she had every Friday night since she'd been on campus.

"Something tells me," he said as they headed out onto the sidewalk and started walking back toward campus, "that hanging out with you would be good for my GPA."

"What's your major?"

"Baseball." He laughed. "With a degree in Economics on the side."

"As you might have already guessed, I've heard a few things about how great you are at baseball. Are you really going to go pro at the end of this year?"

"I could." He didn't say anything else for a little while, and she let him take the time to get his thoughts together. "But—" When he turned to look at her, his eyes were even darker than usual. "—my mom was pretty big on all of us getting a college degree. I can't help but think if I go pro before graduating, and maybe don't end up coming back to finish one day, that she'd be disappointed."

"I very much doubt," Serena said in a gentle voice, "that there's anything you could do that would disappoint her."

He stopped walking and reached for her hand. "The way I acted with you last weekend...she would have been disappointed with that."

"You've already apologized, Sean."

"But I shouldn't have treated you like—"

"How about," she interrupted, "we agree to forget what happened last Friday night? We were both in a weird space and nothing really bad ended up happening, so I'd hate to ruin today by going back to that again."

He searched her face for several long moments. Finally, he agreed, "Okay, I'll try to forget the bad stuff, like what a dick I was. But I can't guarantee I'll be able to forget everything." He moved closer, close enough that she could have easily pressed her lips to his before taking her next breath. "Because I really, *really* liked kissing you, Serena. And I'm really glad you agreed to come get pizza with me today."

She knew she was blushing as she said, "I've really enjoyed hanging out with you today, too. You made a bad day so much better. Thank you."

"You don't have to thank me for anything, Serena. I'm just glad I was able to be there for you when you needed me. And if you ever want to talk about what happened this afternoon, I'm here."

Could anyone be sweeter? Not to mention that the

way his low voice sizzled through her veins made it hard to think about anything other than her desperate need to kiss him again.

And yet, it was that very desperation that scared her enough to need to take a step away from him. Of course she wanted to experience magic and passion, but at the same time she didn't have any experience with these kinds of intense feelings. Feelings that had all come on so suddenly...ones that felt like they could zoom ahead really, really fast. She needed a little time to think, to process, to try to figure out if she could actually manage to do well in school and date, too. Especially given that any guy she was dating was sure to find his face in a tabloid photo pretty darn fast, which also meant that her mother would find out, too.

"I wasn't trying to blow you off last Friday when I said I needed to study," she tried to explain. "It's just that I really need to do well this quarter. That's why I've got to work so hard all the time, even tonight."

"If I kissed you again now, something tells me you might change your mind about studying tonight."

Oh God, when he looked at her like that, with so much heat and desire, she couldn't look away from him, couldn't move. All she could do was wait for his mouth to cover hers, and for everything else to fade away beneath the inevitable persuasion of his kiss.

Only, right when she could almost feel his lips against hers, he was the one suddenly taking a step back and letting go of her hand. "Damn it, I'm doing it again. Trying to convince you to do something you don't want to do." He cursed again, clearly pissed off at himself. "I have no right to ask you to forgive me again—"

"There's nothing to forgive." Because the truth was that she'd wanted his kiss just as much. "Any other girl would have been dying for you to kiss her. And," she added with a small smile that she hoped would soften the blow, "I can say from personal experience that they would have liked it very much." She took a deep breath and made herself add, "Maybe one day I won't always have to study quite so hard."

She hoped he knew that was her way of trying not to close the door forever, and thankfully a few seconds later, he smiled again. Unfortunately, it wasn't his normal easy smile, because he was clearly still upset with himself. And when he dropped her off at the library a short while later, he was careful not to do anything that could be misconstrued as hitting on her again.

So then, Serena wondered as she headed to her usual spot on the third floor, if he'd just given her exactly the space she'd told him she needed by not kissing or even hugging her, why did her little corner of the library suddenly feel lonelier than ever?

CHAPTER SIX

"Dude, no wonder you weren't partying this weekend with everyone." Kurt looked positively gleeful. "You were too busy making your moves on that supermodel again."

Sean looked up from the bench press. Sure, he'd spent the weekend fantasizing about Serena, but he hadn't seen her.

"How'd you convince her to let you into her pants?"

Sean didn't blink, didn't think, just dropped the weights and approached his frat brother and teammate with murderous intent. "What the fuck are you talking about?"

Belatedly seeming to realize he'd said the wrong thing, Kurt shoved his phone at Sean a beat before he could knock a fist into his jaw. "Zane's new girlfriend just told us she saw this."

Sean looked down at the screen. It was one of those gossip sites, full of pictures of Hollywood stars. What he saw had him nearly crushing the phone in his fist.

Someone had taken a picture of Sean standing with Serena on Palm Avenue, just after they'd left the pizza joint. His hand was on hers and it was obvious from the way they were looking at each other that he wanted to kiss her—and that she wanted to kiss him right back. He scrolled down and saw that the second picture had been taken through the window of the pizza place, only this time her hand was on his arm while he'd been talking about his mom. There was also a shot of the two of them laughing together while on their way to get the pizza, when he'd been telling her about his brothers and sisters.

No wonder Kurt believed they were an item. Seeing the pictures and the title—*The Supermodel and the Baseball Bad Boy!*—Sean was hard pressed not to believe it himself.

Quickly scanning the story, he read that he was not only the top-ranked college baseball player in the country and was related to tech wonder Grant Morrison and rock star Drew Morrison...but that he also had a long and varied track record with women as a major campus bad boy.

Unfortunately, that was the end of the valid part of the story, as it also suggested that Drew was the one to introduce Serena to Sean and that they were now "inseparable." It even went so far as to claim that Sean was the reason Serena had given up the glittering life of a supermodel—so that she could stay by his side to make sure he didn't cheat on her with another girl.

She'd told him her life was strange, and he'd acted like he understood because his brother Drew had been open with their family about the difficulties of fame. But Sean suddenly realized the kind of spotlight that his brother had been under so far was absolutely nothing compared to this ridiculously intrusive bullshit that Serena had to deal with.

Without another word to Kurt, Sean grabbed his bag

and shot out the gym door. If by some miracle she hadn't yet seen it, he hoped he could figure out some way to help soften the blow.

She hadn't given him her cell phone number on Friday after they went for pizza, so he ran across campus to her dorm in record time. When no one answered the door, Sean belatedly realized where he should have thought to look for her first.

Green Library was much closer to her dorm than the gym had been and within a handful of minutes he was inside, his slightly labored breathing loud in the otherwise quiet building. Sean stopped in front of the information desk. "Have you seen Serena come in?"

The woman took in his T-shirt and shorts, the sweat dripping from him, and raised an eyebrow. "I'm sorry," she said in a slightly frosty voice, "what is it you would like to know?"

"Serena Britten. I really need to see her and I'm pretty sure she's here." When the woman started to shake her head again, he added, "You couldn't have missed her if she's been in today. She's beautiful."

"There are many beautiful women that come to the library," she replied in biting tones. "I don't see what that has to do with *you.*"

He hated having to reduce Serena to nothing but a supermodel, but he had no choice if he wanted to find her. "This is Serena." He held out his phone to show the woman the part of the online story where one of Serena's modeling shots filled the screen. When the woman's eyes lit with recognition, he asked again, "Have you seen her come in today?"

"Why?" Frost had turned to suspicion as the woman used her finger to quickly scroll through the story and obviously read the headline.

"I just found out about this and need to make sure she's okay. They took her picture without her knowing about it."

Finally, the woman nodded. "She's here. I don't know exactly where, however."

"Thank you for letting me know she's here. And if she comes out before I can find her, I'd really appreciate it if you could let her know I'm looking for her. My name is Sean Morrison and here's my number." He wrote his cell number on a piece of paper and handed it to the woman. "Please don't mention these pictures to her, just in case she hasn't seen them yet. I really don't want her to be upset."

He made a pass of the ground floor, before heading up the stairs. Man, this place was big. He'd been in the campus library before, of course, but it wasn't his regular stomping ground by any means. Mostly, he'd come to look through the amazing photography archives in the basement. He'd even brought his mother with him once, because she'd wanted to see the Ansel Adams shots he'd raved about.

"Your pictures are this good, honey." He'd known it was nothing more than a mother thinking her kid was great at everything, but her encouragement had meant a ton to a guy whom everyone else had always thought of as nothing more than a jock, the brawny Morrison twin.

Grief had him stumbling on the stairs for a moment. Righting himself, he worked to block out the thoughts of never being able see his mom again, or show her another picture, or have anyone else ever see inside of him the way she always had. Instead, he concentrated on looking for Serena, searching every corner, every desk, every row of tall bookshelves.

Thirty minutes later, he was nearly at the end of his

search—and the hope that he'd actually find her in the maze of rooms and shelves and desks—when he saw the top of a baseball cap in the farthest, most remote corner of the third floor.

The books were especially musty smelling up here, and he doubted many people ever made it this far into the building. But, he thought with a smile, Serena had. Without her telling him, he guessed it was her hideout. Her one special place that would be hers and hers alone when it probably felt like everyone was trying to grab on to a piece of her.

He stopped halfway to her, noting the way the light streaming in the window made her glow like the angel he'd thought she was the first night he'd met her. He hadn't wanted to touch a camera for three months, but the way the light was hitting her suddenly made him wish he hadn't smashed it to smithereens.

Wait, what was he thinking? He didn't want to take pictures anymore, had given that up.

It was simply that Serena was so beautiful, how could anyone *not* want to take her picture, if only to try to hold on to her rare and precious beauty for a little while?

Except now he knew just how invasive those pictures could be. And he hated that he would be the one to bust into her private spot. But he needed to talk with her about the pictures someone had taken of the two of them together, and couldn't risk waiting any longer.

He moved to where she could see him, but when she didn't look up, he realized she had her earbuds in and was totally absorbed in the book she was reading. Not wanting to scare her, he knelt by her side and gently touched her shoulder.

She jumped with a little yelp and immediately yanked out her earbuds. Fortunately, within seconds her surprise gave way to a smile that made him feel like he'd just won the World Series. Despite the bullshit they were about to deal with, he couldn't keep from smiling back. It had only been a couple of days since she'd left him outside this library, but he'd missed her.

"Sorry about scaring you like that. You were pretty into what you were reading."

She flushed slightly as she looked down at her book then back at him, her eyes bright and—he hoped—happy to see him. "I should be studying for my geology test, but I found this new book on my way in. I just can't resist biographies about the Brontë sisters."

"I'm like that with the photography archives downstairs." The words were out before he realized it.

Her head cocked to one side. "They've got photo archives in here?"

Knowing he couldn't pretend he hadn't brought it up, he nodded. "In the basement."

She looked at him a little more closely. "Cool. I'll have to go check them out."

He wanted to offer to show them to her, but he couldn't. Not when the memories of the last time he'd been in there with his mom would surely hit him. And not when he had something else he needed to talk to her about right now.

She smiled at him. "Are you here to study, too?"

God, he loved to see her smile. Hear her laugh. See her look carefree and happy. She'd looked like that for a little while on Friday when they'd been heading into town for pizza and he'd been telling her about his family and then later when she'd been talking about why she loved books so much.

The rest of the time, he now realized, she seemed to be on guard.

Yet again, he wanted to reach for her. Not just because he wanted her more than he'd ever wanted anyone else, but because he also wanted her to feel safe.

"Actually, I was looking for you." He knew he couldn't stall any longer, but damn it, he *hated* having to put his phone on top of her book. "One of the guys showed this to me."

Her smile immediately fell away and the color drained out of her face as she stared at his phone. He watched her scan the story, saw the way she lingered over the three photos of them together, noticed the way the pulse at the side of her neck was jumping faster and faster. Until, in a blur of sudden action, she was shoving her books into her bag, pushing her chair back, and making a beeline for the stairs.

"Serena, wait!"

She didn't say anything, just shook her head, and he knew from the way she'd pulled her cap down even harder onto her head and tucked her chin into her chest as she jogged down the steps that she was horribly upset.

He followed right behind her and when they got down to the ground floor, he caught the concerned look from the woman behind the information desk right before he flew out the front door after Serena.

"Serena," he called again, but she didn't stop walking. And even though all she probably wanted to do was get away from him—from everyone—right now, he couldn't let her leave when she was this upset. Reaching out, he gripped her hand in his and made her stop and face him. "I'm sorry," he said softly. "I wish the magazine hadn't written this story. I wish whoever took those pictures hadn't done it. And I know you still don't totally trust me, but you've got to know that I would never have tipped anyone off for this."

But when she didn't respond right away, he realized he couldn't force her to believe that he was on her side. Especially given the way things had begun between them at the frat party, when he'd been exactly the kind of scum she'd been trying to evade her entire life.

CHAPTER SEVEN

She'd been so happy to see him.

Ever since Friday night, Serena had been thinking about Sean, replaying their conversation on Palm Drive when he'd wanted to kiss her and she'd wanted to kiss him, too, but hadn't let either of them do it.

She'd been asking herself why she hadn't all weekend, why she'd felt compelled to hold him off, to take things so incredibly slow.

Now she remembered why.

Because no matter how much she wanted it to be, her life wasn't her own. It never had been, but she'd stupidly hoped going to college would be different. Plus, when her mother saw these pictures, she would automatically assume she was right about Serena chucking in her career for a boy.

What if she never forgives me even though none of this is true?

Even as she thought it, Serena tried not to dwell on the fact that she had, quite possibly, already started to fall for Sean Morrison.

For a moment, when he'd shown her the pictures on

his phone, she'd thought she was going to start crying in front of him. But then, before she could shed so much as one single tear, anger pushed them away. Anger that she'd never let loose because she'd never felt like she had an alternative to the life she was living. But now? Now that she'd tasted freedom? Now that she'd finally met an amazing guy whose kisses had finally shown her what real passion felt like? Now that she'd found out what it was like to be taught by the most brilliant academic minds and had started to think that maybe, just maybe, she could be like them one day if she just worked hard enough and focused on following her dreams?

She couldn't stand the thought of having those dreams ripped away.

"Serena?" Sean still had her hand in his. "Are you angry with me?"

"No, I'm not angry with you. After what you told me about your brother Drew having a hard time dealing with his fame, I just can't see that you'd do that to someone else."

"Does this mean you've decided to trust me?"

She stared into his eyes, wondering if everything the story had said about his being the biggest player on campus was true. Trusting Sean Morrison might very well be the stupidest thing she could do. And yet, whenever she thought about his obvious love for his family, she couldn't quite make herself believe that he was a bad person.

No one bad would ever love his siblings, his parents, that much.

"Maybe."

The corner of his mouth quirked up the slightest little bit on one side. "Well, I guess that's better than a flat-out no."

"It's not you, it's me," she told him, even though it was a total cliché. "After we had pizza and talked on Friday, I thought maybe we could be friends, but now everyone will think we're more than that." They'd all think that she was precisely the slutty model they had assumed she would be based on some of her racier photo shoots.

"Who cares what everyone thinks?"

Being in the public eye for so long, she knew better than to think she could control what people thought of her. But when it came to what her mother thought—how could she possibly explain these pictures?

Of course, that was right when her phone rang. After quickly verifying that it was Genevieve, Serena turned off the ringer and shoved it back into her bag.

"Was that someone else from the press?"

He looked like he was a heartbeat from yanking the phone out of her bag and avenging her in any way he could. Yet again, she was struck by how surprisingly sweet he was. Especially since she'd never had anyone stick up for her before.

"It was my mom."

He looked confused. "But you didn't pick up."

"Like I said before, it's complicated."

Serena needed to be better prepared to figure out a way to explain things to her mother that wouldn't upset her more. At the same time, she also needed to make sure she didn't end up caving and agreeing to leave Stanford just to make Genevieve happy. Because somehow, some way, she hoped the two of them could find some middle ground. A place where Serena could thrive by following her dreams without leaving her mother disappointed and angry. Unfortunately, where that middle place was, she didn't yet have a clue.

"These pictures and what they wrote about us will really upset her."

"Can't you just explain how the pictures were taken totally out of context and that they made up the rest?"

"I hope so. I just need to think about how I'm going to do that." Of course, the problem with waiting was that it would only give her mother more time to fuel her flames of fury over the recent decisions Serena had made. In her frustration, she didn't think before saying, "It was all so normal. We walked like normal people. We talked like normal people. We had pizza like normal people. And now—" She looked down at his phone. "—this."

"You keep talking about wanting to be normal." He looked confused. "But I don't get why would you want to be anything other than as extraordinary as you are?"

She wished she'd learned enough in her English classes already to have the right words to explain things to him. To her mom, too. When she didn't answer him because she didn't know *how*, she could read his frustration loud and clear. She expected him to keep hammering away at her until she explained why she was such a freak.

But instead of pressuring her, he simply said, "If you want normal, I'll give you normal."

It was the nicest thing anyone had ever said to her, and her surprise at his offer—one that showed he already understood so much more about her than anyone else ever had—made her momentarily speechless.

"As soon as I get back to my frat house, I'm going to set everyone straight about us so that they know this story is bogus and that we're just friends. I'll make sure they spread the word."

"That's great," and he was too, "but we couldn't even go get pizza together without it making the national news."

"You said you were starting to trust me, right?" When she nodded, he said, "So now how about you let me actually *be* your friend."

She wanted so badly to take everything he was offering at face value, but what if her mother was right? What if all men did was use and lie and hurt?

"Why would you want to do this for me?"

"In the past year, since we found out my mom was sick, it's been…" He swallowed hard and looked away for a moment. "It's been pretty rough." He brought his gaze back to hers and held her spellbound in his green depths. "But when I'm with you, I forget to feel bad."

Everything he said was so sweet, and so heartfelt, that as all her fears temporarily fell away, she couldn't keep from saying, "When I'm with you, I forget about all the craziness, too."

He grinned at her. "Does this mean you're going to let me show you what it's like to be a normal college student?"

Maybe she was being crazy to open herself up to him like this, but her heart was whirling and twirling around inside her chest too fast for her to do anything but smile back at him and say, "Yes."

As they stood there smiling at each other outside the library, amazingly, what she felt between them was as powerful as his kiss had been at the party. Only, this time she wanted to be the one to pull him against her so that she could kiss him.

The thought had barely passed through her brain when his expression suddenly heated and his gaze dropped to her lips. She could almost taste his mouth on hers when he drew back.

"You weren't done in the library, were you?"

Swallowing her disappointment, she said, "Not quite."

"How about I walk you back inside?"

"Okay," she agreed, before she decided to be brave and add, "but only if you'll take me down to the photo archives and show me around first."

When he'd mentioned his interest in the archives to her upstairs, she'd been more than a little surprised— though if anyone should know better than to take someone at face value, it should be her. Sure, Sean Morrison was a sizzling hot baseball player and frat boy. But just because that was all he normally let people see, didn't mean that was all there was to him.

And the truth was she was so drawn to him that when he let her in, even just that little bit, she couldn't help but want to see more of the *real* Sean.

Only, when his eyes immediately filled with grief at the mere mention of the archives, she belatedly realized that she'd pushed in exactly the wrong place. He looked that same way every time he spoke of his mother, and she felt her own heart swell beneath her breastbone in empathy with his pain.

"I'm sorry," she said quickly, desperately wishing she'd never opened her big mouth in the first place. "You don't have to show me anything. I can go take a look by myself some other time."

But instead of agreeing that they should forget all about it, he squeezed her hand tighter and said, "Actually, I want to take you down there."

"Are you sure?"

His eyes met hers, dark and serious and sweet all at the same time. "You're trusting me to give you normal, so I'm going to trust you with this."

Yet again, she felt the intense pull toward him that

had been there right from the very first moment they'd met on the dance floor. It would be the easiest thing in the world to kiss him, but at the same time it wouldn't be right. Not yet. Not when they were still getting to know each other, just starting to trust each other.

He was silent as they began to walk back toward the library and she didn't push him to tell her about the last time he'd been into the archives. Not when it already felt like he'd given her so much of himself just by agreeing to take her there.

How much deeper would he let her go?

As the question bounced around inside her head, she was shocked to realize that she was, for the very first time in her life, actually starting to lower her walls around a guy. The fact that it was coming on the heels of a tabloid story about the two of them...well, maybe that was crazy. But then, so was the fact that she knew she'd pull it up on her phone later, if only to study the pictures of the two of them together more closely.

She needed to know—had he been looking at her only with desire? Or had there been emotion there, too?

The library had been her own special hideout for the past three weeks. But as Sean held the door open for her and they headed back inside together, it felt perfectly natural. Just as it had when he'd interrupted her reading upstairs, like she'd simply been waiting for him to show up.

He spoke softly to the woman behind the desk. A moment later, she was pulling a set of keys out of a drawer and leading them to the elevator.

"We normally ask you to make an appointment to view the archives," the woman told them as they stepped into the elevator, "but it's quiet enough today that I can make an exception. I can spare about twenty minutes right now, but if you'll make an appointment for a future day, you can stay for up to an hour."

For three weeks, Serena had said little more than hello and good-bye to the people who worked at the library because she'd been afraid of saying or doing the wrong thing. But now that it looked like connecting with Sean might not be a mistake, did she really need to be so careful all the time? Besides, how much worse could things get, considering there were already photos circulating of her and Sean?

Granted, she *really* wasn't looking forward to returning her mother's call...but she wouldn't think of that right now, would just shove it down deep where she was used to shoving things she didn't want to face.

"I'm Serena. I should have introduced myself to you earlier."

She was pleased when the woman shook her hand and smiled. "My name is Janice. And it's always nice to see a student who enjoys being in the library as much as I do."

The elevator doors opened and Janice stepped out to unlock the door to the archival rooms. Serena was about to follow her when she realized Sean hadn't yet moved from where he was standing, his eyes clouded as if he were somewhere else entirely.

She put a hand on his arm, gently bringing him back to the present. "We don't have to do this today."

She watched as he forcefully shook away the darkness. "You know how you feel about the Brontë sisters? That's Ansel Adams for me. They have a few of his early Yosemite prints down here. Have you ever seen his work up close?"

"No, only in magazines and coffee-table books."

He put his hand on the small of her back to direct her

toward the photos. "Get ready to experience pure genius."

"These three rooms house the main photo archives," Janice told them. "We are very lucky that the man who started the photography program at the university in the early seventies was not only a friend of Ansel Adams's, but also collected his work from the very beginning. Obviously, please don't touch anything or take any flash photography. I will be in the far room using the computer if you need me to answer any questions during the next twenty minutes."

Serena was immediately drawn to a majestic black-and-white photo of a waterfall cascading over a rocky cliff. She'd spent much of her life with photographers, and had a deep respect for them, but there was no question that these were more than just photos. They were works of art.

"Adams wanted his photographs to feel like watercolor paintings," Sean explained. "He was also passionate about the environment."

"There's so much clarity and depth to his pictures. It's amazing."

"I know," Sean agreed. "He pioneered something called the Zone System. It's why the exposure and contrast are so perfect."

She loved learning new things like this. Ansel Adams had just jumped up her list of people to research while here in the library. But at the same time, she was responding to more than just technique.

"It's almost like his photographs are vibrating with energy," she said, not letting herself overthink everything, even if what she was going to say might sound a little nuts. "I feel like I can hear the sound of the falls crashing just by looking at the picture."

As she spoke, she could feel Sean's gaze on her,

rather than the photograph. He didn't even need to touch her to make her skin feel warm all over.

Finally, he turned back to the photo and said, "That's exactly how his photographs have always made me feel. Six months ago, I stood in Yosemite, right where he did, to try to capture it the way he did." His voice suddenly sounded a little raw again and she sensed his trip to Yosemite had something to do with his mother. "It was a good hiking trip, anyway."

"You love it, don't you?" Knowing that he was going out on a limb by bringing her down here made it easier for her to step out onto one with him, too. "Not just taking pictures, but aiming for something big. Something that will touch people the way his photos do?"

"The last time I was here, I was with my mother. She—" He stopped, his expression full of such grief it broke Serena's heart. "It was right before she was diagnosed. She hadn't been feeling well and had a pretty bad headache that day, but she didn't let it stop her from coming with me. I went to Yosemite for her, to try to take this picture, to try to bring her back here again somehow."

She didn't say anything, couldn't have found the words even if she'd tried. All she could do was reach for his hand and hold tightly to him.

"She asked me to frame one of the shots and hang it on the wall facing her hospital bed. She said it made her feel good, and happy, every time she looked at it."

It wasn't enough anymore just to hold his hand, she needed to put her arms around him, too. But before she could, he took a step back.

"We've only got a few more minutes. I should show you a few other things before we leave."

She knew what he was doing, that he'd gone as deep as he could just now, had shared as much as he was able, and that if he didn't pull back he'd risk breaking apart. Fortunately, though, instead of letting her go completely, he kept holding her hand as he brought her to the other side of the room and shared what he knew about Ansel Adams's other framed photos on the walls.

And as she soaked up his passion and knowledge, she realized that maybe she didn't need to study the pictures of the two of them online to know what he was feeling for her, after all.

Not when the way he was holding her hand told her so much already.

CHAPTER EIGHT

They had just thanked Janice for taking them down to the archives when the alarm on Serena's phone beeped. She couldn't believe she'd almost forgotten about her appointment with her professor. It was just that so much had happened between Friday when she'd left his classroom and this afternoon...all of it centering around Sean Morrison and her growing feelings for him.

"I have to go," she told Sean. "I have a meeting with one of my professors in the English building."

"I've got a class in that direction, too. Mind if I walk with you?"

"That would be great."

As they headed out of the library and toward the English building, her bag across his shoulder along with his own, he said, "Any chance I can convince you to give me your number so that I don't have to hunt you down in the library the next time I want to see you?"

She laughed, loving how he made things so easy when she would only have made it awkward. She told him her number and he typed it into his phone, then called her so that she had his number, too.

"By the way," he said after he'd slipped his phone back into his pocket, "have you ever thought about embracing the digital age and losing some of these hardcovers you carry around all the time? It'll save your back."

"Or yours," she said with a grin, "since you're the one carrying my bag everywhere lately."

"So, what's your meeting about?"

She'd been so nervous about this meeting with her professor, but being with Sean helped keep those nerves at bay. "I'm giving my professor feedback on some new material he's put together for my class on novels. I pored over everything he sent me to look at this weekend and I'm hoping I can deliver whatever it is he's looking for."

"I'm sure you'll do great."

She knew Sean probably didn't want to talk about his mother any more than he already had, but she needed him to know, "The archives were really great. Thank you for taking me down there. I loved learning more about photography." *And about you.*

"Given what you've done your entire life, I can't imagine there's much you don't already know about the subject."

"The pictures people took of me were meant to sell things," she explained. "But what you showed me today—that was magic." She now realized she'd never truly appreciated the magic of photography, not until today, when she didn't have to be or do or act like anything for the pictures. All Sean had wanted her to do was appreciate their beauty.

She could tell from the way he was looking at her that he wanted to ask something more about her comment, but they were already at her professor's door. She knocked, but there was no answer.

"Maybe he forgot about our meeting." Honestly, though it was an amazing opportunity to get to work with Professor Fairworth, she was more relieved than anything. Perhaps he'd changed his mind about working with her and had chosen one of the upperclassmen instead?

"Serena." Her relief was short-lived as she turned to see the professor walking toward them. "My last class ran long. I apologize for keeping you waiting."

She was surprised when Sean stiffened beside her as the other man approached. "Professor Fairworth, this is my friend Sean Morrison."

"Yes," the older man said as they shook hands, "the brilliant first baseman. And your hitting has been off the charts, too. I thought last year might have been your last playing for us."

Everything he said was complimentary, yet Serena couldn't help but feel that he didn't particularly care to see Sean with her.

"There were a lot of reasons to stay," Sean told him.

Professor Fairworth opened up his office door and when Sean took a look inside the room with the small leather couch and one tiny window, he turned to Serena and said in a low voice, "I'd be happy to stick around until you're done."

Incredibly tempted, she made herself shake her head. "Thanks, but you've got a class to go to, and I don't know how long we're going to be."

While her professor was booting up his computer, Sean leaned even closer and said, "Call me if you need me."

Could he see how much she did? And not just because her professor gave her the creeps?

With obvious reluctance, he put her bag down on the couch. She hadn't been able to give in to kissing him outside the library, but now she had to press a kiss to his cheek in a silent *thank you.*

As soon as the door closed behind Sean, her professor said, "Your boyfriend is very protective of you, isn't he?"

"He—" She stopped herself a beat before she could deny that she and Sean were dating. Because if her professor was actually having creepy thoughts about her, might it help for him to think she was already taken? Besides, the whole world already thought she and Sean were an item based on the tabloid story. "He's great."

An expression she couldn't quite read flashed across her professor's face. But then, amazingly, for the next hour that they reviewed the proposed class notes he'd sent her, he remained perfectly professional. So much so that she found herself wondering if she had, in fact, manufactured his predatory interest in her in her head simply because her mother had trained her to look for the bad in every man.

Or...could it be that seeing her with Sean had deterred Professor Fairworth from trying something?

Either way, despite the tabloid pictures and knowing her day wouldn't end until she'd dealt with her mother, Sean had turned what might have been a really terrible day into one that was at least a thousand times better just for getting to see him smile and hold her hand.

* * *

Serena got to the dining hall right before they closed for the night. She'd been so busy with her two back-to-back late afternoon classes that she'd forgotten about the tabloid story, but when the guy at the cash register looked at her a little funny as he scanned her meal card—as if he now knew *precisely* how easy she was since she was spreading it for a horny baseball player—it came crashing back to her.

Where other freshmen could have a crush that only their close friends knew about, her crush on Sean was a wide-open target for the whole world to gossip about. But as she carried her tray over to one of the dining tables, she knew it was a battle she needed to stop trying to fight because she would never, ever win it. All she'd do was keep frustrating herself.

"Who cares what everybody thinks?"

Sean's voice echoed in her head as she began to cut the rubbery piece of chicken on her plate. And he was right—coming to Stanford had been a step in the right direction, but she needed to stop worrying and truly start living her life and following her dreams.

At the same time, after all the years she'd spent trying to be perfect for agents and photographers and fashion designers and her mother, she wasn't foolish enough to think that she could just shake off the weight of everyone's expectations in one night. Change—real change—took time. Maybe, she thought for the first time, she needed to give herself some room, some space, a little leeway, to make those changes. Not all at once, perhaps, but as she felt ready to tackle them one at a time.

By the time she got back to her room, Abi was sitting with her feet up on her desk, slicking on a layer of bright blue nail polish. "Hey, I'm glad you're back earlier than usual! Guess you didn't get my text about grabbing dinner together tonight?"

Serena shook her head. "Sorry, my phone is buried somewhere at the bottom of my bag and I didn't hear it going off." She'd left it there on purpose because she wasn't yet ready to deal with listening to her mother's message. Or messages, as the case probably was all these hours later. "Is something wrong?"

Abi put down the nail polish and turned to face Serena with a clearly concerned look on her face. "I was kind of worried about you."

"You were?"

"I know we haven't gotten to know each other that well yet—" Abi looked a little uncertain. "—but when I saw those pictures of you and your walking orgasm of a boyfriend online today, I realized I should have thought more about how hard it must be for you to deal with that kind of stuff all the time. It's just that I've never known anyone famous like you before. I guess I've kind of been afraid to say the wrong thing."

Serena was floored by what Abi had just said. Plus, she knew she was doing a terrible job of trying to hide her flushed cheeks at her roommate's "walking orgasm" comment. Especially when the vision of Sean kissing her came so suddenly—and so clearly—that she didn't have a prayer of containing her reaction to it.

"Sean and I, we're just friends," she tried to clarified.

But Abi reminded her, "I saw you two kissing at the frat party. It was *hot.* And FYI, I have no problem if he wants to stay the night with you in here."

"Don't worry," she told Abi, "he won't be staying over here." In fact, she was sure her roommate would be shocked if she knew just how *far* they were from sleeping together, considering she wouldn't even let him kiss her again.

Feeling awkward, she said, "I know it's not the easiest thing in the world rooming with me. And you haven't said anything even remotely wrong to me."

"But I might have thought it…because I kind of hated you at first for being so much prettier than me," Abi admitted.

"I'm not prettier than you," Serena said earnestly. She'd never be the all-American beauty that her roommate was. "And you're so much fun. Everybody likes you."

Abi smiled at her, obviously thrilled by the compliments. But then she asked again, "Are you okay? You know, about that story that came out today?"

Serena had risked being open with Sean and so far he'd proven to be a really amazing guy. What if Abi turned out to be just as great? Could the two of them become friends? Real friends instead of just roommates who did their best to stay out of each other's way?

Taking a deep breath, Serena admitted, "Showing up in those pictures with Sean...well, it wasn't the best thing that ever happened."

"Why, was he mad that you guys had been outed?"

"No." He'd only been worried about her, and how she'd react to the story and pictures. He hadn't, she now realized, seemed to give one thought to how the article would impact him. "I think it's more that if Sean and I were starting something, we would both want it to be just between us."

But Abi was shaking her head. "I know it's on a larger scale because you're famous, but even if you weren't, it would still be a *really* big deal if people thought you were dating him. Sean Morrison is pretty much the hottest thing at Stanford, so people would still be talking, probably as much as they are now."

Serena hadn't thought about it that way. And, surprisingly, it made her feel better rather than worse about everything. "Thanks, that helps actually."

"No problem. And, hey, anytime you want to talk or hang out, even if you seem *way* too into your classes," Abi said with a grin, "I'm around. Who knows, maybe I should even tag along with you to the library so my parents don't end up killing me over my grades."

"I'd love that," Serena said, meaning it wholeheartedly.

But though Serena really wanted to end the day on this high note, she still had one more thing to deal with. The hardest thing of all...

CHAPTER NINE

Serena knew her mother's routine down to the tiniest detail. By eight p.m., if they weren't at an industry event, Genevieve would have poured herself a glass of wine. By eight thirty, the bottle would be half empty and she'd take the rest of it with her to the bathtub, where she'd relax and finish her final glasses. By nine fifteen she'd be beneath the covers snoring with her eye mask on and her earplugs in. Serena was always supposed to be asleep by nine, too, so that she didn't wake up for early calls with dark circles under her eyes. But once she got old enough to realize that her mother never stirred once she passed out from the combination of alcohol and hot bath, she'd only pretend to go to sleep before staying up reading under the covers. Or, as the case had been this past fall, filling out college applications.

Grabbing her phone, she left her room and headed down the hall to find a private spot outside in the middle of the deserted parking lot to listen to her mother's message and then finally call her back.

But when she finally looked at the screen, she was surprised to see a text from Sean. She smiled as she ran her fingertip over the screen, wishing she could actually touch him by doing so.

HOW'D YOUR MEETING GO?

She knew he'd been worried about her when he'd left her with Professor Fairworth, probably because she'd clearly been freaked out about being alone with him in his small office. Thankfully, it looked like it had been another situation she'd read wrong.

GOOD

She paused, tried to think of something fun or flirty she could add.

HOW WERE YOUR CLASSES?

She groaned the second she sent her text. Seriously, she didn't have the first clue how to flirt. Abi probably could blow a guy's mind in five words, no problem. Maybe she should ask her roommate for lessons?

LONG ENOUGH FOR ME TO PLAN OUR FIRST OFFICIAL "NORMAL" OUTING

Their *first* official normal outing? Did that mean he wanted there to be others?

Suddenly, she remembered what Abi had said about Sean being the hottest guy in school, the one everyone wanted. Why, she had to ask herself again, would he want to be with a girl who was awkward and studious, not to mention a total pain in the butt to hang out with when cameramen tended to follow her every move?

But before she could text back to let him off the hook, he wrote:

NOT GOING TO TELL YOU WHAT WE'RE DOING, BUT DON'T THINK I'M LETTING YOU OUT OF IT

Her smile was so big it almost hurt her cheeks as she texted him back.

VERY MYSTERIOUS

And sweet, too. If the rest of the girls on campus knew that Sean Morrison wasn't just gorgeous, but nice, as well, they'd never leave him alone. Jealousy rose swift and hot at the thought of anyone else with him, even though he wasn't hers.

Not yet, anyway. Because she kept pushing him away.

But what if she stopped doing that?

What if she pulled him closer, instead?

FRIDAY NIGHT AROUND 5?

After she quickly texted back to let him know that time would work, he sent one more.

I'LL PICK YOU UP AT THE LIBRARY

Her laughter rang through the parking lot at how well he knew her already, that she was likely one of the only students on campus who would choose studying in the library over hanging out and listening to a band play outside on a sunny Friday afternoon.

And just as he'd made her forget her nerves about going into her meeting with her professor, she now felt much less tense when she finally pressed the play button on her mother's voice mail. After all, everything else that had been worrying her today had ended up going so much better than she expected. Maybe her mother's phone call would, too. In fact, maybe Genevieve had finally realized during the past three weeks in which she hadn't responded to any of Serena's phone calls or emails that she wasn't trying to hurt her or rebel. She was just trying to live her own dreams.

Of course, as soon as she heard her mother's voice, she realized just how stupidly hopeful she'd been. Because Genevieve Britten was very upset with Serena. Very, very, very upset.

"How could you?"

Her entire message was those three little words. But she'd managed to convey every last nuance of how she felt with them.

With a shaking hand, Serena dialed her mother's number, and it wasn't until voice mail picked up that she was able to unclench her teeth and take in a full breath.

"Hi, it's me. Sorry I didn't call you back earlier, but I was in the library and then in a meeting with a professor and classes until now."

She tried to make her voice sound relaxed, but not like she was actually having fun at college. *Especially* not having fun with a boy in his bed, since she knew from her mother's message that was where Genevieve's brain had immediately gone. Likely it had been a two-bottle night.

"I was just as surprised as you were to see those paparazzi pictures, but I swear it's not what it looked like. I promise you that he's just a friend and we were just grabbing a bite to eat."

She didn't bother trying to deny the fact that she and
Sean had been eating pizza and drinking Coke, not when
her mother had surely already cataloged every sin in the
pictures, including the dumpy clothes and baseball cap
Serena had been wearing.

Hoping that short and sweet was better just in case
she accidentally said too much, or ended up sounding too
guilty, she closed with, "Everything's fine here and I'll
keep sending you emails about my classes and what I'm
learning."

Serena wrote Genevieve a long email every week
about her classes, and even though her mother hadn't
responded to any of them, she hoped she was at least
starting to realize that Serena was serious about staying in
school. And that she loved what she was learning.

Hope was a funny thing. Because even after she'd
spent nineteen years with her mother acting in one
specific way—namely, putting Serena's career before
absolutely everything else, including the true happiness of
either of them—she still kept wishing things could be
different.

And that maybe one day, if she could just find the
right way to frame things, her mother might actually see
the real *her*.

CHAPTER TEN

Sean kept looking at his phone, the first time he'd ever waited for a girl to text him back, but Serena was obviously done sending him messages for the night. At least it had ended on the victory of her agreeing to go out with him on Friday. Especially after the crazy day it had been.

Blindsided by seeing his pictures—and partial life story—online. Trying his best to talk Serena off the ledge about it. Forcing himself to leave her alone with a drooling professor that he didn't trust as far as he could throw the guy. Then dealing with his team at practice— and his brothers in his frat house—all wanting to know what was up with him and Serena.

That, at least, had been easy. He'd warned them to watch their mouths because Serena was special.

So special that he'd actually taken her into the archives and talked to her about photography. She'd gotten it, too, not just the brilliant technique in the photos, but the passion behind them.

Just the way, he couldn't stop thinking, she seemed to get him.

There weren't a lot of people outside his family who knew he was into photography. And it sure as hell had never come up with any of the other girls he'd been with.

But ever since this afternoon, he'd found himself looking at things differently, as though through the lens of his camera, studying and framing the world the way he always used to. Before his mom died.

He hadn't purposely blocked the camera lens in his brain, hadn't made a conscious decision to never take another picture. It had happened all on its own. Every day that she'd gotten closer to going, it had been harder and harder for him to take pictures to bring back to her hospital room to show to her. And still, he'd known he wasn't hiding anything from his mom, that she could see just how hard it was for him to find the beauty in everything for her. He'd just kept digging as deep, as far down, as he could up until that final day.

The day when he'd stopped being able to see the beauty in anything.

From that day forward, he'd only been looking for *numb.* And for the past three months, that was all he'd gone for to replace *grief.*

Until Serena had appeared, like a beautiful angel, before him.

He'd thought his love for photography had died when his mother had, had known he couldn't possibly take another picture without being able to show it to her. But now, suddenly, he found himself wondering, could he do it again? Could he take a picture one day and not feel only the pain, the helplessness, of watching his mom slip away? Because just as he'd been overwhelmed by the urge to capture Serena's beauty on film in the library with the sunlight shining down on her, the same intense yearning had come over him again in the photo archives when she'd been studying Ansel Adams's photo, *Bridalveil Fall*.

The knock came at his door a beat before he heard a female voice say, "Sean? Are you in there?"

Olivia? What was his sister doing here?

Of course, it wasn't hard to guess that she must have seen the magazine. His little sister, Maddie, had been the first to text him to ask if he really was dating Serena Britten and to find out if she was as pretty in person as she was in magazines. He'd given her both answers, first that he was trying to convince Serena to date him—and also that she was a thousand times more beautiful in person. His two older brothers were likely too busy taking over the business and rock 'n' roll worlds to have seen the story yet, and no doubt his twin had been locked inside a lab all day and hadn't even seen the sunlight, let alone some paparazzi pictures.

But Olivia...she noticed everything. Worried about it all, too. And if his fastidious sister was willing to pick her way through empty beer bottles and smelly frat guys to come and see him, that meant she was *really* worried.

He opened the door. "Welcome."

"I really don't know how you can stand to live in a place like this," she murmured as she walked into his room. Never one to waste time getting to the point, she sat down on the edge of his bed and pulled out her phone to show him the story he'd already seen too many times today. "A friend of mine showed this to me tonight at dinner. And since I can see that you're not surprised, I take it you've already seen it."

He sat in the chair behind his desk and swiveled it to face Olivia. His room was one of the biggest in the frat house—and one of the only ones that came with its own bathroom and shower—but with his sister's concern sucking up all the oxygen in the room, it suddenly felt way too small.

"A good dozen times."

"I thought Drew was the only one we were going to see in things like this—at least, until you went pro."

Sean instantly tensed up at the assumption that he was definitely going to play pro baseball. He was used to strangers bringing it up, but a part of him wished his sister knew him better...even though he hadn't actually said or done much to make her think he might want to pursue a different path in life.

"Is it true? Are you dating the supermodel?"

Olivia only had his best interests at heart, but he still didn't like the way she'd boiled Serena down to *the supermodel.* "Her name is Serena." He forced his frustration back, knowing none of this was his sister's fault. "No, we're not dating." Not yet, anyway. "But we're friends."

"Really? You're not dating?" She looked down at the pictures, seeing what everyone else must have—a guy and a girl on the verge of a kiss, both of whom were dying for it. "Because you two look pretty close for just being friends."

"Look, just because we're not dating yet doesn't mean I don't wish we were. She's pretty skittish about getting involved with anyone."

"Well, I'd say you're both pretty darn involved now, whether you want to be or not." She pinned him with her clear blue gaze, so much like his mother's that it shook him. "I don't want you to get hurt, Sean." Of his five siblings, Olivia had always been the caretaker. If his parents weren't around, she was the one who'd pull out the first aid kit and make them hold still while she cleaned their playground cuts.

Giving his head a shake so that he was seeing Olivia sitting on his bed instead of a ghost, he said, "You don't have to worry about me, sis."

"You really like this one, don't you?" At his look, she amended *this one* to, "Serena."

"Serena is different. You'd like her." He could so easily see Serena and Olivia hanging out, talking books. "You'd like her a lot, actually."

"Are you sure you don't just think she's great because she's so pretty? I mean, even another girl like me can see how beauty like hers could blind someone to anything bad she might be hiding."

There was no question in Sean's mind that Serena was hiding things. Things he hoped she'd eventually trust him enough to share. Like why she'd really given up her old life. Why she'd looked so sad when her mother had called that afternoon. Why she hadn't told her lecherous professor where to stick it when he looked at her so inappropriately, like he wanted to devour her.

And why she was so afraid to let Sean kiss her again.

But whatever her secrets—and her reasons for keeping them—he already knew for sure that she wasn't a bad person.

Not bothering to weigh his words first, he flat-out told his sister, "She's just as beautiful on the inside, Olivia."

His sister's eyebrows went up as she stared at him in stunned silence for several long moments. "In that case, what are you going to do when she leaves?"

Even the question had his gut clenching tight. "She isn't going to leave." Easily able to read his sister's disbelieving look, he said, "I've never seen anyone as serious as she is about school. Not even Justin." And he thought he knew why. It wasn't that his twin was any less interested in the intellectual stimulation, it was that he'd never had to fight for it. It was basic human nature that people valued the things they couldn't easily have, that they had to work for, more. "Serena wants to be here more than you or I could ever understand."

"It's hard for me to believe anyone in her position would feel that way, but since you know her and I don't, I can only take your word for it. But the thing is, even if she wants to be here, someone like Serena Britten..." She paused, clearly hesitant to say something that would upset him. "I can't help but think that she's too famous, too necessary a player in the world she came from for everyone not to need her back for their ad campaigns, or fashion shows, or catalogs, or music videos, or movies."

He was surprised to realize just how much his sister knew about Serena. He'd thought Maddie was the only one in his family who read the kind of magazines his picture had been in today, but now he wondered if his more serious sister had secretly been reading them, too.

"Because," Olivia continued, "even if she doesn't want to go back, even if she wants to stay here to learn and even date you when you get your way like you always do," she added with a small smile, "what if something comes up that she can't say no to?"

For all that his sister had said so far tonight, it was what she didn't say that was clearest of all: She was worried that if he actually went and fell in love with Serena and then she left him...wanting to be *numb* would only be the tip of the iceberg for him. Because obviously, over the past months, Olivia had noticed his drinking. His partying. And she was clearly worried that if things didn't work out with Serena, he'd take things even further. Even darker.

Forcing away the thought that his sister might be

right about the risk of falling for Serena, he said, "How about you wait until I convince her to actually call what we're doing this Friday night a date before you go all worst-case-scenario on me?"

"Mom would—"

"Have wanted to meet Serena before she made any decisions about her."

Olivia finally stopped protesting. "You're right, she would have."

And he was also right that it was becoming increasingly difficult for his sister to try to fill their mom's shoes. Olivia was awesome. But no one could be Lisa Morrison.

He could also see that while his sister clearly didn't like his determination to continue moving things forward with Serena, she also knew when it was pointless to try to hold him back.

"So, when will I get to meet her? When will all of us get to meet her?"

"Hopefully soon. Actually, since you're here, I've got a question for you. Ever played Frisbee Golf on the campus course?"

She looked at him like he was insane. "No. I didn't even know it was still there. I mean, who actually *plays* Frisbee Golf anymore? Even in the seventies people could barely bring themselves to play it."

He grinned. "Something tells me the sport is about to make a comeback."

"You're weird," she said, but she was grinning as she stood up to leave, and he was glad to see his sister smile again. The first one he'd seen on her face in far too long.

CHAPTER ELEVEN

Sean didn't believe in picking a girl up late for a date, but he'd never been fifteen minutes early, either. Still, something told him Serena probably wouldn't mind if he came up to her spot on the third floor of the library a little ahead of schedule. At least, he hoped she wouldn't, and that she'd lost at least some of her well-honed concentration to thinking about him. Because Lord knew he'd lost plenty this week thinking about her.

"Hi, Janice. How's your week been?"

The woman behind the information desk smiled. "Good. Are you here to book more time in the archives?"

He started to shake his head, when he realized it was one hurdle he didn't have to worry about jumping again. All because of Serena. And though he probably wouldn't be picking up a camera any time soon, that didn't mean he couldn't at least enjoy looking at some of the best photographs in the world.

"I came to pick up Serena, but booking more time is a great idea."

After they'd arranged for an hour midweek when she would be personally available to bring out some of the hidden gems people rarely got a chance to see, he jogged up the stairs. The second he saw the top of Serena's baseball cap, he smiled.

The library was the last place in the world that should have been romantic, or felt special. But when he looked at her, he realized it was both. Even better, late on a Friday afternoon, no one else was around and it felt like it was all theirs.

"Hey, beautiful."

She jumped slightly in her seat, the way she had before when he'd surprised her reading with her headphones on. Next time he'd have to figure out a better way to get her attention.

"Hi. I set my alarm to go wait for you downstairs, but I guess I didn't hear it go off."

"I'm early." If he'd been smart, he would have taken the extra fifteen minutes and just stared at her from a distance to try to get his fill of her beauty. "Do you need to finish up?"

"No." She closed her book. "I've kind of had a hard time concentrating this afternoon." Her cheeks flushed at the admission. "I couldn't stop wondering what you had planned for us."

He reached out to tilt up the brim of her baseball cap so that he could better see her face. "You'll never guess, so you shouldn't even bother trying." When she looked a little worried, he added, "But I'm pretty sure you're going to have fun."

Her face was such an open book—happy to see him one minute, a little worried the next, and then trying to trust him when he asked her to. How the hell he was going to keep from kissing her today, he didn't have a freaking clue.

All he knew was that the next time they kissed had to

be because *she* wanted it, not because he couldn't keep from reaching for her again and crashing his lips against hers.

When he picked up her bag, he was surprised by how light it was. "Finally given up carrying around bricks all day?"

She laughed. "I might have bought a couple of ebooks this week. Just to try them out, mind you."

As they headed downstairs, it would have been perfectly natural to take her hand. But at the last second, he stopped himself. They hadn't talked boundaries, hadn't discussed public perception, hadn't yet worked their way around to whether this was really a date or just two friends hanging out. For the first time, he understood what it must have been like for the girls he'd been with over the years, not knowing where they stood with him. No doubt they'd all love to see the tables turned on him now.

But since he'd been worrying all week about the way her professor had been looking at her before her meeting with him, first he had to ask, "How'd the rest of your week go? I kind of got a weird vibe from that English professor."

She shot him a slightly surprised look before saying, "I felt the same way at first, but, actually, this week has been totally fine. And I guess he already got what he wanted out of our meeting on Monday, because he hasn't set up another one since then."

Serena didn't say that she was relieved, but he could hear it in her voice. And she wasn't the only one. All week, he'd had ugly visions of what that professor probably dreamed of doing to his supermodel student. Now, thankfully, it looked like Sean didn't have to worry about it anymore, since the guy had decided to back off. Had him showing up with Serena at his office and her kissing him on the cheek played a part in the professor's sudden about-face?

"And has anyone on campus given you grief over the story about us?"

"Well, since no one knew it was all made up, I'm pretty sure all the other girls on campus aren't too happy about me stealing the most wanted guy at Stanford." She wasn't saying it to flirt with him, he realized, she was simply telling him how the week had gone for her. "But apart from that, I'm already such a freak that, honestly, I don't think anyone really blinked an eye over it."

"You're not a freak."

"When I was five years old and in kindergarten, I was already taller than the third-grade boys."

"Okay," he said in a teasing voice, "maybe that *is* a little freaky."

He was glad when a surprised laugh bubbled out from her lips. "How tall are you?"

"Six-four."

"I actually have to tilt my head to look up at you. That hardly ever happens."

They were, he already knew, a perfect fit...and again, that urge to thread his fingers through her silky hair and drag her into him for a kiss almost overpowered his better sense.

"What about you? I know it must have been weird for you to find pictures of yourself online like that. I was so shell-shocked by it on Monday that I didn't think to check in about how you were doing until you were already gone, and I didn't want to bug you with texts."

He could feel an apology coming on, but since none of it was her fault, he cut her off at the pass. "First, you should text me whenever you feel like it. And, honestly, it wasn't that big a deal. Except for having to tell people that we weren't actually dating. That sucked."

"It did?"

Seriously, did she not have any sense at all of just how amazing she was? Not just beautiful, but easy to be with, and so warm, that she'd actually managed to melt some of the ice that had frozen his heart this year.

"Big time. But if you'll agree that tonight is a date and not just two buddies hanging out, that might help me get over it."

When she didn't say anything back, or give even the slightest hint of a smile, he knew he was moving too fast again. Hell, hadn't she already told him a half-dozen times that she wasn't here to date? Why didn't he actually *listen* for once?

On a low curse, he said, "I know I've got to stop trying to push you like that."

"No," she said softly, "it's actually really nice, the way you keep asking me out. It's just..." She flushed. "I can't believe I'm about to tell you this, because then you'll know *exactly* how much of a freak I really am, but I haven't exactly been out on a lot of dates."

"First of all, stop calling yourself a freak. It's really starting to piss me off. And second, guys must have been falling all over you for years, so I don't get how you not dating is even possible."

"I've always worked a lot," she explained. "And I haven't been to a normal school since I was a really little kid. This is the first time in my life that my mother hasn't been with me pretty much all the time."

He frowned. "She couldn't have been with you every second of every day."

"She was extremely protective. And—" She scrunched up her face as if she was embarrassed. "—I never really tried that hard to push the boundaries with her. Not until I decided to give up my career to go to school." She took a deep breath and turned to face him, brave and beautiful. "Ask me again, Sean."

The late afternoon sun was at her back and she was so radiant that for a few seconds, he almost couldn't remember how to form words. He didn't have his camera with him, but that didn't stop him from taking a picture in his head.

"Will you go on a date with me tonight?"

"I'd love to."

* * *

Fifteen minutes later, Sean led them into the middle of a field. "We're here. Welcome to your first official *normal* college student experience."

The green sign in front of them was faded enough that Serena had to step close to it and squint to make out the words. "Stanford University Frisbee Golf Course." She looked from the sign to Sean. "*This* is what normal college students do on a Friday night?"

"According to my parents—" When he paused, she watched him fight back the wave of grief that tried to get in as he pasted a grin on his lips. "Frisbee Golf used to be really cool back in the day."

"Which day was that, exactly?"

They both laughed, and she was glad to note that it sounded less and less rusty every time he did. Sean Morrison had been born to smile and laugh. But he clearly hadn't done it nearly enough lately, and it broke her heart. Especially when he'd obviously worked so hard to think of something "normal" that they could do in a totally off-the-grid setting where they wouldn't have to deal with people looking at them or taking more pictures.

Because she was pretty darn sure that they were

going to be the only two people out on this Frisbee Golf course tonight...

He walked toward an oak tree and pulled out two Frisbees from behind it, one red, one blue. He presented the red one to her as if it were a rose. "The rules are the same as regular or miniature golf. A stroke is counted every time the Frisbee is thrown and we stop counting once we make it in. We don't have to keep score if you don't want to."

"You're not the only competitive one," she told him, even though she'd never thrown a Frisbee in her life. How hard could it be? "Why don't you show me how it's done?"

His stance was at once precise and effortless, and when he let the Frisbee go, it sailed through the air with a little whistle then landed smack dab in the middle of the faded blue metal basket around the silver pole.

She couldn't stop smiling as she looked at him, and it wasn't just because he was breathtakingly handsome in his jeans and T-shirt. Seeing how pleased he was at getting a hole in one was super cute, too, and she could easily see him as a little boy with his parents as they showed him how to play this strange game.

A little cocky now—with a blush, she imagined several other things he probably had to feel cocky about, all of which she was suddenly longing to experience—he grinned at her and said, "Your turn."

She stepped up to the marker he'd dropped on the grass, turned slightly to the left, put her weight on her right leg, pulled the Frisbee back toward her chest, and let it rip.

Straight into the tree a good ten feet to the right of the basket.

She could hear him trying to muffle his laughter as

she headed over to the tree to pick it up.

"Did it slip at the last second?"

She could barely keep her own laughter at bay as she said, "What do you think?"

But they were both laughing by the time he said, "Why don't you try again? Hold up a sec, though, so I can get out of your way first." He moved halfway behind another tree. "Go for it."

Again, she tried to copy what she'd watched him do. This time, it went better, landing on the grass only five feet away from the basket without hitting any trees or bushes.

"I have an idea," he said as she picked it up a second time. "Since you've obviously never thrown a Frisbee before—" He ignored her faux scowl even as a grin continued to play around the edges of his mouth. "—maybe it will be easier if I help you get a sense of what it should feel like."

Stepping behind her, he put his arms around her and reached for her hands. "Is this okay?"

Instantly consumed with the delicious heat of his body against hers, and how good he smelled, all she could manage was a quick nod.

He had her shift her hips slightly to the left, then used his right foot to scoot hers up on the grass. "It should be an effortless glide of your arm from here—" He brought their right hands back toward her chest, careful not to touch her inappropriately in any way. "—to here."

She felt the muscles of his forearm and bicep ripple against hers as he moved their arms back out, both of them still holding on to the Frisbee.

"And don't forget," he said, his breath dancing across her earlobe so that she had to work really hard to fight back a shiver of need, "this is supposed to be fun. Keep breathing and relax your muscles."

She had learned at a young age how to make her too-long arms and legs move in a seemingly effortlessly coordinated manner as she walked down a runway. But it was one thing to do that around a bunch of other women and gay men with cameras. It was another entirely to do it around a ridiculously hot guy who sent her system into such disarray that she could hardly remember her name.

"Ready to give it another try?"

Actually, she was mostly fighting the urge to spin around in his arms, drop the Frisbee, and lace her fingers through his hair so that she could drag his mouth down to hers for another one of the kisses she hadn't been able to stop thinking about. But she forced herself to follow his lead, instead, and together they threw the Frisbee.

It landed right in the middle of the basket.

"Good job."

His arms were still around her as she laughed, and this time she couldn't stop herself from turning to face him, her hands pressed flat to his chest between them, his heart beating steady and strong against her palms. "You did all the work, you know."

"It was both of us."

She was tall enough that his mouth was right in front of hers when she tilted up her face to look at him. She could feel her breath coming faster and his heartbeat picking up against her hands. "Maybe I should try one by myself this time."

"Maybe." His gaze dropped from her eyes to her mouth. "Or maybe you should kiss me."

CHAPTER TWELVE

Serena surprised them both by not hesitating at all before she softly pressed her lips against his. Heat instantly enveloped her, both from his hands tightening on her waist and the sparks that shot from just one sweet kiss. She hadn't forgotten the pleasure of being in his arms at the frat party. And still, she was stunned by the intensity of her attraction to him.

"Again."

His request was deep and hungry. And it was her own hunger for him—and pure feminine instinct—that sent her hands up from his chest to twine around his neck. Her mouth had barely touched his again when his lips came crashing down onto hers.

His groan, her gasp, they were both one hundred percent pleasure at a kiss that was at once rough yet sweet, possessive yet gentle. And when he moved one hand from her waist up to cradle her cheek, she felt warm and cherished as he slowly angled her jaw so that he could take the kiss deeper.

His tongue slicked out across her lower lip, leaving a sensual path of fire in its wake. One that could only be quenched by another taste, and then when that wasn't enough, the slow slide of his tongue against hers.

Desire crashed into her just as his mouth had, exploding at the tips of her breasts and the vee between her legs. She felt hot, desperate, achy.

Wanted.

But she'd been her mother's daughter for too many years to be able to sink into passion without worrying about consequences. She'd been taught her entire life that all men were evil and only wanted one thing. The very same thing she suddenly realized she *desperately* wanted herself.

Overwhelmed by it all—by so much heat and desire and *need* that every last part of her felt swamped by it—she abruptly pulled away.

"Serena?" She was surprised to see that he looked as overwhelmed as she did. "Are you okay?"

She put her hand over her racing heart as if to try to slow it, and to keep from reaching for him again. "Every time you kiss me, I..."

She loved words, but right then she couldn't find any of the right ones to explain what his kisses did to her. Not when she was only beginning to understand just what a truly powerful force desire could be.

But Sean didn't seem to need her to finish her sentence. "I know. When you kiss me, it's like that for me, too."

If he had reached for her again just then, the truth was that being overwhelmed or confused couldn't have stopped her from letting him take her into not only another kiss, but more. So much more.

Anything he wanted...because in that moment she would want it, too.

Instead, with what looked like major reluctance on

his part, he walked away from her. It took her a few long moments to realize that he was grabbing her Frisbee from the basket.

"Ready to try again?"

She took the red plastic disk from him, working to keep her hand steady. "Sure." Her voice was still too breathy, her lips still tingling. But now that he'd made an effort to give them some space, she needed to make an effort, too, to keep enough distance between them that she could figure out what she was, and wasn't, ready for.

She knew how to throw the Frisbee now, remembered precisely how he'd moved her hips and feet and arms a few minutes earlier. Focusing every ounce of her attention on the basket across the field, she drew her arm back and was about to it fly when a bee suddenly buzzed against her nose.

Giving a small scream as she jumped back so that it wouldn't sting her, she couldn't quite keep her grip on the Frisbee before it went sliding out of her fingers.

Straight toward Sean.

"Look o—" Her warning dried up in her throat as the Frisbee slammed into the center of his forehead.

She ran over to where he was lying on the ground with his hand over his forehead and got down on her knees beside him. "Oh my God, are you okay?" When he didn't say anything, just groaned, she tried to explain, "I'm so sorry, I didn't mean to hurt you. There was this bee and I was about to throw the Frisbee and the next thing I knew it was flying in the wrong direction."

"Nice velocity."

For a moment, she was sure she must have heard his half-spoken, half-moaned words wrong. He couldn't have just complimented her on her throwing, could he? Especially not after she'd just felled him.

"It was an accident, I swear. I'm so, so sorry!"

He uncovered his eyes, and she was horrified by the red bump starting to grow on his forehead as he reached up to wind a lock of her hair around his fingers. "I know it was an accident. And I've been hit by plenty of harder things on the baseball field and lived to see another day. But none of the guys throwing those things at me were as pretty as you. Or had hair quite this silky."

Though her heart was still racing from the thought that she'd hurt him, he always knew how to make her smile. "But almost as silky?" she teased. When he laughed, rather than groaning again, she said, "Let me help you up."

"Probably best if I lie here for a little while longer."

The next thing she knew, he was tugging her down to lie next to him on the grass...and he didn't let her hand go the entire time that they lay watching the puffy clouds transform from one shape to another in the slowly darkening sky.

* * *

"So," Sean said as they were heading away from the field, "when are you free for our next normal date?"

They'd continued playing until the sun had set. At the middle basket, he'd pulled some cheese and crackers and salami and sparkling water out of his bag. They'd sat with their backs against a tree to have a really nice alfresco meal before making their way through the course. Surprisingly, after her terrible beginning she'd actually started to get pretty good at the game. And, not nearly as surprising, she'd really enjoyed spending time with him, especially when he told stories about his brothers and sisters and growing up in the Bay Area. She'd even told him some funny things that had happened during her years of modeling.

Though it was dark now, there were enough lights on campus for her to clearly see the bump on his forehead. It hadn't gotten much bigger, but it hadn't gone away, either.

"Are you sure you want to risk potential injury again?"

"One day when we're old and gray," he said with a grin, "it will be the perfect first date story."

How did he do that? By now, she expected him to steal her breath away with his kisses. But he'd just done it with one simple, beautiful sentence.

In that moment, she realized just how easy it could be to do exactly what her mother had warned her about: give up everything for a guy, forget all about why she was really here, forget that she was still on probation and needed to get great grades. She didn't want to wait one more day to spend time with him again, to laugh and play and kiss. Heck, she didn't even want to say good night to him in a few minutes when they got back to her dorm...not when it would be the easiest thing in the world to let him take her back to his place so that she could spend the entire night in his arms. A night that she knew wouldn't stop with just kisses, either.

Which was why she made herself say, "Next Friday."

It seemed to take him a few moments to realize what she'd said, as if he'd been lost in exactly the same fantasy of tangled limbs and desperate kisses.

"You want to wait a whole week to see each other again?"

God, no, she didn't *want* that. But she needed to be smart about this. As smart as she could be, anyway, with the limited number of brain cells and synapses that she could actually get to fire when he was standing this close to her.

"You're busy with your team and classes and your family."

"I can figure out how to juggle all those things and you, too, Serena."

"But I don't know if I can." She put her hand on his arm to try to take the sting out of putting on the brakes. "You know how I told you I didn't get a chance to go to school much as a kid? Well, that meant I didn't have a normal transcript with the same tests and grades as everybody else. Honestly, I was shocked when I found out Stanford had accepted me on the strength of just a few tests and essays, but the thing is, it's only a probationary acceptance. Whether or not I get to stay here for the next three and a half years depends on how I do this quarter. I've got to nail every single class."

He slid his hand over hers. "You will."

"I really hope so. This has been my dream my entire life."

"I know you love learning," he said as he reached up to play with a lock of her hair the same way he had on the Frisbee Golf course. "And now that you've told me this, I understand that you've got even more pressure than the rest of us to excel. But—" He tucked the lock of hair behind her ear, then moved to stroke her lower lip with the pad of his thumb. "—I also know that you're brilliant enough to succeed at whatever you choose to do. And that this is your way to keep me from moving too fast with you."

"Sean—"

He pressed his thumb over her lips to quiet her. "And you're right. Because even knowing you need to go slow, I want to push you fast. So damned fast." He lowered his gaze to her lips and she shivered with need. "I want to kiss you for hours and hours, nowhere but that sweet mouth of yours, until you're begging me for more. Pleading with me to kiss you anywhere I want. Everywhere *you* want."

Her breathing grew ragged from nothing more than just listening to him.

"So even though I hate having to wait a whole week to see you again, I'm not going to ask you to change your mind. And I won't text or call or come by or get in your way while you're studying this week, because something tells me that would be just as bad a distraction for both of us, and I could never forgive myself if your grades slipped because of me. But if you need me for any reason, I want you to know that I'll drop everything for you."

His lips were close enough now that she could practically taste them. "What if I just changed my mind?" She knew it was unfair of her to flip-flop like this, but she couldn't find a way to stop herself from doing it. "What if I told you I don't want to wait until next Friday night to see you again? What if I said I want to go back to your room with you tonight?" *And all the other nights you'll have me.*

"You don't know how much I want that." And she could see from the heated desire in his eyes that he meant it. "But I still wouldn't let you do it, Serena. Because even though I know how good it's going to be between us, and even though I've never wanted anyone the way I want you, I also know you'll end up hating me if we move too fast."

Her breath rushed out, ragged and shaky. Seeing that they were close to her dorm, it was up to her to make things easier on both of them. "I had a great time tonight, Sean. See you next Friday."

She made herself walk away, but this time she turned

back to smile at him over her shoulder. And when he smiled back she realized she'd never felt happier in her life.

CHAPTER THIRTEEN

The next Friday, Sean showed up early again. But Serena was clearly expecting him this time, because as soon as he made it to the top of the stairs, she pushed her chair back and flew across the floor toward him.

He dropped the black duffel bag he'd brought with him and caught her in his arms. The clean, fresh scent of her hair and skin sent his system reeling even as the press of her curves against him made it nearly impossible to think straight.

All week long he'd thought about her. Wanted her. Waited for her. And now that she was in his arms...God, it was the *best* feeling in the entire world.

He could feel her heart beating hard as she wrapped her arms around his neck and pressed her mouth to his in a sweet, yet hungry, kiss. It took every ounce of his self-control to let her lead, but when she moved from simply pressing her lips against his to slicking her tongue against his lips, he didn't have a prayer of holding back.

Two steps forward for him, two back for her, and he had her pressed up against the wall at the top of the stairs. When one of her legs automatically moved to wrap around his calf as she tried to pull him even closer, he grasped her thigh and lifted her leg so that he could feel the heat of her even through their two layers of denim.

When he'd kissed her at the frat party four weeks ago, and then again last Friday night, her kisses had been tentative and full of a surprising innocence. It all made sense now that he knew she'd hardly dated. But this time, as she threaded her hands through his hair and drew his mouth down even closer to hers, she seemed to know exactly what she wanted.

Him.

All he'd done for the past week was think about her, so who the hell knew what would have happened next if the voice hadn't come over the speakers just then: *Marie, you're needed at the special membership desk.*

The library. Jesus Christ, he'd actually forgotten where they were.

There was no one else up on the third floor on a Friday afternoon, but that didn't mean someone couldn't have shown up any second. Being caught grinding against each other at the top of the stairwell would blow their photo spread from last week out of the water.

Still, it wasn't easy to make himself lower her leg from around his hips rather than pull her even closer. Her striking blue eyes were foggy with passion as she blinked up at him and he had to press his mouth to hers again one more time before he finally stepped back.

"Hello, beautiful."

"Hi." Her gaze had finally cleared, but she had lifted one hand to her mouth as she stared back at him, running her fingertips lightly over the place where he'd just been tasting her.

Wanting desperately to be the one touching her like that, but knowing there was no way he'd be able to pull himself back twice, he made himself shove his hands into his pockets instead. "It's been a long week."

"It really was," she said softly.

More than once during the past week, he'd wished he could have already had her with him, warm and soft and gasping with pleasure in his bed while he made every fantasy a reality for both of them…and that he finally knew what sounds she made as she came apart in his arms and he made her his. Finally his.

But now he belatedly realized that they'd been right to wait. Not just because she truly hadn't been ready and would likely have ended up hating him for taking too much too fast. But also because this anticipation they were both feeling was actually really hot.

And when they finally did come together…

Hell, even letting himself think about it right now was a dangerous road to go down.

Forcing himself back on task, he asked, "Are you ready for another totally normal Friday night on campus?"

For a moment, she looked a little surprised by the way he'd deliberately tried to bank the heat between them. But then she nodded as if she was determined to pull off the same shift in herself.

"I am." She looked down at the bag he'd just picked up off the floor. "Did you come from working out?"

"Nope, these are our outfits."

She raised an eyebrow. "Outfits?"

Of course, he could read her mind—and her newly flushed cheeks—enough to know that she'd immediately assumed he must have brought something sexy for her to change into.

"I'd be lying if I said I didn't like your dirty mind," he said with a grin. "Probably comes from reading all those books, doesn't it? They give you more ideas, more possibilities, than other people."

He expected her to protest, to say she didn't have a dirty mind. Instead, she shrugged and said, "I have read about quite a few things over the years. Really interesting things. In fact, those ebooks you suggested I start downloading make it pretty easy to read *all* kinds of books without anyone ever knowing what's on my screen."

He barely held back a groan. Jesus, she was sexy. Not just her face and body, which were enough to scramble him up every time he looked at her, but the way her mind worked. All those brains. All those thoughts.

Sean tried like hell to shake the vision out of his head, but it was pretty much impossible. Fortunately, she took pity on him by asking, "Can I see what the outfits are?"

He walked over to the table in the corner where she'd been working and put the bag on it, then unzipped it and pulled out a Cardinal red Stanford Football long-sleeved T-shirt and a pair of matching sweatpants with the word *Stanford* running up the left leg. There were two of everything and he hoped she'd be laughing by the time he laid it all out, but instead she was biting her lip.

"It's not that I don't like the idea of going to a football game tonight. My roommate Abi said they're lots of fun, and I'd love to experience it, but—"

"No one is going to recognize us, I promise. No more pictures of us are getting out. Not unless we want them to."

"Even if we both wear all of this—" She gestured to the big pile of Stanford themed clothes he'd taken out of the bag. "—I can't see how people won't be able to figure out who we are."

He unzipped a side pocket and pulled out a small,

thin container. He flipped the top open to show her the palette of red, white, and green face paint.

"Face paint?"

He grinned at her incredulous expression. "And don't forget these." He held up a set of Cardinal red Stanford hats and sunglasses that had a sideways "S" curving around the frame.

There wasn't another girl on the planet he would have done this with. No one but Serena.

She wasn't just the girl he wanted the most...she was also the one he liked the best.

But she was still shaking her head. "You don't actually plan on both of us dressing up like over-the-top Stanford Football fans *and* painting our faces with their colors, too, do you, while wearing *these* sunglasses?"

"It's going to be great."

That was when she started to laugh. "People would never guess it from looking at you, but you're kind of weird."

"Funny," he said with a grin, "my sister Olivia was telling me that just the other day."

* * *

Thirty minutes later they were ready. And he'd be lying if he didn't admit to enjoying the hell out of painting up Serena's face in greens and reds when they'd locked themselves in the bathroom for their transformation. It was another excuse to touch her. And to be closer.

"Wow," she said as she looked at their reflections in the mirror. They'd both done such a thorough job with the face paint that even Sean could barely recognize either of them now that they both looked like Stanford Football obsessed kooks. "We look…" She started laughing too hard to finish her sentence.

"You wanted normal," he said around his own laughter. "And it's my pleasure to give it to you."

Again she laughed, shaking her head as they walked out of the bathroom. "I asked my roommate if she knew there was a Frisbee Golf course on campus and she looked at me as if I'd lost my mind. I hope it's okay with you that I told her we went out last week."

"Why wouldn't it be okay?" He'd shout it from the rooftops, if he could.

"I don't know. I've never done anything like this before."

"Neither have I, Serena."

"It's just...I don't know what the rules are."

He reached for her hand and tugged her closer. "There aren't any rules. The only thing that matters is that you feel good about what we're doing." But when he could see that she was still conflicted over the whole thing, he added, "And just for the record, the only reason I'm not going to kiss you again right now is because it will seriously screw up your face paint. Especially the green lipstick."

Again, laughter transformed her wildly painted face and he nearly messed it up by kissing her anyway. But they had a Friday night football game to get to and he didn't want her to miss a second of the normal college experiences he was giving her, so he stuffed her bag into his empty one, slung it over his shoulder, then headed down the stairs with her hand in his.

Janice looked up from the information desk as they walked by and gave them a thumbs-up. "Go Cardinal!"

"Have a great weekend," he said to the only person on campus who knew who was behind the crazy outfits and face paint.

"Oh, Serena," Janice called out when they were almost out the door, "I almost forgot to tell you that the transfer for the Ansel Adams books you requested should be coming in tomorrow morning. I'll send you an email once I've got them."

He swore he could see Serena flush even through the thick layer of dark makeup. "Thanks, Janice." She waited until they were outside before telling him, "When I looked at his pictures with you, it made me wonder about the man behind the camera."

"I always did, too. Ansel Adams is a very interesting man."

She didn't say anything for a moment. "It didn't just make me wonder about him, though. It made me wonder about you, too." She turned to meet his gaze. "About your photos. Because you take them, don't you?"

He knew she was waiting for his answer, but he didn't have a good one to give her. "Yeah, I used to be pretty into photography." Knowing that his *used to* stuck out like a sore thumb, he added, "But my photos weren't anything special."

"I wish I could just request a book of them so that I could see for myself," she said softly. "But since I can't, I guess I'll have to wait for you to want to show them to me, won't I?"

He hated disappointing her, especially when she was putting her trust in him each Friday night. Sure, playing Frisbee Golf and dressing up like crazies to see a football game wouldn't normally be huge things, but if he were to slip the information to a tabloid or photographer—if he called up a journalist and told them about how all Serena Britten wanted was to be normal—these little things they were doing together would become huge stories in an instant.

So since she was trusting him with so much, it wasn't fair for it to only go one way. But he hadn't even talked much with his brothers and sisters about his feelings over losing their mother.

Then again, maybe answering Serena's question about his photography didn't have to be about his mom. Maybe he could just tell her about himself and that would be enough. For now, at least.

"My sister Olivia had one of those little toy Barbie cameras as a kid. I stole it from her and wouldn't give it back." He liked hearing Serena's laughter. It made it feel easier to talk to her about things. "At first I mostly took pictures of the sky. Trees. Water. Bugs. People came last, and only because when I was a kid they reminded me of bugs."

"They did?"

"Sure. Some are social. Some are solitary. But everyone's just trying to stay alive. And when you get a good up-close shot, they all look pretty funny."

"What kind of pictures do you like taking now?"

"I haven't taken any in a while."

She was quiet for a few moments, but he could practically hear the gears in her head working. Finally, she said, "You know, if you ever want..." She paused, clearly uncertain about what she was about to say. "I know bugs are a much better subject than I could ever be, but if you—" She paused to swallow hard again. "—if you ever want to use me to practice working with light or shadows or whatever, I'd be happy to help."

The thing was, by that point he'd started to get a pretty clear picture of the fact that after nearly two straight decades of modeling, she didn't much care for being photographed. But before he could reply, a stranger walked up to them with his phone out.

"Hey, any chance I could get a pic of the two of you for my Stanford Football blog?"

With everything in this section of the campus close together, they'd quickly gotten close enough to the stadium to be surrounded by other football fans. Tailgates were wrapping up in the parking lots all around them and the smell of barbecues and beer permeated the air. Fortunately, until now, no one had so much as looked over at them with any recognition whatsoever, given that there were just enough other crazy football fans in similar getups that they barely stood out.

But even though he doubted the guy with the blog had a clue who he was talking to, when Serena immediately flinched and turned away from the camera, Sean told him, "Actually, there's a group of about ten guys over there who would be way better for your blog. One has even painted his entire body like a tree."

The blogger bounded off, but Sean could see that Serena was still tense. She'd actually cringed at the thought of the guy taking her picture. That was how much she hated it.

And yet she'd offered to model for him?

"Hey," he said, reeling from the knowledge of just how huge her offer had been—and how tempting the thought of photographing her was even though he never thought he'd want to pick up a camera again, "it's okay. He didn't know who we were."

She stepped out of the way of a couple of girls who were taking a selfie. "Thanks for throwing that guy off our scent."

He knew she was trying to change the subject, but first he had to know, "If you didn't like your job, why did you do it for so long?"

"I liked it at first, or at least I thought I did because

everyone was so nice to me when the pictures were good. But by the time I realized I didn't want to spend the rest of my life standing in front of a camera..." She paused. "So many girls dream of being on magazine covers and in Paris fashion shows that I always felt like a snot when I wanted out, so I tried to stop wanting it. But then I realized I couldn't keep ignoring my own dreams forever. I just couldn't. So that was when I made the decision to apply to college."

"Sometimes baseball feels like that for me."

"It does?"

He could see that he'd surprised her. Hell, he'd surprised himself, too, not only by admitting that, but also by saying it out loud.

"I'm good at it. Really good." It wasn't bragging when it was the truth. "And when we're winning and everything is clicking and the crowd is going nuts, I'm not going to lie and say it isn't pretty damned fun."

"Being on the runway was like that sometimes. If the designer was really spectacular and I knew fashion history was being made that day, it was pretty cool. But every time I met people who had real passion for clothes and fashion, I'd end up feeling like a fraud for not being one of them."

"Most of the guys on the team, especially the ones who are good enough to go pro, they live and breathe the game. So I know what you mean about feeling like a fraud sometimes."

Just then, the campus mascot—a seven-foot-tall redwood tree made out of sewn-together pieces of felt— danced by them with the Stanford band not far behind. The campus band was notorious, not only for their crazy outfits, but also for their shocking antics. Tonight it looked like they were going to be putting on one of their better shows, as the guys were all dressed in drag and they were playing a dirty "alternate" version of *Come Join the Band.*

There was no way Sean and Serena could have kept from laughing at the perfect break in what had become far too serious a conversation for a Friday night football game. He wanted to get to know her better, but he was just starting to realize that sharing didn't go one way. He couldn't just dig into her past, her secrets, her fears and dreams without letting her do the same to him.

The things was, he thought as he handed the girl at the gate their tickets, he didn't know if he was ready to go there yet. But could he do it for Serena?

CHAPTER FOURTEEN

"Wow," Serena said as they stepped into the stadium, "this place is huge. And loud. Really, really loud."

Deliberately shaking off the dark cloud of his thoughts—his worries about the future and his grief over the past—Sean made himself focus on the here and now.

His family had been coming to games for as long as he could remember, and they'd worked their way up over the years to sweet seats right at the fifty-yard line. But if he and Serena sat there, it would make their disguises pointless. Which was why he'd sucked it up and bought a couple of crappy seats in the nosebleeds.

Clearly, though, she had no idea that their seats were terrible as she looked around her with such wonder on her face that he could read it from behind her sunglasses. "This is *so* great."

He'd taken girls to games a couple of times in the past and had always regretted it. They were too cold, too hot, too bored, too annoying. But Serena was already perfect.

"How much do you know about football?"

"Nothing."

He'd assumed as much, guessing that a supermodel with an always-there mother and no dad in the picture probably didn't have many chances to watch football on TV or live at a stadium.

"The game's pretty easy to understand. You have an offense trying to score and a defense trying to stop them. The offense has four chances to go ten yards to get the first down. If you don't get at least those ten yards, the other side gets the ball. You score by getting the ball in the end zone, or depending on your field position you can try to kick the ball through the uprights for a field goal."

"Surely it's more complicated than that."

"There are a bunch of extra details I could add in like penalties, turnovers and safeties, but if you just remember that the offense is trying to get the ball in the end zone, and the defense is trying to stop them, you've pretty much got the point of the game." He waved over a teenager who was selling concessions. "I'm thinking popcorn, hot dogs, candy, and Coke. What kind of candy is your favorite?"

"If I had to guess, I'd say all of it."

If she had to guess? Hadn't she grown up eating teeth-rotting candy like the rest of them?

He told the teenage girl to give them one box of each kind of candy, along with loaded hot dogs, a huge bag of popcorn and two bottles of Coke.

"Tonight must be costing you a fortune," Serena said when he came back with the pile of junk food in his hands. "I want to pay next time."

He loved that she was talking about next time. "Nope. I asked, I pay."

"Then I'll just have to ask you first, won't I?" Before he could interject, she said, "Will you go out with me next Friday?"

He had to mess up her green lipstick then by kissing

her. "You know," he said when he made himself draw back, "that means you're in charge of finding something normal for us to do."

That seemed to take the wind out of her sails a bit. "What if I blow it?"

"I have faith in you."

She stopped then and stared at him as if he'd just blown her mind. But before he could say anything else, the ref blew the whistle for the opening kickoff. Together, they sat back in their seats, his arm around her shoulders, her head nestled into his chest, and both enjoyed forgetting about everything else in their lives for a few hours.

Everything but each other.

* * *

Serena quickly picked up the game and by the end she was so into it that she was screaming and jumping out of her seat along with everyone else when Stanford won in the final seconds of the fourth quarter.

She threw her arms around Sean. "We won!"

Who cared about the game? He felt like the biggest winner in the stadium just for getting to be with her. Her smile was so big and wide that he could see the face paint cracking at the corners of her lips. "Let's go take off this goop so that I can kiss you properly."

That was all it took for heat to rise between them. He grabbed her hand and pulled her out of the stands and down the stairs to the exit. For three hours he'd been close to her, had gotten to hold her hand and put his arm around her shoulders.

But it hadn't been close enough.

Thank God their Friday night date wasn't over yet. Not even close.

"Where are you taking me now?"

She was slightly breathless from the speed at which he was making them walk as they headed across the street from the stadium to the empty baseball field and the locker rooms.

"I've got this fantasy," he teased her, "about you and me...and an empty locker room."

She laughed, but it was a nervous sound. One that had him stopping in the middle of a patch of grass to tell her, "You know I'm kidding, right? I just figured it would be a private spot for us to take off the face paint and hang out for a while until the crowds thin out. I meant it when I told you that I would never do anything to hurt you. And I won't do anything you don't want, that you're not ready for, either." Even if he was beyond ready for all of it.

For all of her.

"I know you won't. It's not you, it's me." She gave another shaky laugh. "That didn't come out right. I need to explain and hopefully, I won't just end up making it worse."

It was nearly completely dark out by then and they were far enough away from the crowds that she finally slipped her sunglasses up to the top of her head so that he could see her eyes. He'd missed being able to look into them. Missed being able to see what she was thinking, what she was feeling.

"My mom had a pretty hard time with my dad. It's weird to even call him that, when he was more like an accidental sperm donor. When he found out she was pregnant, he split. And even before him, I don't think she'd ever been with a guy who treated her well. All my life, she's been worried that the same thing will happen to me. That some guy will use me or hurt me." She shook her head. "Even though I know her experience with men is colored by what she's been through, and that all guys can't be bad, the truth is that it's hard to forget what she's taught me my whole life." She paused before adding, "And it's hard not to be scared that she's going to be right."

"I've been that guy," he admitted to her. "I mean, I haven't gotten anyone pregnant," he clarified, "but I've been a dick who only thought with mine. I don't want to be that guy with you, Serena. Let's forget the locker room, okay?"

She surprised him by tugging him in the direction they'd been going. "I don't want to forget it."

"Are you sure?"

"I've had an amazing time with you so far tonight. I know this part will be just as good."

"I figured there was a pretty good chance that when you saw the clothes and face paint you were going to tell me to forget this whole Friday night normal-date thing."

She looked down at her sweatpants, tracing the *S* on her thigh with her fingers. "No one has ever tried this hard to make me happy." She looked up at him, her eyes shining. "Thank you."

Five minutes later, they were walking into the empty locker room. "Welcome to my world." He'd never taken a girl here before, just as he'd never taken one to see the Ansel Adams photos.

"I did a photo shoot in a locker room once. They stuck me in an expensive couture dress and had a couple of football players hold me up." At his look, she said, "It didn't seem as strange then as it does now that I'm telling you about it."

"Those poor guys, I'll bet they were both in love with you by the end of the photo shoot." When she flushed lightly, he knew he'd hit it dead-on. "They asked you out, didn't they?"

"They seemed like nice guys, but—"

"You weren't allowed to date."

"No, I wasn't. But there's no one here to stop me now."

He'd planned on waiting until they'd taken off the face paint, but he couldn't keep from putting his hands on her hips and dragging her close. "Thank God."

He lowered his mouth to hers and kissed her. Tried to, anyway, but the paint started cracking off into their mouths the second their lips met.

"We've got to get this stuff off."

"No kidding. I'm really good at taking off makeup. Let me do it." A few seconds later, she was wetting a clean towel from a small stack in the corner. "Close your eyes."

Her hands were steady and sure as she quickly wiped his face clean, and by the time she told him he could open his eyes, his skin was back to normal. Before she could do the same for herself, he said, "Let me."

She closed her eyes and let him gently run a new wet towel over her skin. Everything about her was flawless, but he was always careful not to stare too much, not to let on that he was shocked by her beauty each and every time he looked at her. Not when he could tell that being the most beautiful girl in the world hadn't always been easy for her, and that it hadn't always made her feel good or happy. But here in the locker room, just as he'd been able to stare a little longer than usual as he'd put on her face paint, he was able to run his fingertips over the curves of her cheekbones, the hollows beneath them, the sweet arches of her eyebrows, and the sensuous curve of her lips.

He took his time restoring her skin to its usual

smooth, soft glow. When he was done, he threw the towel into the linen basket across the room and straddled the long wooden bench. She moved one leg across it to face him. Her skin was flushed, the pulse at her neck racing. She looked nervous. But also aroused.

And happy...most of all she looked happy. It was how he always wanted her to be.

"Kiss me, Sean."

He slid a couple of inches closer and reached up with one hand to cup her jaw. Gently, and oh-so-softly, he leaned in and pressed his lips against hers. Their kiss was barely more than a breath against each other's lips, but he could feel the impact of it all the way down in the deepest part of him.

He wanted to take. Wanted to ravage. Wanted to possess. At the same time, he also wanted something he'd never known he could want before: for their kisses to be as emotional as they were sexy. And for each one to be more than just foreplay. More than just a way to tease, to tempt.

But though he could tell Serena was as affected by these kisses as he was, he also knew from the way her body was winding tighter with each one that she was hungry for more. He'd felt her hunger last week, too, but she'd hadn't been ready for more than kisses. And even now that he swore he could feel the heat radiating from her, he didn't want to make the mistake of pushing her too fast. But, he wondered as she made a little growly sound at his next super-soft, super-sweet kiss, could it finally be time to start gently leading them down the road in the direction they both obviously wanted to go?

"Is this how you want me to kiss you?" Yet again he pressed his lips against hers, no tongues, no teeth, just the sweet, simple pleasure of being close to her.

Her hands had moved to his thighs by then, and he didn't know if she realized how tightly she was gripping him, her fingers loosening every time he kissed her, then tightening when he drew back.

"I really, really like it," she whispered against his lips a beat before she surprised him by saying, "but I want you to kiss me like *this*."

CHAPTER FIFTEEN

As her mouth crashed against his, he moved his hands to her hips to drag her even closer. Instead of pulling away, she wrapped her legs around his waist and bucked against him as she moaned into his mouth.

Layers. There were too many layers of clothes between them. He didn't stop to think before he found the hem of her long-sleeved Stanford Football shirt and yanked it up over her torso. Clearly as desperate as he was to get rid of at least one of the cotton barriers between them, she helped him get it over her head and toss it onto the bench.

He stroked her nearly bare back, only her bra left on her upper body now. She was so warm, and when she arched into his touch, he finally saw what he'd uncovered.

"You're—" *Beautiful* didn't even come close. *Gorgeous* was just a word. "A miracle."

Apart from that night at the frat party, she'd always worn baggy clothes. He'd been careful tonight to make sure that the shirt he'd bought for her to wear at the game hadn't been too fitted, either. But now, with her breasts swelling over the top of the surprisingly sexy silk bra, he wanted to touch, wanted to stroke, wanted to taste.

But when he looked up at her face, he could read every one of her fears, every bit of her hesitation. And he also finally realized that he was gaping at her like a horny idiot.

"Serena, you don't have to be frightened." Instead of touching her breasts, he threaded his fingers through her hair. "You don't have to worry." He pressed his lips to hers, slow and soft and sweet. "It's me." He kissed her again. "I won't hurt you." Their lips brushed, tongues licked, teeth nipped. "We're only going to go as fast as you want to go." He was reminding them both. "We can put your shirt back on if you want to. If you need to."

"No." She moved closer. "I don't want that. I don't need that."

"What do you want? What do you need?"

But instead of answering him, she put her hands over his and moved them to cup her breasts over the silk. He had to close his eyes, had to take a breath, and then another, to try to keep his shit together.

So good. She felt *so good.* Soft and warm and round and perfect.

"This," she whispered. "I want this. I want you to touch me like this. I *need* you to touch me like this."

Her nipples were pebbling against his palms through the silk, and thank God she'd just told him she wanted him to do this, because he didn't know if he was strong enough otherwise to stop himself from brushing his thumbs over both gorgeous peaks.

A low moan emerged from her throat. *"Again."*

It was just what he'd said to her at the Frisbee Golf course when she'd surprised him with a kiss, and he loved that she was the one saying it to him now as he cupped her breasts in his hands. She held on to him as he stroked her nipples so that they grew even harder against the pads of his thumbs.

"More. I want *more."*

He knew what she wanted, knew what she was asking for, but still he hesitated. It would be so easy, too easy, to just take and take and take from her. But it wouldn't be worth it if he only ended up losing her once the rush of pleasure had passed.

But then, as if in slow motion, he watched her drop her hands from his and reach around to her back. He heard the soft click as the latch of her bra came undone, almost undoing him at the same time.

"Please."

She'd not only just given him permission to strip her bra completely away, but had also made it perfectly clear that she wanted him to touch her skin to skin, without anything between them for once. Not even the thin layer of silk.

And yet...he still didn't lift his hands from her silk-covered breasts. Didn't give in to the urge to see her naked chest completely revealed. Because for as much as he needed it, for as desperate as he was to make her his, he needed this to be about more than just two horny college students copping a feel in a deserted locker room.

"Why?" He knew he wasn't being clear, wasn't making sense. "Why me?"

"Because I trust you." Something flashed in her eyes, something that he thought looked like a lifetime of wondering about the motives of everyone around her. "You're the only one I've ever trusted."

He shifted his hands so that her bra fell in a soft heap of fabric between them, but he still didn't drop his gaze from her eyes. "I'm going to keep earning your trust, Serena, every single day."

Her mouth was sweet and hungry beneath his and when she twined her arms around his neck, the full, soft, sexy-as-hell press of her bare breasts against his chest short-circuited what remained of his nearly lapsed control. He couldn't stop himself from putting his hands on her shoulders and drawing her back from him.

His mouth watered as he saw that her breasts were as perfect as the rest of her. Gently, he moved his hands from her shoulders to cup the full, soft undersides. Her nipples were rose-colored peaks that tipped up slightly, almost as if they were begging for him to lower his mouth to taste them.

His erection throbbed almost painfully as she leaned in toward him, pressing her breasts more firmly into his hands. "I love it when you touch me. I love feeling your hands on me. My hair. My face." She paused to lick her lips as she took in the view of his big tanned hands over her. "My breasts."

He had to kiss her again, had to make sure she knew just how happy, how good, she made him feel. He could have waited longer for her to let him be with her like this if she'd needed him to, but he was damned glad she hadn't.

"I want to kiss you," he said softly. "Here." He kissed her again on her mouth. "And here." He slowly slid each of her nipples between his thumb and forefinger. Her gasp of pleasure rolled up from her rib cage and then through her lips. "But only if you want me to."

"I've never wanted anything more."

Sean's groan reverberated throughout the room, bouncing off the metal lockers. He'd barely gotten to first base and she was already just about killing him. His breathing uneven, he lowered his mouth to her breasts. Her nipples grew even harder the closer he came, and when he cupped her soft flesh in his hands so that he could slick his tongue across both peaks, she made a little whimpering sound that drove him nearly to the edge.

He had her fully on his tongue a moment later, first one breast and then the other. Laving. Sucking. She shifted her hips to press even harder against his and wound her legs tightly around him so that they were full-on grinding against each other. Everything was a blur as he laid her back on the bench, one hand behind her spine to cushion it, the other still playing with her breasts, wet now from his tongue.

If he'd been able to think straight, maybe he could have stopped himself from sliding his hand down her stomach, past her belly button, and beneath the fabric of her sweatpants. But there was nothing left for Sean in that moment but how good she tasted and smelled, the sweet little sounds she made as she took everything he was giving and wordlessly begged for more.

Lord, was she wet. So damned wet and soft and *hot,* that as she gave a little cry and arched into his hand, he instinctively slid his fingers into her.

He felt the change in her just that quickly. Open and willing one second. Closed and tense the next.

"Serena?" He immediately drew his hand away, laid it flat on her stomach. He swore as he moved to shift them back up into a sitting position. "I'm sorry. I should have asked first." He knew it didn't count, but he still had to tell her. "I meant to ask."

She stopped his apologies with a hand over his. "I liked it. Everything we were doing. Everything you did." She shook her head, obviously a little embarrassed by what she was about to say. "I think that was why I just freaked out. Because I liked it *too* much."

Relief swamped him, just as lust had moments

earlier. Still, he knew— "I moved too fast." Worse, he'd done it right after he'd promised that he'd always be careful with her.

"You didn't."

He brought his mouth nearly to hers. "I did." After one more soft kiss that he wished could undo his mistake, he picked up her bra and T-shirt and handed them to her. "I should take you back to your dorm."

She looked disappointed, but didn't disagree with him. Which was how he knew that he was right about stopping things where they had. After making his own adjustments—and using every single mind-control technique he could think of to will his erection away before they headed back outside—he got up and held out a hand to her.

She took it, but didn't move for a few moments, just looked at him with an expression he couldn't read. "I've never felt like this before. I don't think my heart has ever beat this fast." She moved his hand to her chest so that he could feel her rapid heartbeat. "I never thought I was a very sensual person..."

He knew he needed to let her go, and that he should keep his distance for another week, but he couldn't keep from pulling her into his arms. "If you were any more sensual, I wouldn't have a prayer of surviving you."

Her answering smile was utterly radiant. "Really?"

"Really." He picked up his bag and tugged her out of the locker room. "Now let's get you back to your dorm room so that you can get into bed and finish what I started." Just as he expected, her cheeks flushed. "And just so you know, I'll be thinking of you while I do the same thing."

He was glad when her laughter joined his as they headed out into the darkness.

CHAPTER SIXTEEN

"Abi, can I ask you a question?"

Serena's roommate looked up from her book. They'd just finished going over some calculus equations and Serena hoped her explanations were helping Abi a little bit, at least. Her roommate's parents had come down on her pretty hard in the past week over not studying hard enough, which definitely sucked. Although, somehow, Serena couldn't help but think that Genevieve's complete and utter freeze-out—apart from the three-word phone call about the pictures online—was worse. At least Abi's parents cared enough about her to want her to do well. Whereas Genevieve didn't seem to care at all about Serena now that she was no longer doing what she wanted her to do.

"Sure, what's up? Is it about your gorgeous secret boyfriend?" When Serena nodded, Abi shoved her books and laptop aside and focused every ounce of her attention on her. "You're going to sleep with him tonight, aren't you?"

Serena felt her entire face go up in flames. But that was nothing compared to the way her body heated up at the mere suggestion of sleeping with Sean. As if she hadn't thought about it all week long since the football game, and wondered...

"No, I—"

"I don't know how you can stand it," Abi exclaimed before Serena could say anything else. "Sean Morrison is *so* gorgeous. And he obviously just freaking adores you if the past couple of dates are anything to go by, because I don't know any other reason he would take you to play Frisbee Golf or paint his face and dress up like a total dork for a football game."

Serena was really pleased that her decision to trust her roommate had been a good one. Abi hadn't leaked anything to anyone about Serena and Sean, not even to the other girls in the dorm. And it was so nice to finally have a confidant.

"I just don't get why you're holding out on him like this. Not just by not doing the most doable guy on campus, but by only seeing him once a week. If it was me," Abi said with a wicked smile, "I'd be living in his bed twenty-four seven. Hey," her roommate added as if she'd just thought of something, "doesn't he have a twin? Wouldn't it be fun if we dated Morrison brothers?"

Serena didn't know what to say. She really liked Abi, and yet she definitely didn't feel equipped to play matchmaker. Not only because everything with Sean was so fresh and new, but also because she hadn't even met his twin yet.

"From everything Sean has told me, Justin sounds great," she said carefully, "but—"

"Or maybe I should go for his rock-star brother, Drew," Abi said with a dreamy look on her face. "He's *crazy* hot and his music is amazing." Without taking a break to let Serena answer her initial questions about why she wasn't yet sleeping with Sean, Abi said, "Have you met any of them yet?"

"No."

She hadn't expected to, either. She and Sean were still slowly getting to know each other. Okay, she thought as she tried to fight back a flush that Abi was sure to comment on, so maybe the way he'd been kissing and touching her last Friday in the locker room hadn't exactly been *slow*. Although the way he'd stopped when she'd freaked definitely had been.

Did he have any idea how much more his stopping made her trust him? Especially when she knew he'd wanted to do anything but.

"I'm sure you'll be meeting them soon," Abi said with perfect confidence.

Not for the first time, Serena wished she could be like that, so sure of her place in the world and what she wanted from it. Abi was planning to go into politics and Serena had no doubt she'd get the internship she wanted in Washington, D.C.

"Anyway, remind me why you haven't slept with Sean yet?"

Even though Abi had proved herself to be completely trustworthy so far, Serena was still scared to tell her something so intensely personal. Namely, that she was a nineteen-year-old, world-famous virgin who had only experienced a guy's hand in her pants for the first time last Friday...and that it had fueled every single one of her private fantasies since then.

"We both want to take it slow."

Abi snorted in disbelief. "I don't know *any* guys who want to take things slow. There's got to be another reason."

Serena thought about the way she'd thrown herself at

Sean both of the last Fridays. *"What if I said I wanted to go back to your room with you tonight?"* and *"More. Please."* Each time he'd been the one with the self-control to make them step back from the edge.

"He knows I'm not ready."

"Like I said, I don't know many guys who would care whether you're ready or not. If you ask me, there's only one reason he'd be willing to take things slow." Abi cradled her chin in her hand and sighed. "He's in love with you."

"In love?" *With her?* Serena shook her head, so fast and hard that she nearly fell off the bed. "No. He can't be."

"Why not? Like I said before, when the housing office let me know that you were going to be my roommate, I was ready to totally hate you. But not only were you not all stuck up or into yourself the way I figured you'd be, you ended up being nice and real and helpful with my classes. If I were a guy—or swung the other way—I'd be all swoony over you, too."

"Swoony?"

Abi grinned at the way Serena repeated the silly word. "Swoony *and* smitten." There was a little pause before she shifted slightly on her bed so that Serena couldn't quite see her hands or face anymore. "Besotted. Bewitched. Captivated. Enchanted. Enraptured. Hooked."

Serena grinned. "I think I get what you're trying to say without the online thesaurus."

"How'd you guess?"

"You were saying the words in alphabetical order."

Abi tossed her phone back onto the bed. "What about you? Are you in love with him, too?"

Serena reeled from the pointed question, even though she'd known it had to be coming. "We only met a few weeks ago."

"So what? Are you telling me you don't believe in love at first sight? Or that it can last forever?"

That was just the thing—Serena didn't know what she believed. For nineteen years, her mother had taught her that love wasn't real, that no one would ever love her the way Genevieve did, and that her mother was the only person she'd ever be able to trust. At the end of Serena's first frat party, it had looked like all of those things were true.

But in the past few weeks she'd come to trust Sean in a way she'd never trusted anyone else. Even going so far as to offer to model for him if it would help him get back into photography after the break he'd taken since his mother's death.

She inhaled a deep, shaky breath, before blowing it out. "I'd like to believe it's real. And that forever is possible with someone."

For once, Abi didn't have a snappy comeback. Instead, all she said was, "I'm pretty sure we all would." But before the moment could get too deep, she added, "Hey, didn't you have a question for me?"

With thoughts of love dancing around inside her head, it took Serena a few seconds to rewind to the beginning of their conversation and remember her question. "I'm the one who asked Sean out this week, so I'm in charge of planning our date on Friday night. I was wondering if you'd be able to help me with what I was thinking of doing."

Abi's smile grew as Serena explained her plan, and when she was done, her roommate said, "Of course I can help you. But if you ask me, this plan is bound to send you straight into Sean's bed. Which means you must be more ready for him—and for falling in love—than you think."

* * *

"How did you sneak this stuff in here?"

Sean's voice was low enough that only Serena could hear it. As he quickly zipped up her backpack to hide the small bottle of tequila, shot glasses, penknife, and lime she'd packed for tonight, her stomach twisted. Had she already screwed up this date night?

"I'm here so much that they don't check my backpack too carefully when I come in."

He sat on the edge of the work table and stared down at her, his expression unreadable. "I know I'm always asking you this, but are you sure this is what you want to do tonight?"

It would have been easier to shake her head, to laugh it off and tell him the contents of her bag were a joke. But what could be more normal for a college student than getting drunk on a Friday night?

So instead of backing down, or apologizing for following her instincts, she told him, "I've never been drunk before. And according to my roommate and every college movie I've ever seen, it's an important—and very normal—rite of passage for a freshman. The thing is...there's no one I'd trust with it but you. Especially since I have no idea how I deal with drinking—" She almost held the rest in before deciding to spit it out. "—and I *hate* always feeling like I'm a dozen steps behind everyone else."

"You've had experiences, and know how to do things, that ninety-nine percent of people on this campus will never know. Will never deal with. Will never achieve. Getting drunk is nothing special—take it from a guy who knows firsthand. But I get that you want to know that for yourself." He took her face in his hands and gently stroked her cheekbones. "And you'd better believe that I don't want you drinking with anyone but me."

She'd missed his lips on hers all week long, and it was with such relief—and pleasure—that she pressed her mouth to his. Just like always, their kiss quickly spiraled from soft and sweet to desperate and wild.

Finally, he tore his mouth from hers. "So, where are you thinking about getting me drunk?"

He was teasing her, but she'd be lying if she didn't admit that the thought had occurred to her that perhaps Sean might be a little less careful with her under the influence. It wasn't that she didn't love how concerned he was that every step they took should be the right one for her...but at the same time a part of her wondered what it would be like if they both just threw caution to the wind.

"Abi mentioned a path up at the Dish that's off the regular trail." Her roommate had said the park in the foothills at the edge of campus where students and faculty went to exercise would be perfect for the two of them to find a private spot. "I thought we could kill two normal birds with one stone tonight, since I've never hiked the Dish either."

"Your roommate knows about your plan?"

"She's the one who got the bottle for me. She's been really awesome about keeping everything I tell her private, actually." *And she thinks you're in love with me.* The thought flustered Serena so that she started saying, "If you think there's a better spot, we could go somewhere else. Or we could just forget about the whole thing, since I know it's a crazy idea, and there are probably lots of other normal things we could do together."

"The Dish is perfect." He stood up and held out his

hand. "Shall we?"

Loving the way he said it, as if they were going out for an elegant night of dinner and dancing rather than hiking up to a secluded spot on the top of a hill to pound shots, she answered him with a kiss.

CHAPTER SEVENTEEN

Serena had to stop halfway up the hill to lean over with her hands on her thighs and suck in large gasps of oxygen. "Abi forgot to mention," she said around her panting, "how steep this path is."

"Why do you think it's such a secluded spot?" Sean teased.

Despite the fact that the climb was practically vertical, he wasn't even breathing hard. She knew from looking at him—and having touched his rock-hard, rippling chest and abs—that he was in great shape, but shouldn't he at least be sweating? So much for any plans she might have had for seducing him. Who in their right mind would want to get sexy with her when she was like this?

"You knew how hard this was going to be, didn't you?"

He surprised her by lifting her into a standing position and dragging her damp body against his. Before she could protest, he licked her neck just below her earlobe. "Mmm, you taste a little salty." When she went to pull away, he kept her against him. "I like it." As if to prove it, he ran his tongue across the other side of her neck, making her shiver despite how warm the hike had gotten her. "A lot."

"I can't believe you even want to touch me when I'm all wet like this."

His eyes darkened as he looked down at her. "Promise me you won't talk about being all wet again once we start drinking," he said in a low voice that only intensified her shivers. "Because if you do..."

It was, she realized, a sign of just how incredibly safe she felt with him that she found herself wanting to do just that. To talk about being all wet again, but to mean something else entirely...and then to finally find out what he was going to do about it.

"I've got my breath back now," she told him, even though being in his arms had made her lose it all over again. "Let's keep going up to the top."

She was already heading up the path when he called out, "You didn't promise."

Feeling light and flirty and *fabulous* for the first time in her life, she threw him a deliberately sensual look over her shoulder. "I know."

* * *

Sitting on the blanket she'd brought, he let her do it all—unscrew the top of the tequila bottle, put out the salt shaker between them, pour the shots, cut up the lime—and she knew why. Yet again, he didn't want her to feel that he was forcing her to do anything. He wanted to be sure that everything she was doing was her decision.

But while she hadn't changed her mind about her plans for tonight, and the tequila thankfully smelled better than she'd expected it to, that didn't mean she felt all that confident about how to actually drink it.

"I looked up several ways to do the shots on the Internet," she admitted. "But I'm sure you have some favorites."

He reached out and brushed his thumb across her lower lip. "I do." His gorgeous mouth tipped up into a smile. "But I'll need you to come closer so that I can show you what they are."

Every inch of her wanted every inch of him already. It had been that way from the first moment he'd held her in his arms at the frat party, but now that she knew how amazing he was...well, she was barely a heartbeat from shoving aside all the drinking paraphernalia and tackling him.

"Care to share some of what's going on inside that big brain of yours?"

She looked up at him in surprise, feeling as if he'd already read her mind. And since she guessed that even if she didn't say it aloud, he'd know, she said, "I'm having trouble concentrating on my goal of learning how to drink tequila when all I want to do is kiss you."

His mouth curved up wider even as his eyes grew darker. "Who says you have to pick one or the other?"

He poured tequila into one of the shot glasses, quickly drank it, then drew her onto his lap so that she was straddling him. He slid his tongue into her mouth and she instinctively knew to suck the liquor from it, then lick his lips clean, too.

"How was that?"

She was almost too breathless to reply. "Good." She couldn't drag her gaze away from his mouth. "So good."

He poured another small amount into a shot glass, then held it out to her. "Your turn."

She brought the glass up to her lips and tasted it, unable to stop her nose from wrinkling at just how strong it was.

"It's usually better if you just toss it back," Sean coached her. "Although I'm perfectly happy to quit the drinking part of the evening now if you want...and just get back to the kissing part."

Oh, but she was tempted. It would be so easy to skip over this rite of passage. Only, she knew it would keep bothering her that she'd never experienced something that was a part of nearly every other college student's *normal* vernacular.

Taking a deep breath, she tilted her head back and tossed the shot down her throat. Oh God, she thought as her eyes watered, it burned like fire...but then Sean was there with his fingers tangling in her hair and his mouth on hers as he sucked at her tongue the way she'd sucked at his. As the fire immediately moved from her throat to her breasts and the vee between her legs, the shot glass dropped from her hand and she wrapped her arms around him to try to get closer.

"What did you think about that?" His mouth was still so close to hers that his question felt like another kiss.

"It was hot. But I'm not sure how much of the way I'm feeling has to do with the tequila."

A low sound of pleasure came from his throat as he nuzzled the curve of her chin and into her shoulder. "Do you want to do more?"

She couldn't quite manage to get her lips to form the word *yes* when what he was doing to her sent thrill bumps running all across the surface of her body, but she could nod.

"You're a hell of a lot more addictive than booze," he murmured as he poured another shot. "And I've got a serious thing for your neck tonight. Tilt your head to the side for me, beautiful."

Her heart raced as she made her neck completely vulnerable to him, and though she wasn't cold or nervous, she actually started to shake as he lightly brushed her long hair over to her other shoulder. His tongue slicked out across her neck, warm and slightly rough, and then he picked up the saltshaker and dropped a few grains onto her skin.

"Doing okay?"

She loved that he was checking in with her, not just with his question but also by running his free hand down her arm in a reassuring way.

"I'm great," she said, and she really was. Simply because she was with him, and he made her happier than anything or anyone else ever had.

His mouth descended to her neck and he sucked on her skin, taking the salt. If she hadn't already been aroused, that would have done it, and when he lifted the shot glass to his mouth, she wished she could be there on his tongue instead.

In a flash, the memory of his mouth on her breasts the previous Friday night hit her and she was nearly moaning aloud by the time he put the lime between his teeth and sucked the juice from it. She was so jealous of all of it—the salt, the tequila, the fruit—that she didn't think, couldn't stop herself from giving in to the urge to tackle him.

She attacked his mouth with hers, her weight over his pushing him onto his back on the blanket. And when his arms came around her back and hips to drag her closer, she realized it was the first time they'd ever lain down with each other. Every other time they'd kissed, they'd either been standing or straddling the bench in the locker room. How easy would it be, she wondered as he nipped at her lower lip, for them to strip off each other's clothes and make good on the sensual desperation that was driving them both to distraction?

But before she could so much as reach for the hem of his T-shirt to find out, he'd rolled them over so that she was beneath him. "Slow." The word came out on a harsh breath. "We're taking things slow."

Remembering what Abi had said, that the only reason he'd want to take things slow was if he was in love with her, she said, "Sean—"

He cut off her protest with a kiss, even as he brought them both back into a sitting position. "It's your turn to do another shot now."

When he poured it for her, she noticed his hands were shaking slightly. At least she wasn't the only one who felt like she was rapidly approaching the edge of insanity.

"How do you want it?"

"Your stomach."

She was as honestly surprised by her answer as he seemed to be. It was just that after reading online about people doing body shots off one other, she'd been unable to shake the idea of doing a shot off Sean's abs.

"Okay." He shifted so that he was leaning back on his forearms. "Go for it."

His T-shirt was already mostly out of his jeans and belt, and she was almost unbearably excited as she reached for the cotton to draw it up and expose bare skin. A few heady moments later, she was staring in awe at his beautifully tanned six-pack.

No, there were more muscles than that, she thought as she momentarily forgot all about drinking her next shot to run her fingertips over his abdomen. His muscles rippled beneath her touch and when she looked up at him, his eyes were darker and more intense than she'd ever seen them.

"Your body is a work of art," she told him earnestly. "You could make a fortune modeling."

He laughed, but it sounded slightly choked. "Good to know." He closed his eyes for a brief moment, as though searching for control. Finally, he opened them and said, "You know the drill, right? Get my skin wet, drop the salt on, then lick it off and pound the shot, chasing it with the lime juice."

She nodded, her nerves making a sudden reappearance at the shocking realization that she was just seconds from licking a guy's stomach. She'd never done *anything* like this before, and even the way Sean had played with her breasts the previous Friday somehow felt different because *he* had been the one doing everything and all she'd had to do was let herself enjoy it.

Whereas right now, it was all up to her.

"Serena, it's okay," he said gently. "You don't have to do this."

The warmth in his voice calmed her, and brought her back to her original purpose. "I know," she said, "but I really want to."

With that, she leaned forward and breathed him in for a moment before she slid her tongue over his abs. The muscles tightened as she licked them one by one, and she could see his hands fisting tightly at his sides.

As a model, she'd sold an illusion of sensuality to consumers hundreds of times. But though she'd been taught to be a master at playing her part for the cameras, she'd never before witnessed, live and in person, just what her genuine sensuality was capable of doing to a guy. Or just how much she could make him want her with nothing more than a few kisses, a few touches. Or that Sean's obvious hunger for her would fuel her own for him so strongly.

Though she'd already gotten his skin wet enough to shake on the salt and move on to the shot, she couldn't resist leaning close one more time to lick him again. His groan came as a clear enough warning that he was nearing the end of his rope, so she finally stopped teasing him and shook salt onto his abs.

She pressed her mouth to his stomach and sucked on him just as he had on her neck. It was with no small regret that she finally lifted her mouth from his skin and put the shot glass against her lips. This time, the tequila went down much more smoothly, and when she pressed the lime slice between her lips it was deliciously cool and the perfect mixture of sour and sweet.

Feeling warm and loose all over, she smiled at Sean. "Yum."

He grinned at her as he sat up. "Starting to develop a taste for tequila?"

"Maybe." She licked her lips. "Or maybe it's you I've developed a taste for."

"That makes two of us, then." He pulled her back onto his lap. "How are you feeling?"

The shot hadn't just made her limbs feel warm and fluid, it also made it so much easier for her to admit, "Like I can't stop wanting you. Like I don't ever want to stop wanting you."

For all his obvious arousal, his kiss came sweet and soft. "And the tequila?" he asked, his deep voice rolling through her like warm waves of a tropical ocean. "How's that treating you?"

"Good." She nibbled on his earlobe. "But I don't think I'm drunk yet."

"No?" The short word came out a little strangled, as if he was just barely managing to rein himself in.

Instead of answering him, she leaned over to pour

herself another shot. She didn't bother with salt or lime this time, just tossed it down her throat and got back to what she really wanted to do: kiss Sean.

And as he whispered her name against her lips before kissing her back just as passionately, she realized maybe she *was* ready for more.

Not just for hot sex...but maybe even for falling in love.

CHAPTER EIGHTEEN

Sean was glad that the back entrance to his frat house was deserted as he brought Serena inside a couple of hours later. Like every Friday, there would be another party tonight. Already, the bass pounded so loudly from the speakers downstairs that the walls were actually shaking. But he wasn't planning on either of them making an appearance.

She giggled, leaning into him while they walked. "This place smells bad. Like rotting socks."

"Alumni say it's smelled this way for more than a hundred years," he told her, making her laugh again, the sound slow and warmed by all the tequila she'd put away.

She was an adorable drunk. A ridiculously sexy drunk.

But still drunk, nonetheless.

Up on the hill when they'd been making out, the more she drank, the more she'd lost her inhibitions. Even knowing ahead of time that the evening was going to wreak serious havoc on his self-control, he'd still had to steel himself not to take advantage of her when he'd wanted her so badly.

Lord, was he glad he'd been there for her first drinking experience. He hated to think about what pretty much any other guy on the planet would have done as her defenses fell one after the other.

He hadn't planned on bringing her back to his bedroom tonight. But when she'd gotten a whole lot drunker, a whole lot faster than he'd expected, there'd been no way that he could just take her back to her room and leave her there. Not when neither of them knew how the post-drunk period would treat her. If she needed him, he needed to be there for her.

Luck remained on their side as he took her up the narrow, empty stairwell. His room was just a couple of doors down the hall and once he got her inside, he let out a breath of relief.

It wasn't that he didn't want to be seen with her—of course he wanted to claim her as *his* in front of the entire world. But since they still hadn't made an official decision about how public their relationship should be, he didn't want to make a misstep and upset her with more pictures and gossip spreading throughout campus—and beyond.

"I've been wondering for weeks what your room looked like." She shifted slightly against him so that her breasts pressed against his chest. "And I've been wondering what it would have been like if I'd come up with you when you asked me that first night—especially now that I can guess how good you would have made me feel."

Like he said, she was a sexy-as-hell drunk. But he made himself press a kiss to her forehead rather than her lips as she swayed even tighter into him.

"Come over here, beautiful."

"It's different when you say it."

He walked her over to the bed and gently sat her down on it. "What's different?"

"When you call me *beautiful*." She whispered the last word as if it were a bad one.

"Why?" He knelt in front of her, needing so badly to understand what made him different to her. "Why is it different when I say it?"

"My face, my body—all they are, all I am, is money to the people I've been around my whole life." She licked her lips as if she was afraid she wasn't making sense. "They call me beautiful to get something from me. They want me to be beautiful to get something for themselves. For their companies." She looked straight into his eyes. "But when *you* say it, I believe it might actually be true. And that it isn't bad. That I don't have to keep wishing it away."

"You *are* beautiful, Serena. So damned beautiful," he told her in a raw voice, not thinking, not weighing any of his words. Just knowing that they needed to be said. And heard. "All of you, Serena. Not just your face. Not just your body. *Everything* you are is beautiful."

He pulled her against him, breathed her in as he held her tightly. He'd taken care of his sisters, had his brothers' backs, watched over his mother and father, but that was his family. When it came to girls, to romance—to love—he'd never wanted to be a knight on a white steed for anyone, had always thought those fairytale stories were ridiculous. But now, he understood each and every one of them.

Because if he could vanquish Serena's demons, he would.

Stunned by the force of his own feelings for her—and by the fact that *love* was the only way he could describe them—he gently set her away from him. "Why don't you lie down for a few minutes?"

"Are you going to join me?"

God, he was tempted, especially given the half-innocent, half-budding-seductress way she'd asked. But he knew better, knew that the very last thing in the world he should do was kiss her, strip off her clothes, and make her his while she was drunk.

No, he wanted her to be one hundred percent with him when that happened.

"I should have made sure you ate before we went up to the Dish, but since I didn't, I'm going to go down and make you a plate of food to soak up some of that tequila you guzzled on the hill."

She moved as if to sit up. "I'll go with you."

He could only imagine the way word would spread if she wobbled into the kitchen downstairs. Like a freaking wildfire.

Plus, he needed a few minutes to try to get his head on straight. Or, more accurately, to figure out if he'd fallen in love with Serena. Because, at this point, even the idea of falling in love felt like being hit by an earthquake from out of the blue. Exciting to the part of him that wanted to believe there would be no collateral damage. Terrifying to the rational part that knew there probably would be.

And the thing was, if he really had gone and fallen in love with her, then he needed to figure out just what they were going to do about it. Starting with whether she loved him, too.

"I think you should stay up here."

"Kiss me first," she requested as she rolled over to put her arms around his neck, "and then maybe I'll stay."

He loved when she kissed him. With every kiss it felt like another meaningless hook-up from his past disappeared. One day, he wondered, would there only be her?

He could easily have kept kissing her all night long, but made himself draw back, stroking her silky hair with one hand as he pulled away. Her eyes had closed and there was a smile on her lips as he told her, "I'll be right back."

She nodded into his pillow, wrapping her arms around it. "I'll wait here." Her words were soft and slightly slurred.

Closing the door behind him with a soft click, he ran into Zane in the hall. "Hey, didn't think we'd see you tonight. Ready to party with us again?"

Sean hadn't been to one of his frat's parties since the night he'd met Serena. In truth, he hadn't enjoyed them for a long time, but he'd been so desperate to escape what was in his own head and heart that he'd kept going along with the same ritual as everyone else. But drinking, partying, picking up random girls, even working out until his muscles burned, hadn't helped him feel better.

Only being with Serena had been able to do that.

"Nope, just heading down to grab something to eat."

Zane looked at him like he was nuts. "What's up with you, man? You've been living like a monk for weeks. Ever since those pictures with you and the supermodel—" At Sean's hard look, he remembered not to call her that. "I mean, the pictures with you and Serena came out in that magazine."

Damned glad that no one knew she was upstairs right now, Sean walked into the kitchen, grabbed a plate, and opened the fridge. "You should have told me you were missing me this much. I would have brought you some roses, taken you out for a nice dinner somewhere."

"Asshole," Zane muttered good-naturedly, but Sean

was glad to see that he was already past his questions about Serena and was uncapping a bottle of beer.

It turned out, though, that Zane wasn't the only one who wanted to shoot the shit tonight, and in the end, Sean figured it was better to stick around for a little longer rather than make them wonder why he was in such a rush to get back up to his room. A dozen off-color jokes later, he finally picked up the plate of food and a bottle of water and took it upstairs. Stepping inside his room, he locked the door behind him so that they wouldn't risk one of his frat brothers barging in on them, and put the plate down on his desk.

"I brought some of every—"

His words fell away as he realized Serena was fast asleep. His heart turned over in his chest at just how soft and sweet and vulnerable she looked cuddling his pillow against her chest. Her long eyelashes dusted the tops of her cheekbones. Her full lips were slightly parted. And her hair was spread all across his pillows like someone had posed her for a sexy magazine shoot.

But no one had orchestrated the picture she presented for him. She just really was that beautiful. So beautiful that he could still hardly believe she'd chosen him to date, to kiss...and to trust.

Clearly, she wasn't going to be eating anything tonight, but at the very least he could make her more comfortable while she slept. She barely stirred when he unlaced her shoes and pulled them off. Though he knew most girls didn't like to sleep in their bras, and that no one liked to wear jeans to bed, he didn't let himself take either excuse to strip off anything more.

But he did need to get her beneath the covers, which meant the pleasure of lifting her into his arms so that he could pull back his covers and slide her onto the sheets.

"Sean?"

"Shhh." He breathed the word against her cheek as he slowly let go of her so that he could pull his dark-blue comforter over her. "I'm here if you need me."

Her eyes opened and they were such a clear, striking blue that he knew no photo, regardless of how talented the photographer or how good the equipment, would ever do her justice.

"I do need you," she whispered. "So bad that it hurts sometimes."

And when she held out her arms for him, how could he do anything but give her what she needed? By the time he'd gathered her into his arms, her head nestled into the crook of his arm, she was fast asleep again.

He doubted he'd be able to get much sleep of his own tonight, but he wasn't complaining. Not when holding the girl he loved, and feeling her heart beat against his, was the best thing he'd ever felt in his life. So good that even the thought of collateral damage no longer mattered.

Whatever came, he'd deal with it.

They both would.

* * *

Serena woke just as the sun began to rise outside the window. Years of early shoots to catch the sunrise still made it impossible for her to sleep in...even when her head felt like someone had been hitting it repeatedly with a sledgehammer. She groaned as she lifted her hands to her face, but the sound died in her throat when she realized she wasn't alone in her bed.

And that it wasn't her bed.

Her heart immediately started to race as she slowly turned her head on the pillow and saw Sean sleeping beside her.

Oh God, yesterday had been her big "let's get drunk together on tequila" plan. Obviously, given the throbbing in her head, she'd managed the *get drunk* part, no problem.

But what else had she done while she was at it?

Like, say, Sean Morrison?

Just as panic started to whip up inside her, she belatedly realized that she was still wearing her sweatshirt and jeans. Relief promptly stole away her panic.

Last night she'd thought that she might be ready to sleep with Sean, but the morning after, she now knew that doing it after drinking would have been the world's worst idea.

Not, she thought as her brain started to slowly fill in the gaps, that she hadn't given seducing him a shot. Surely she'd provided him with at least a couple of good openings to sleep with her if he'd wanted to. But that was exactly why she'd felt safe enough to take her first-ever drinks with him—she could always trust him to make good decisions, even if her own judgment became impaired.

For weeks she'd been wondering what it would be like to come up here, to his room. To his bed. Of course, she thought with a small smile, she hadn't thought it would finally happen because she'd been too tipsy to make it back to her own.

Smiling made her realize just how dry her lips and tongue were, and that she was desperate for a drink of water. She didn't want to wake Sean—not when he looked to be sleeping the sleep of the truly exhausted—so she moved as carefully as possible from under the covers he must have pulled over her last night.

But once both feet were on the floor, instead of tiptoeing into his adjoining bathroom right away, she couldn't stop staring at him while he slept. And all the while, her heart tumbled in her chest.

Was this what love felt like?

From the start, she'd been stunned by the strength of her feelings for him. Still, it might have been easy enough to convince herself that it was nothing more than a physical reaction to his kisses, especially when he was so amazing at giving them to her.

But this morning, she couldn't deny any longer that her feelings went far deeper than just bodies and kisses. And she couldn't fight the desire to want to go even deeper, to know him even better. So much better than she did right now.

For the past few weeks they'd grown more and more comfortable with each other on their Friday night dates, and had definitely shared things with each other that they didn't share with others. But at the same time, they'd also both been careful to keep their biggest secrets to themselves.

When her head began to pound in earnest, she headed into his bathroom to splash some cold water on her face, guzzle some down, and brush her teeth with some toothpaste on her fingertip. Feeling a thousand times better from that alone, her stomach was growling by the time she tiptoed out of the bathroom.

It only took her nose a few seconds to zero in on the plate of food on Sean's desk. She had a vague memory of his telling her he was going to get her something to eat to soak up the tequila. She smiled as she picked up the plate full of crackers and cheese and salami. The food looked a little the worse for wear by this morning, but not bad enough that she'd turn it down when she was this starved.

After that night they'd shared slices of pizza together, salami and sharp cheddar cheese had become two of her new favorite things to eat. She happily sat down on the chair in the corner of his room with the plate on her lap. But for all the grace she'd had to learn as a model, this morning her limbs were getting away from her enough that she accidentally kicked a plastic box beneath a side table. Hard enough that the top slid off and landed on the floor with a thud.

Her gaze flew to Sean, but thankfully, he didn't so much as stir. Carefully putting the plate on the table, she was bending to pick up the top of the box when she caught sight of its contents.

Pictures.

Dozens of pictures, in both black and white and color, all piled in the box under his table.

And the top picture on the pile was of his mother.

CHAPTER NINETEEN

Serena knew she should put the top back on the box. She knew she should get back on the chair and eat the food he'd brought her. She knew she had no right to pry into Sean's life, especially without his permission. She knew she should wait for him to want to share these pictures with her.

But all the things she knew, and how badly she wanted to know him better, got so blurred inside her head that she couldn't stop herself from sitting cross-legged on the floor and reaching for the pictures.

Her hands were shaking as she stared at the woman in the photo. Serena recognized Sean's smile on her face, so easy, so captivating. Because even though his mother was far too thin in the picture, and there was pain behind her eyes, when she smiled into her son's camera, pure, sweet love shone through.

How many times, Serena wondered, had Sean taken out this picture to stare at it? And how many times had he wished that his mother had survived?

A tear fell unnoticed down her cheek as she carefully laid the photo down and reached into the pile for another.

A large family stared back at her, their smiles slightly forced, but beautiful nonetheless. His three brothers were all big and handsome like him. His two sisters were incredibly pretty, the older one more elegant and serious, the younger obviously full of spunk.

But his father...all she could think, as she stared at the photo, was that his father looked broken. As if he simply couldn't imagine going on without the woman he loved.

Serena hadn't been able to see anything but the love in his mother's eyes when she'd looked at that first picture, but as she laid the family photo down on the floor beside it and picked up another photo of the ocean tide on a smooth, sandy beach, she realized just how talented a photographer Sean was. Not, of course, that she was surprised. Everything he did, he did well, from schoolwork, to baseball, to kissing her.

But even though each of the three photos was very different—a candid of his mother, a portrait of his family, and a nature shot—each had a distinct perspective. Technically, they were all excellent, but it was the emotion in every one of them that held her captive.

One picture after another, she learned about the man she'd fallen for. Saw not only how much his mother and his family meant to him, but also how much he saw all around him. He'd joked about taking pictures of bugs as a kid, but now she knew that he saw even the smallest things that most everyone else—including her—never noticed at all. Things the rest of them never even thought to look for. It was just how she felt whenever he looked at her, whenever he called her *beautiful*, like he saw everything she was trying so hard to keep hidden. Not just from everyone else, but even from herself.

But it was a photo near the bottom of the pile that made her forget not to gasp out loud.

Sean's mother was sleeping in the picture. She was in a hospital bed, with wires and tubes all over and around her. She was painfully thin and pale. So horribly pale that it was obvious there was nothing more to be done for her. Serena stared at the picture, her heart breaking for him all over again.

"What the hell are you doing?"

She was still holding the picture of his mother in the hospital as she slowly turned to face him. The utter despair on his face almost made her lose her voice. But though she'd totally screwed up and needed to apologize, she first needed him to know how much she cared for him. And that she wanted so badly to help heal his pain.

"I'm so sorry, Sean. Your mother—" She looked down at the heart-wrenching photo in her hand. "—she's beautiful."

In a flash, he ripped the photo from her fingers. Roughly, quickly, he gathered them all up and threw them back into the box.

"Careful!" she pleaded as she came to her feet. "Those pictures you took, they're precious. You shouldn't ruin them because you're angry with me." Despair had turned to fury in his dark eyes as he swung around to face her. Her chest, her stomach, all of her hurt, as she said, "I'm sorry. I didn't mean to look. I swear I didn't. I accidentally kicked the box and when the cover came off—"

"It sure doesn't look like a goddamned accident to me, you sitting there with my pictures on the floor all around you."

He was right. Even though finding the pictures had been an accident, poring through them hadn't been. "I shouldn't have looked at them. I know I shouldn't have, not when you weren't ready to show them to me." She wanted to reach out to him, wanted to touch him again, wanted to try to close the huge distance that was growing between them. Especially when she'd never seen him look so anguished. "But I..."

He shifted just out of range of her fingertips. "But what? You thought you'd do it anyway just because you felt like it? Because you've always gotten everything you wanted so you figured this was one more thing that should be yours?"

She sucked in a shaky breath even though all the oxygen in the room had been sucked out by her stupid decision to pry into his past, his emotions, the most painful part of his life.

"I care about you, Sean, you know that I do," she told him in a voice barely above a whisper. "And when I saw the picture on top, when I realized it was your mother, I—" Her voice broke on the single syllable. "I'm sorry."

"How could you?" But he didn't give her a chance to try to answer. "I thought I knew you."

"You *do* know me."

"Do I? Or was I just being an idiot, blinded by your face like everyone else?"

It stung, God, how it stung, to hear him talk about her looks right now, and to blame his feelings on them. Especially after the way she'd told him last night that he was the only person in her life who didn't look at her face as a commodity.

"I'm so sorry for looking at the pictures without your consent, sorrier than you'll ever know," she said again as she tried to push away his heated words, words she didn't want to believe he could possibly mean. He was grieving and in terrible pain over the loss of his mother, and her actions had obviously brought all of those feelings back up before he was ready to deal with them. "But I've seen the way you look every time your mother comes up and I want so badly to be there for you."

"So this is how you thought you'd do it? By snooping through my things?"

Why couldn't he see that she hadn't meant to hurt him? That she'd only done what she had because she cared so much about him? And that it also hurt her the way he was shutting down, shutting her out so completely?

"You asked me from the start to trust you. You said it was okay to be scared, because you'd make sure that I didn't get hurt, and that we wouldn't move too fast. I've tried to keep trusting you, tried so hard that sometimes I actually think I've succeeded at conquering some of my own demons. But now, with these photos which obviously mean *everything* to you, why can't you trust me, too?" When he didn't say anything, even though something way down deep inside of her it felt like everything was starting to shatter, she still couldn't let herself give up on him. On them. "I know I can't understand what it must be like to lose your mother. But if you can just try to let me in a little—"

"How many times have you spoken to your mother since you've been on campus?"

"I..." Her throat felt as raw as if she'd been crying all night rather than sleeping in Sean's arms. "I haven't."

"Do you know how many times I would have given anything to talk to my mom again? You haven't even talked to yours at all, but now you want me to open up to you about mine being dead?"

She knew he was hurting terribly, but for everything he thought she didn't understand about him, there was just as much he didn't understand about her. And what he didn't know about her mattered. Mattered a lot, even if it wasn't life and death.

"Do you know why I haven't talked to my mom? Because she won't call me back. She won't write me back, won't have anything at all to do with me, because she's so mad at me for finally making my own decisions about everything. But even though she doesn't understand why I need to make my own decisions for once in my life, I've been trying so hard to make sure they're the right ones." God, she could hardly think it, let alone say it aloud, but she had to. "Now you're making me think I haven't. Now you're making me wonder if the dumbest thing I ever did was trust you with myself. With my heart." Her breath was coming fast and her ears were ringing as if she was in the front row of a hard-rock concert. "I'm sorry. I'm so sorry, so impossibly sorry that you're hurting. I'm so sorry you lost your mom. I'm so sorry I pried into your private things. I shouldn't have done it. I shouldn't have kept looking at your pictures. One day I hope you'll be able to forgive me. But most of all, one day—" She could barely get the words out around the tears that clogged her throat as she reached blindly for the doorknob, needing to run so he wouldn't see just how broken she felt about opening up her heart to him just in time for him to break it in two. "One day I hope you'll find a way to be happy again. Because there's nothing I want more for you than that."

CHAPTER TWENTY

It had been a huge shock to see Serena going through his pictures. But it had been an even worse shock to see the photos of his mom again.

Sean hadn't just stayed away from his camera since the day his mom died. He'd completely avoided his box of pictures, too, not even letting Olivia dig into them for the funeral when she'd needed some extra photos to display for the hundreds of people who had come to pay their final respects.

Just hours earlier, he'd fallen asleep holding Serena in his arms, and it was her absence that had woken him up. He'd been so glad to see that she was still there. But then, when he'd realized what she was looking at, it had felt like all his skin had been ripped off and there was nothing left of him but blood and bones and guts in front of her. That was why he'd reacted so harshly. Too harshly. Like a complete idiot who couldn't stop things he didn't even believe about her from spewing out of his mouth.

Not until she'd turned to walk away from him and it finally got through his thick skull that she was leaving.

Leaving him.

Because he'd hurt her.

"Please." He caught her halfway down the back stairs. "Please don't go. I'm sorry for everything I just said. I'm sorry for everything I just did." He didn't care who heard them, who saw them together. All that mattered was that Serena knew he was sorrier about what he'd said to her than he'd ever been for anything his entire life. "If I could talk about my mom with anyone, it would be with you. I didn't mean what I said. *I swear I didn't.*"

For several long, painful moments, she didn't move. Didn't speak. And he thought for sure that he'd lost her.

But then, when she finally turned back to face him, he was brought nearly to his knees. Because instead of looking at him with hate...all he could see was the pure truth of how much she cared about him. Just like she'd said over and over when he'd been blinded by grief.

"I know you didn't," she said softly. And then, though he didn't deserve it after what he'd said, after the way he'd behaved—when anyone else would already have been gone by now—she slid her arms around him and laid her face against his chest. "And I know you would."

"Don't leave. Please don't leave me, Serena."

She didn't answer him with words, simply slid her hand through his and led them back to his room.

Desperate to make right everything that he'd nearly destroyed, he begged, "Forgive me." His words were muffled against the top of her head where he was pressing one kiss after another to her hair. Hell, she should leave him for this alone, if only to get away from a guy who wanted too much from her, who needed more from her than anyone else ever had. "I shouldn't ask you to forgive me again, not when I promised never to screw up like I did that first night, but I can't stop myself from asking. And I can't stop hoping that you will."

She turned her face up to his so that his next kiss landed on her mouth instead of her hair. "I already have. Especially since I should have waited until you were ready to show the pictures to me and talk about them, too." She slid one hand up between their chests and laid it over his racing heart. "I..." He could see that she was nervous about what she was about to say. "I care so much about you. So, so much, Sean."

He badly wanted to tell her what he'd realized last night—that he was in love with her. So in love that he could hardly think straight anymore. But he'd already done enough to screw things up for one morning. If she didn't feel the same way, if she wasn't yet ready to move from caring about him to loving him...hell, the last thing he needed to do at this point was risk pushing her even further away by coming on too strong.

Still, for all that he was trying to hold back so that he didn't scare her, when he said, "You're amazing," the two simple words came out so strong, so raw, that he knew he wasn't hiding much at all from her.

When her lips found his at the same time his took hers, their kiss was more passionate, more intense, than he'd ever known a kiss could be. Her mouth on his tangled his senses, made him ache way down deep in the center of his chest.

"Please," she whispered against his lips. "Please don't stop with just a kiss today. Not when I need you so badly. Not when I need to know that we're still real and that nothing has changed because both of us are sorry and both of us are forgiven, too."

Needing all the same things, he captured her mouth

in another searing, mind-bending kiss. Gripping the bottom of her sweatshirt and her T-shirt and her bra all together in his fists, he yanked at them so roughly that he nearly tore them as he pulled them over her head. And then...sweet Lord...she was standing there in front of him, bared from the waist up and so shockingly beautiful that the final threads of sanity he'd been trying to hold on to were lost in a rush of desire so strong it actually did take him to his knees.

"Serena." He whispered her name in the exact moment he took her nipple onto his tongue. His hands cupped, caressed, teased her breasts even as his mouth took, feasted, craved.

"Please," she begged again, breathless now as she threaded her fingers into his hair and arched into his mouth. "Oh God, please don't stop."

No. He wouldn't stop. He couldn't stop. Didn't ever want to stop kissing her. Didn't ever want to stop tasting her. All he wanted to do was claim her as his. Only his. Not only today. Not just this morning. But over and over and over again.

Forever.

He moved his attention to her other breast and licked over her with deliberate slowness, knowing that if he didn't force himself to take his time, he'd later regret not savoring every single second. Not just of getting to be with her, but getting to be her first.

He knew by now that she'd never been with another guy...because she wouldn't have trusted anyone the way she trusted him.

Earn it. He swore again to himself that he would earn her trust. Even more so in the aftermath of having lashed out and hurt her just minutes earlier. She'd just forgiven him again, and he'd make damn sure she wouldn't regret opening herself up to him. That she wouldn't regret being there for him. And that she wouldn't regret staying.

He'd always made sure to stop them before things went too far. But today, the boundaries had shifted. Far enough that he wouldn't stop at the edge today, but would take her all the way over it. No matter what else happened, he'd make sure she knew pleasure. The deep, amazing pleasure that she deserved...and that he was so damned lucky she trusted him to give her.

Finally rising from his knees, he kissed her long and deep before pulling back to look into her eyes. Just as he had every time they were together, he needed to make absolutely sure that he wasn't moving too fast.

"Is it too much?"

"No. God, no. It isn't nearly enough."

He slowly moved his hands to the top of her jeans. "What about this?" He slid the button out of its hole. "Will this be too much? Because I'll stop if you need me to."

On a little frustrated growl that shot straight to his groin, she slid her hands from his hair to cover his over her zipper, and yanked it down. The next thing he knew, she was shimmying out of her jeans...and was standing before him in nothing but little white lace panties, at once both totally innocent and the sexiest thing he'd ever seen.

"I can't think when I'm looking at you," he confessed in a half-whisper, half-groan. "I need a second to get a grip."

But instead of giving him a chance to pull himself together, she put her thumbs in the slim sides of the lace that barely covered her. "I've wanted this with you since that first night. Since our first kiss."

"I have, too," he told her, but he still made himself cover her hands with his so that she had to hold the lace up against her hips rather than pull it down. Because once she was naked...

When she realized he wouldn't let her strip off her underwear, she looked up at him with equal parts frustration and desperate lust. "Then why haven't you? You've been so gentle, given me so much space and room it's nearly driven me completely crazy. Especially knowing that you've done this with so many other girls, but not with me."

"You're not like the others, Serena. You'll never be like the others." She made him want to be a better man. "You're special. You need to know how special you are."

"You've always made me feel special." She shifted her hands beneath his so that they were palm to palm. *"Always.* Even that first night, the way you held me, the way you kissed me, the way you looked at me...I'd never felt like that with anyone else. "

This time when they kissed, there was more than just need. More than just desire. More than just desperate lust. And when he touched her, when he made her come, he knew it wouldn't just be about giving her physical pleasure...it would be about making her happy in ways and places that even the best sex in the world couldn't reach.

Still kissing her, he slid his arms around her shoulders and beneath her legs, then lifted her. He felt her smile against his mouth, loved the soft sound of her happiness as she laughed in his arms while he carried her over to the bed. But after he laid her down and finally slid the lace from her hips and down her legs, never once did his gaze leave her eyes. Not until she put her hand over his and slid it up her bare thigh to her hip bone.

Knowing that she was finally giving him permission to touch her made him feel like his heart was going to rip out of his chest, it was beating so hard. "Show me," he begged her. "Show me what you want. Show me what you *need.*"

His name was on her lips as she slid both of their hands over her sex. The moment he caressed her slick, hot flesh, her breath left her lungs in a hard rush, her free arm clinging tightly to him as she buried her face in the crook of his neck.

"So soft." He barely knew what he was saying, just that he had to tell her what touching her like this did to him. "So wet." He had to slide one finger down over her once, then twice, then a third time. "So perfect."

She pulled him even more tightly against herself, trembling from the force of trying to get closer to his hand as he stroked her. "I've dreamt of you coming for me," he whispered against her ear. "Of how you'd sound. Of how you'd feel." He nipped at her earlobe. "And of how you'd beg me to make you just keep coming, again and again and again."

"*Oh God.* I feel—" She didn't finish her sentence, but the way she opened her thighs even wider for him, then bucked up into his touch, told him exactly how she was feeling.

Tangling his free hand in her hair, he pulled her head back, gently, but far enough that her eyes met his. "I need to see you," he ground out from lungs that felt like they'd never be able to take in enough oxygen ever again. At least not when Serena's naked body was wrapped around his. "I need to know that everything I do, that everything we do together, feels good."

"Good," she gasped against his lips a beat before he covered hers to pour all of his pent-up, barely controlled need into a kiss. "So, so good."

Her eyes were dilated nearly to black when he finally

allowed himself to slip one finger inside.

"Oh!" The sound caught in her throat, and broke into several pieces as he slowly moved over her clitoris, then just as slowly slid back inside. *"Oh God."*

He built the rhythm as deliberately as he could given his wild, insane need to make her come apart beneath him. Soon, she was rocking against him, growing even wetter, even hotter, so that he almost forgot to be careful, almost forgot not to tear off his own clothes and just *take*.

But he would never let himself forget that this morning was about Serena. About showing her pleasure. And even more important, proving to her that she could trust him—that she wasn't wrong to have forgiven him for doing and saying all the wrong things.

Between the breathy little sounds she was making and the way her inner muscles were clenching around his finger, he knew she was close. Brushing back the hair from her face, he cupped her cheek gently in one hand as he played over her with the other.

"Come for me, beautiful."

Her eyes had fluttered nearly closed before they suddenly flared open with so much pleasure that it floored him to watch her give herself over so completely, so incredibly, not just to her climax...but, amazingly, to him, too.

CHAPTER TWENTY-ONE

Everything was perfect, and Serena felt like nothing bad could ever happen to her again. Not when she was feeling like *this,* all softly melting and brilliantly sparkling at the same time.

And still...there was more. More she wanted. More she needed to finally experience.

She'd been naked plenty of times in her life as she changed backstage at fashion shows, and while designers had pinned and draped fabric over her. Her mother had always been there to watch the proceedings like a hawk, so there had never been the slightest bit of sexuality to her nakedness while she worked. On the contrary, she'd always felt as if she was no different than a plastic mannequin standing cold and lifeless while waiting for someone to dress her in the latest fashions for a display window.

Being naked with Sean was a revelation. He looked at her with so much heat, and with seemingly unquenchable, never-ending need. He couldn't keep his hands off her as he stroked and caressed, so sweetly gentle and then perfectly rough just when she needed him to be. And when his tongue had slicked across her nipple and he'd drawn her in between his lips?

Delicious shivers wracked her body as arousal set up high and heavy in her bloodstream just from remembering how good it felt. Her eyes were still closed but she could feel his fingertips lightly dancing over her eyelids, then down the bridge of her nose and over her lips and neck, until he laid his large palm flat between her breasts, right where her heart was still beating so fast for him.

"Serena?"

She knew he was probably concerned about having pushed her too far. But didn't he know that he shouldn't have one single thing to worry about right now on her behalf? Not when she felt better than she ever had in her entire life.

"That was—" She was about to say *amazing*, but the word didn't sound right in her head. What they'd just shared, what Sean had just shown her, was so far beyond *amazing* that all the seven-letter word did was make it sound trite, rather than the most beautiful, wonderful, incredible thing that had ever happened to her.

So instead of trying to find the right words, she opened her eyes, smiled, and kissed him.

She kissed him to show him how much she loved him, even though she was scared to say it so soon.

She kissed him to tell him just how good he'd made her feel.

She kissed him as an open invitation to taking all of her, body and soul, with nothing held back anymore.

"Make love to me, Sean."

She whispered the words between kisses. And when he groaned and kissed her back, she didn't let herself overthink things, just reached for the button of his jeans to strip away the denim barrier between them. But just as he had when she'd been about to take off her own clothes, he put his hand over hers to still it.

"I want you, Serena. You can't possibly imagine how much I want you right now. To take you and make you *mine*. But—"

"I already told you," she interjected, "you don't have to wait. *We* don't have to wait."

She was begging, but she didn't care. Not when he'd just given her a taste of something more beautiful than she could ever have imagined and she now knew that a taste could never again be enough. She had to have *all* of it— all of him, and herself, too.

"Earlier, when I woke up and you were looking at the pictures—"

"I'm sorry," she said again. "I won't pry again. Not until you're ready."

Still holding her close, so close that her breasts were pressed against his cotton-covered chest, he said, "I don't want you to apologize anymore. I'm not angry with you, Serena, I swear I'm not. I meant it when I said if there was anyone I talk about my mom with, it would be you." He inhaled a hard, slightly shaky breath. "Soon." She knew it was a promise. One that he meant. "But not today. Not yet." He paused another beat, before adding, "And if I can't give you everything, then you shouldn't give me this."

If she could have argued against what he'd just said for the sake of pleasure and pleasure alone, she would have done just that. Especially when she knew that he'd had plenty of sex before, with girls he hadn't let into his heart anywhere as deeply as she was already. But it was more than just the fact that he wasn't yet able to trust her with his grief over losing his mother that held her back. Wasn't it true that she hadn't told him everything about her mother, either?

Soon. Just like he'd said, she would tell him soon.

"Okay," she finally said, "but even though I'm agreeing that we should wait a little longer to sleep together, that doesn't mean I want to wait until next Friday to see you again."

"There's no freaking way I'm waiting a week, either." He kissed her, but when the soft press of their lips quickly shifted back to full-on passion, each of them made themselves pull back. "We may have to meet in public spaces from now on, though."

She knew he was simply joking about the fact that they were bound to jump each other if they were alone again, but she needed him to know something. "I'm sick of hiding, Sean. I don't care if every magazine in the world prints pictures of us." She'd been so worried about her mother disowning her for dating someone. But she'd just have to find a way to make Genevieve understand that this wasn't a fling and Sean wasn't using her. It was, at least on her side, *love.* "I want to be your girlfriend. For real. Out in the open so that everyone knows I'm yours."

"Mine." He didn't hold back with the kiss that followed his verbal possession of her, and she loved feeling that possession in the way he ran his hands over her curves, from breasts to hips and then between her legs, too. "One more, Serena. Give me one more before I take you home."

Her lungs all out of breath, her brain all out of words, she told him *yes* simply by wrapping her arms and legs around him and kissing him back with all the passion she possessed.

* * *

A little while later, Serena somehow managed to firm

up her melted bones and fried brain cells enough to put her clothes and shoes back on, even as she was terribly distracted by how aroused Sean still must be. She'd done absolutely nothing to take the edge off his desire, but that was only because he'd stuck firmly to his guns and hadn't let her.

Again and again, she kept reminding herself that he was right—they needed to take the final emotional step with each other before they took any of the next physical ones. The problem was, every time she thought about the way he'd touched her, kissed her, how high he'd sent her flying...it only got harder and harder to remember all the rational reasons to keep taking things slowly.

When they were both fully dressed, he slid his fingers through her hair to comb it back from her face. "Ready to do this?"

She smiled at him. "It's my very first walk of shame. Just like all the other normal Stanford students have already done."

When his face fell, she realized just how stupid her joke had been. "I'm just kidding. I'm not ashamed to be with you, or to leave your room with everyone knowing exactly what we've been doing." She went up onto her tippy-toes to kiss him. "In fact, is it bad that a part of me *wants* all of them to know?"

Slowly, his lips curved up into a smile. "They'll all think and say whatever they want. But the only one I give a shit about is you. Although, if someone says something to you that makes you uncomfortable, I want you to tell me right away."

"If they do say something, I'm not going to worry about it." She looked into his deep green yes. "Not anymore. Because the only one *I* give a shit about is *you.*"

She loved hearing him laugh at her surprising potty

mouth and was glad that they'd managed to break through the tension. He put her bag over his shoulder, then held his door open for her. It figured that she'd barely put one foot over the threshold when she walked into one of his frat brothers.

The guy looked at her, then around her to see Sean standing in the doorway. *"Dude."* He strung out the four-letter word into one long sound.

Sean put his arm around her waist. "Zane, this is my girlfriend, Serena."

She loved the way he said it so easily. "Hi," she said, smiling. "It's nice to meet you."

Sean's friend seemed more than a little bit stunned. "Great to meet you, too."

"Talk to you later," Sean said before his friend could start a conversation. His hand remained on her lower back as he directed her toward the main stairs rather than the back ones they'd come up the night before.

"'Bye," she called over her shoulder with another smile.

One by one they met more of his frat brothers and teammates downstairs, every one of them having a similar borderline-speechless reaction. Finally, when they made it outside to the sidewalk, she couldn't hold back her laughter any longer.

"Wow, my head is spinning at how quickly you got us through there. What exactly did you think they were going to do if we hadn't blasted through?"

"With those guys? Who the hell knows? Trust me, they're all losing their minds over finally seeing you and me together."

"I know I'm not always the most socially adept person on the planet," she admitted, "but I think I could have held my own if you'd let us stay long enough to talk with any of them."

"Of course you can hold your own." It warmed her how he said it, as if it was the most obvious thing in the world. "That's not why I got us out of there so fast."

"Then why?"

"Because they can be a bunch of idiots. And if any of them had said anything even remotely inappropriate to you, I would have had to tear them apart with my bare hands. Right in front of you."

She'd known he was protective, had heard it in his voice when he spoke about his sisters and the rest of his family. And she'd seen it for herself, as well, in how he'd gone out of his way to carefully plan their Friday nights so that she wouldn't be recognized. But this morning, it was amazing to see his protectiveness in action. First, when he'd held them back from making love because he thought they needed to take the final emotional step before they had sex. And now, when he couldn't so much as stand the thought of anyone disrespecting her.

"People are going to say things," she reminded him. "But," she added with a finger to his lips before he could jump in, "I've learned a lot in these past few weeks about not caring what anyone else thinks. And I don't think it's such a bad thing if I learn what I'm actually capable of dealing with and doing."

"*Anything*, Serena. *Everything* is what you're capable of."

She knew she'd never smiled wider, or been so happy as they walked together across campus, hand in hand. And for the first time since she'd started at Stanford, she kept her head uncovered and wore only a T-shirt, rather than her big sweatshirt. Not only had she and Sean started to really solidify things between them, but her routine these past few weeks couldn't have been more boring to any paparazzi that might still have been hanging around. Surely, people's interest in her stepping away from modeling and going to college had finally dribbled away to nothing.

Maybe she didn't need to hide anymore.

Maybe she could finally become the person she was meant to be.

Someone who loved books and learning.

Someone who loved new experiences and trying new things.

Someone who loved an amazing guy...and was loved right back.

* * *

"Thank God," Abi said when they walked into Serena's dorm room a short while later. "I was hoping that's where you were last night." She shot Sean a quick smile, but then frowned at Serena. "Seriously, next time you could at least text me back."

Surprised to realize that her roommate had been worried about her, Serena said, "I'm sorry, I didn't even think to check my phone." And wasn't it amazing that she finally had a real friend? Someone who actually worried about her. Someone who actually cared. Serena silently vowed to do better on her end. "I'll let you know next time when I'm not coming back for the night. I promise."

Thankfully, her roommate was extremely forgiving. On the other hand, she was also clearly extremely interested in whatever had transpired between the two of them. "You two look happy." Serena could feel her cheeks flushing even before Abi asked Sean point blank, "Does your twin look just like you?"

To his credit, he laughed. "Pretty much."

Abi's eyes lit up. "Do you know if he's dating

anyone?"

"I don't, actually. But I could find out."

"That would be awesome. And if he isn't, maybe you could tell him all about your girlfriend's great roommate."

Sean grinned at her again. "Will do."

With that, thankfully, Abi turned back to the book she was reading and stuck in her earbuds. Serena mouthed *sorry* to him. But he was still smiling.

"Speaking of my brother, how would you like to meet him?"

"Are you kidding? I'd love to."

"Good. Because it's my sister's birthday tomorrow and we're all getting together at the house in Los Altos."

His brother had been easy, but the thought of meeting everyone immediately set her heart to racing. *Fast.* "Your whole family is going to be there?"

He was smiling down at her as he brushed a thumb over her lower lip. "Does the idea of meeting all of them make you nervous?"

She didn't even need to think about it. "Yes."

"Don't be. They're all going to love you." His eyes darkened. "Drew might actually love you a little too much. In fact, it wouldn't surprise me if he pulled out all the stops to convince you to dump my ass for him."

"He wouldn't."

"I might have stolen a couple of girls from him back in high school," Sean said in a slightly cocky way. "He's still trying to get payback. But it will never happen."

"No," she agreed, "it won't." Because no matter how great the other Morrison brothers were, she couldn't imagine wanting anyone but Sean.

"Olivia, my middle sister, might be a little slower to warm up than the others. But that won't have anything to do with you. It's just because she worries too much. And

Maddie is probably going to want to trade outfits with you or beg to do your hair, or something. Justin, at least, will be cool. He's really mellow."

Even though her brain was reeling at the thought of meeting them all, she realized he'd left one sibling out of his list. "What about your oldest brother? Will he be there?"

"Sure. But Grant won't try to mess with your head. Not when he takes his role as oldest so seriously. And I'd bet my tuition for the year that my father is going to pull me aside to tell me not to screw things up with you. Be prepared," Sean warned. "He's going to call you a *keeper.*"

Realizing, again, just how close—and fun—his family was, suddenly she didn't feel quite as nervous anymore. Especially when him letting her in like this was one step closer to that final step they needed to take.

"Okay. Tomorrow I'll go meet your family."

He pulled her against him, and she loved the way they fit so perfectly together. Her head tucked right in beneath his chin, and she was tall enough to feel his heart beating against hers, so warm and real.

"I'd better go," he finally said, "before I can't stop myself from dragging you back to my place. Because you've probably got tons of studying to do, don't you?"

"I do," she made herself say. And it was true. She had a bit more preparation to do on her big midterm presentation about the Brontë sisters' novels, and it wasn't going to get done while she was making out with Sean. "You've got studying *and* baseball, don't you?"

He nodded, and when she looked into his eyes, she knew that even one more little kiss would send both of them spiraling off again. "Thank you for an amazing night. And an even more amazing morning."

"Tonight." He didn't say it as a question. "I want you with me tonight. Once you're done studying, text me and I'll come pick you up."

She nodded, shivering slightly at what she knew would happen again tonight. Because even if he wouldn't yet make love to her, he would touch her in other ways that made her burn in the best possible way.

"Tonight," she echoed. A beat later, he was gone.

* * *

"You're glowing."

Serena slowly turned to face her roommate. She felt as if she were dreaming and one too-quick move would break the beautiful spell. "I feel like I actually am."

"So much for taking it slow," Abi said with a wide grin that showed how much she approved of seeing the two of them together.

"We didn't—" Serena began, but there was so much that they *had* done, that the full truth came down to, "I'm still a virgin."

"So technical," Abi teased. "Well, whatever you did with him, you're one lucky bitch!" She sighed. "All the guys I've hooked up with on campus so far have been major creeps. Total losers."

"Sorry." Her roommate was sweet and fun, and Serena wanted only good things for her. "I'm going to be meeting his family tomorrow, so I can check out his other brothers if you want."

"Of course I want! Where are you meeting them?"

"His sister's birthday party."

Abi made an *I knew it* sound. "He is so in love with you."

"He hasn't said anything like that to me."

"Are you kidding? He's saying it to you every way a

guy possibly could. Setting up all these clandestine Friday nights so that you aren't bombarded with photographers. Not rushing you to do him. Taking you home to meet the fam. And I'm not even going to ask you if you're in love with him, too. Nothing has *ever* been clearer than that."

The thing was, Abi was right. Serena *was* in love with Sean. And even if he hadn't yet said the words, he *had* shown her in so many different ways just how much he cared about her. So then why hadn't she let him all the way in?

Tomorrow, she decided. Tomorrow, after she met his family, if she still felt good about everything, she'd finally open up completely to him about her mother and what her life had really been like before she came to Stanford.

And then maybe, just maybe, he'd finally feel comfortable opening up completely to her, too.

CHAPTER TWENTY-TWO

One of the biggest things Serena had learned during the past few weeks was the art of concentration. It would have been so easy to lie around daydreaming about Sean, or even better, to spend every free moment with him. But pursuing her dream of getting a serious education that she could build into a rewarding career was just as important. Close, anyway, she thought, as he drew her closer with his arm around her shoulder to shield her from the cool evening breeze.

For the past eight hours straight, she'd been writing and rewriting her big presentation for Monday. She could practically recite it in her sleep by now, but she'd never had such a big test before. Especially not an oral one in front of her professor and her entire class.

"You sure you're okay with coming over tonight?"

Sean had her things in a bag slung over his shoulder, and they were already more than halfway between her dorm and his frat. But even though she knew turning back was the last thing he wanted, he'd take her right back if he thought that was what she needed.

"Yes. I'm totally sure about staying with you

tonight."

But he didn't just listen to what she said, he made them stop in the middle of the path so he could look into her eyes. "Did you get through all of your work today after I left?"

"I did."

"But?"

Had anyone ever understood her this well, hearing all the things she wasn't saying, making her admit even her smallest fears so that she could finally get over them?

"I feel like I've been preparing for my presentation forever, but I'm still a little nervous about it. Especially since I've never stood up in front of a class to talk before."

"What if you gave the presentation to me tonight? And then after you aren't nervous about it anymore..." He gave her a smile, one full of so much sensual promise it took her breath away. "I'll take your clothes off and make you come again."

She loved that he hadn't just blown off her concerns by telling her how great she was going to do. And she *definitely* loved the way a few hot words from his lips had her entire body burning up even as a cold breeze blew over her. Still, "You don't want to hear me talk about the Brontë sisters and their influence on the modern novel."

"I do."

She laughed, shaking her head. "Nice try, but I'm pretty sure being bored senseless isn't the kind of foreplay every guy looks forward to."

"Screw foreplay. If you just need to stay up with me working on your presentation tonight, that's what we'll do. I want you, Serena. But I want you to be happy more."

It was the most seductive thing he could possibly have said to her.

"Thank you," she said as she kissed him. "But, honestly, I think just admitting out loud that I'm nervous has already helped. Because the truth is that I really *am* ready to ace this thing."

He studied her face for a few long moments before his obvious concern eased. "You really are, aren't you?"

Finally feeling as though she could conquer absolutely anything she set her mind to, even meeting Sean's entire family tomorrow, she said, "I really am. Now, how quickly do you think we can get to the part where you're taking my clothes off and making me—"

His mouth covered hers before she could finish her sentence, his tongue against hers giving her quite a few hints about what he intended for them on their second night together. And she was pretty sure they beat any previous cross-campus speed record as they headed straight for his frat house, making it to the front door in less than five minutes.

Nothing, she was certain, could bring her down tonight.

But as soon as they walked inside the Delta Tau Delta house, it was as if her optimism had turned straight into a jinx when she heard the too-familiar strains of *Crashing Girl*...and realized Sean's frat brothers were all hunched over an iPad.

Watching *her.*

* * *

Sean knew the second he and Serena walked into the house and every guy in the place turned to them with guilty looks on their faces that something was up. Something bigger than how they'd grilled him about her all day.

It hadn't taken much to shut down their borderline

raunchy questions when they'd realized he was serious about her. Not when they knew the kind of damage his fists could do to when he was provoked.

Out of the corner of his eye he'd seen them shove what looked like an iPad under a couch cushion. "What the hell were you just looking at?"

Serena was pulling his hand in the other direction, but he needed to deal with the situation in his house immediately. And in the strongest way possible.

Kurt stood and held up both hands. "It's nothing, bro. Just watching some videos."

"Give me the goddamned iPad."

One of the newer recruits, clearly figuring there was a better chance of saving his ass this way, grabbed it from its hiding place and held it out to Sean.

The screen was paused on an image of Serena on a sandy beach. Tiny scraps of fabric barely covered her and she was wet and covered with sand. It was a music video he'd seen before, for the song that had been playing when they walked inside, but he hadn't remember that she was the girl writhing around so sexily in it.

He threw the iPad across the room so that it slammed into the hardwood bar.

He hadn't let go of her hand, and when she jerked at the sound of the device shattering on impact, he wanted to pull her against him to tell her she didn't deserve every goddamned creep in the world drooling over her. But for the moment, he needed to focus on ripping his frat brothers a new one.

"I thought I already told all of you not to do one damned thing to disrespect her." He had Kurt's throat in his hand and had lifted him up so that his toes were barely touching the floor.

"Sean, it's okay." Serena tugged on his hand again,

hard enough that he had to turn to look at her and break his hard hold on his onetime friend's throat. "It's not their fault I was in that video."

She looked so obviously distraught that it made him even angrier. But at the same time, he could belatedly see that he was only making things worse for her by losing it.

Turning back to the crowd of guys who looked like they were about to piss themselves, he warned them, "If I so much as hear that you're looking at pictures or videos of Serena again—"

"We won't." The scared freshman was the first to make that promise, but all the other guys quickly nodded and echoed it.

Kurt was rubbing his neck with one hand and wiping the water from his eyes with the back of the other. "Jesus, Sean, we didn't mean anything by it."

He was about to launch at him again when Serena said his name. "Please, Sean, it's okay. I'm okay." He watched her take a deep breath before turning to the group. "I know my past is a little weird—"

"It isn't weird!"

She shot him a look that shut him up before she continued. "But if you want to know something about me or the career I had before I came to Stanford, I'd appreciate it if you'd ask me straight to my face instead of doing an Internet search. And things like that video..."

When she paused and he felt her hand shake a little in his, he wanted so badly to jump in to let her know she didn't need to do this, didn't need to be so brave. But for as badly as he wanted to protect her, he swore he could hear his mother's voice in his head and what she'd always told him when he wanted to step in for one of his sisters. *"She needs to do this. She needs to know how strong, how powerful she really is."*

"That video was a part of my career before I came here, but it isn't who I am now. And," she said with a small smile, "I'm going to do my best to convince Sean that he doesn't need to beat up every guy who so much as looks at one of my pictures, because I don't want you all to feel unsafe just walking past a stack of magazines or turning on your computer. But I'm also thinking that maybe you all could do your part by trying not to look."

Right before they walked away, he could see the new respect in the eyes of most of the guys in his house—guys who, until this very moment, had only looked at her and seen a hot girl they wanted to do.

* * *

"I never wanted to be in that video," she told him as soon as his bedroom door closed. "But my mother swore it would be fine, that she wouldn't let them film anything inappropriate, and that it was a really important next step toward making it as an actress."

"How could she do that to you?" Sean drew Serena against him. She needed to get this off her chest, but he couldn't let her explain her previous life to him anywhere but in his arms. "To her daughter who trusted her to help her?"

But instead of answering his questions, she said, "I wanted tonight to be fun. To be good. I didn't want to ruin it with all of this."

"You're not ruining anything, Serena."

"But I already have. Just by being in that video."

"Bullshit. Don't you dare take the blame for something that wasn't in your control. You were just a kid doing what you were told."

"Honestly," she said in a soft voice, "I don't think my mom realized just how bad the video was for a seventeen-year-old girl to be in until it was too late. Once the song became a massive hit, all she could do to justify it was say that at least I'd proven I wouldn't freeze up on screen. And she was right, because the scripts started pouring in. Every single one of them was the same, though, wanting me to play the young, overly sexed-up girl getting in too deep and getting hurt, just like I had portrayed in the video. That was the first time I ever refused my mother anything—refused to audition for any of those directors. She was so angry with me. She said she'd never met anyone so selfish, so unappreciative, in all her life. So when Smith Sullivan came along with a great script and a real character who felt like someone I actually understood, I couldn't say no." She tilted her face up to his. "I got the part in his movie, Sean, and I would be there now filming if the production hadn't ended up on hold indefinitely."

His chest clenched even tighter. One of the biggest movie stars in the world wanted her to be in his film. Sean finally realized just how close he'd come to missing meeting Serena altogether. He couldn't imagine his life without her in it now, but if Smith Sullivan's movie hadn't gone off the rails, Sean would still be searching for *numb*…and hating his life more with every day that passed.

"I'm glad you're here. So damned glad."

"I am, too. But I know it's hard for you to be with someone like me."

"It's not hard."

"It *is* hard," she insisted. "Stuff like what just happened downstairs would never have happened if you were dating anyone else on campus. It's why I never really thought I'd be able to date anyone or live a normal student life."

"Of course you can." He didn't like the direction this conversation was going. Not when they were just starting to figure things out. Not when they were finally dating out in the open. And not when he was *in love* with her. "I don't care if we have to work a little harder at making things work. You're worth it."

"So are you," she said, "but are you sure you want to keep having to deal with things like this? With paparazzi randomly popping up so that you never know when you're going to run into pictures and clips of me that people—especially guys—are going to be looking at? Even your friends?"

"Do you know why I reacted the way I did down there? Not because you were in that video. Sure, I don't like knowing that my friends, that strangers, are drooling over you. But even if you hadn't been a model, I guarantee they'd be doing that. What kills me is knowing just how much you hate that video. What kills me is seeing you tighten up and your eyes cloud over like you're getting lost in a bad memory. I want so badly to be able to go back in time to save you from all of it, but I can't, Serena. I can't and I hate that no one else did, either."

"You know what," she said slowly, "you're right. You're not the only one who's going to need to figure out how to deal with it. I do, too."

"It wasn't fair," he said. "You were just a kid, and if you didn't want to do any of those things, you shouldn't have had to."

"But I did. And they're done. There's no going back in time to undo them. No erasing pictures and video clips that will be around forever." She could have played the victim, but didn't, and he was pretty sure he'd never respected her more than he did in that instant. "I never had anyone to talk to about any of this. Not until you. But at the same time—" She put her hand on his chest, pressing it flat over his heart which was still pounding way too hard. "—when you smashed the iPad—"

"I scared you." He covered her hand with his. "I didn't mean to. I just wanted it gone."

"I know. And I'd be lying if I didn't say I wanted that, too. But do you think that maybe..." She shook her head, but this time after a bit of a pause, she didn't finish her sentence.

"Don't stop talking to me now. I don't want you to be frightened of me because of what I did down there."

"It's not that," she said softly. "I'm not afraid of you now, and I wasn't scared earlier, either. Stunned, but not frightened. You would never do anything to hurt me, or to hurt anyone else, not if they didn't deserve it. It's just that this morning with the pictures...I accidentally pushed you too hard. Too far, too fast. I don't want to make that same mistake again tonight by saying the wrong thing."

His chest immediately clenched tight, even tighter than it was already. But he couldn't shut her out again. Not if he wanted her to actually consider sticking around.

And it was just how badly he wanted her to stay that made it possible for him to get the words out. "No one has pushed me for three months. Hell, all year." He'd thought it would be easier, better, if he buried everything and eventually forgot. But it hadn't worked out that way. "I can't guarantee how far into it all that I'm going to be able to go tonight. Or tomorrow, even. But last night you told me that you trust me in a way you've never been able to trust anyone else. It's the same with me, Serena. I trust you in a way I haven't been able to trust anyone else. So..." He took a breath, forced the oxygen into his constricted lungs. "Push."

She watched him carefully for a few seconds before finally saying, "When you threw the tablet across the room, even though I knew you were upset about the other guys watching the video, I couldn't help but wonder if your reaction—and the fury behind it—wasn't entirely about me. If, maybe, your friends watching the video was just what pushed you over the edge because of everything you've been keeping bottled up inside for so long. Ever since…ever since your mom got sick."

He had to work to let her words in, to force himself to actually think about what she was saying. For so long it had been instinctive to push away his emotions, his grief, the feelings of loss that only seemed to grow bigger each day rather than smaller. Fortunately, from the way she was looking at him, it seemed she understood that he was listening, even if he wasn't capable of responding just yet.

"I've tried to push away my past, too," she said softly. "And even though I know what I've been through is nothing compared to losing your mom, I'm just starting to see that maybe hiding from it hasn't worked...and that trying to turn away from who I've been will never work. I don't want to face it all head on, and it seems like it would be easier not to, but what if facing it is exactly what I've got to do? If I can ever be tough enough to do it, that is."

"You're definitely tough enough considering you just impressed the hell out of the guys downstairs when you laid it down straight for them."

She looked up at him, a small smile finally on her face. "I did, didn't I?"

"They're not the only ones who are impressed." He hadn't planned to tell her this tonight, but there wasn't anything else he could say now. Not when she'd just stripped his soul bare and made him finally face the truth.

About everything. "I've fallen in love with you, Serena."

CHAPTER TWENTY-THREE

Serena felt more than a little overwhelmed by everything that had happened in twenty-four short hours. Spending her first night in Sean's bed. Having a huge fight over his mother's pictures.

And now, hearing that he'd fallen in love with her.

She might have stood there all night, speechless and stunned, but fortunately, Sean knew exactly what to do, and the next thing she knew she was lying beneath him on his bed, her arms around his neck while he traced her lips with gentle—and very arousing—fingertips.

"Did I just move too fast after all my promises not to?"

She wanted to shake her head, wanted to tell him no, but she couldn't lie to him. Not now. Not ever.

"I want," she said, her words seeming to come from somewhere far away, "so badly to believe that it's true, that someone like you could love me."

"How could you doubt it for a second?"

"You know how people have said my whole life that I was beautiful?" God, she hated the way this was going to sound, but she just couldn't hold back. Not anymore.

Not with Sean. "That word. *Love.* Whenever I heard it, whoever said it to me, it felt the same. Like it didn't really mean anything. Because they weren't saying it about the real me."

"But what if they were? What if everyone who ever said they loved you meant it?"

"How could they? How could any of them have ever meant it when no one but you has ever really known the real me?"

"I'll tell you why," he said in a deep voice that rumbled all the way through her. "Your beauty is so much deeper than the makeup, the outfits you wore, the part you played all those years. And your heart is so big, and so damned pure, that anyone would have to be blind not to see it. Not to see you and fall in love with you the way I did from the very start, from that very first night when you looked at me and saw *everything.*"

"I think," she said in a voice that was barely above a whisper, "that I've fallen in love with you, too."

He didn't freak out the way she had when he'd said it to her. No, he simply smiled, a smile that got bigger and bigger by the second. "I thought you might have."

His gentle teasing made it easier for her to relax into the idea of loving...and being loved. "What tipped you off?"

He stroked her hair back from her face and looked at her in a way he never had before. A look so warm, so comforting, so sweet and yet so raw and real that it shot straight to the center of her heart. "Where should I start?"

She loved the slightly cocky edge to his words, the fact that they could laugh and love each other at the same time. She'd never known it could be like this, that passion and desire and deep emotions could be tempered so perfectly with such ease, and with friendship.

The truest friendship she'd ever known.

"Start right here, with this," she said, and then she kissed him, slowly running her tongue along his lower lip, from one corner of his mouth to the other. He was so delicious that one taste wasn't nearly enough, so she took another, this time of his upper lip, and then of his tongue as she slipped hers inside his mouth.

They were both still fully clothed, but she was already wrapped all around him, and his hands were holding her hips tightly. She rocked into him, and knowing *exactly* how good it felt to come apart against him made her feel reckless. Bold.

Her whole life she'd had to hold back, had to make sure that she didn't make a single misstep in front of the camera, but with Sean she didn't need to worry. All he'd tried to do since that day he'd found her in the library so that he could show her the pictures of the two of them online, was love her. And even though she'd been scared to let him, how could she ever possibly have resisted him? Especially when his mother had done such an exceptional job of raising her son.

"You made me feel so good this morning," she told him. "I want to make you feel good, too."

His eyes were dilated nearly to black when he looked down at her. "You already are."

He kissed her again and she almost forgot everything in the wonder of his mouth against hers. Only, in the past ten hours since he'd dropped her off at her dorm room, Serena had realized that she wanted to experience his pleasure as much as she did her own. It had been a revelation to come with his hands on her. And it would, she was certain, be even more of a revelation to make *him* come.

"Let me touch you, Sean." When she ran her hands

down from his broad shoulders to his jeans, she could feel the hard flexing of every muscle in his back, his hips, as he worked to keep himself under control. Slowly, she slid her fingers around to the front of his jeans. "Please."

"Jesus." He inhaled a long breath, then blew it out. She'd heard from Abi that he was a master of control, both around the bag at first and in the batting box. Though she hadn't had a chance to see any of his games, she knew she was witnessing that control firsthand. "Okay," he finally said, "but only if you're naked first."

It was a bargain she was happy to make, especially when she knew just how good he made every inch of her nakedness feel.

"Take off your clothes, Serena."

He'd always stripped her bare before now, and surprise at his sudden request had her hesitating for a split second. Because *oh my God* it was sexy when he gave her a sensual command. To buy herself time to try to get her bearings back, at least a little bit, she said, "What do you want me to take off first?"

His slow smile held as much heat as happiness. "How about we go from the bottom up this time?"

Maybe the thought of being naked from the waist down while still covered up on top shouldn't have been so wickedly, crazily sexy...but it was. *So* insanely sexy.

The first thing she did was toe off her tennis shoes, but she needed to sit up and bend over to reach her socks. And even with all of her clothes on, the way Sean looked at her while she slid the cotton from her feet was so freaking hot that she practically came right then and there.

She'd only just dropped her socks onto the floor beside his bed when he took one of her bare feet into his hands and ran his thumb up her arch with the perfect pressure to make her moan from the pleasure of the impromptu massage. By the time he did the same to her other foot, she was shocked to realize that *every single way* he touched her only aroused her more.

"What are you going to do with those amazingly talented hands once I take my jeans off?"

His grin grew wider...and wickeder. "Take them off and I'll show you."

Fumbling now to find out exactly what he had planned, she yanked open the button and zipper of her jeans and shoved them off. But he didn't seem to care about her non-striptease because his eyes were trained on her underwear.

When she looked down, she saw why: the pink fabric was clearly damp...and getting wetter by the second.

"My God, Serena," he said in a raw tone, "you blow my mind."

Wanting so badly for him to touch her again, any way he wanted to, any way at all, she slid the thin layer of cotton off. She'd never had any experience with seducing anyone before, but it was suddenly the most natural thing in the world for her to say, "What about now?"

He answered her with a kiss, but not on her mouth. Between her legs.

Obviously guessing that she would be equal parts nervous and excited by what he was doing to her, his hands were soothing as he took hers in his and laid them together over her hip bones. Once more, he pressed a soft kiss to the damp flesh between her thighs, before lifting his head and meeting her gaze. "If you want me to stop—"

"No." *God no!* "It feels so g—"

Her final word was lost on a gasp of pleasure as his tongue slicked over her. *All* of her. Again and again he laved her with his tongue, and she spun out further and further as pleasure took over every last inch of her. She knew she was gripping his hands tightly, too tightly, but as he took her higher and higher, she desperately needed something to hold on to, some way to try to keep it together when she was going to split apart into a million little pieces any second. At the same time, somewhere in the back of her head she couldn't help but be frightened by how intimate this was...and that somehow in her stupid inexperience she might be doing something wrong.

She'd just started to tense up when Sean shifted over her, just enough to say, "Let go, Serena." His breath was warm over her sensitive skin, his lips brushing over her with each word he spoke. "Let go for me."

And in the end, it was knowing that he could read her innermost thoughts almost before she could that made it not only possible for her to let go as he swept his tongue, his lips, even the edges of his teeth over her, but also to know that it was okay for her to break apart into a million pieces.

Because he'd be right there to help put her back together, even stronger, and better, on the other side.

* * *

"Was that okay?"

Sean hadn't been planning to take things so far, so fast tonight. Sure, he'd wanted to, but he'd promised they'd go slow. Only, when she'd said she wanted to touch him...well, his brain had basically shut down and he'd acted without being able to think it through. Apart from that one moment when he'd asked her if she needed him to stop.

Thank God she hadn't.

"Better than okay." She made a happy little sound. "Perfect." But then she amended that to, "Almost perfect.

Because there's still that small matter of my doing the exact same thing to you."

Hell, he thought, that was nearly the end of it for him as he twitched hard against his zipper from nothing but the thought of her mouth on him.

"Clothes." The one word was strangled, and he had to struggle to string it into a sentence. "You still have clothes on."

She huffed out a breath. "Fine. I'll take off the rest of my clothes first, but you'd better not distract me this time."

He'd been ridiculously attracted to Serena when she was shy and uncertain and just trying to feel her way around their kisses and his hands on her curves. But now that she was starting to own her sexuality?

Luckiest. Guy. Ever.

"Me? Distract you?"

She laughed softly, but he was the one currently being distracted by the way she was now lifting her T-shirt over her head. After tossing it on the floor on top of her other clothes, she said, "You *love* distracting me."

Before she could lower her hands to the clasp of her bra, he grabbed her wrists. "You're right," he agreed. "I do. I *love* it." He bent his head so that his lips were barely a breath from hers. "And you. I love you, Serena." He swallowed her echo of his words with his kiss.

A long while later, when he knew he wasn't being fair, he finally let her up for air. "Okay, no more distractions."

Her eyes were cloudy with arousal, and he liked seeing how long it took for them to clear to the point where she could actually form the word, "Okay," and then a few beats later, "You'd better not."

Of course, when she took off her bra, he was hard-pressed to stick to his promise. Fortunately, the next thing he knew, she was pushing him back down on the bed and levering herself over him so that the only reasonable place for him to put his hands was over her breasts. Not because he was trying to distract her, of course.

The way her breath stuttered in her chest told him just how much she liked the way he was touching her, but he could see the determination in her eyes, too. "I like your hands," she said softly as she moved her attention to pulling up his shirt. "How big they are." Her fingertips— deliberately, he decided—lightly tickled over his abs as she lifted the cotton. "How they're a little rough on my skin."

That was right when she pulled the shirt over his head and he had no choice but to take his hands off her, at least until she tossed his shirt onto the floor. And he might have gone right back to teasing her again if he hadn't caught the look in her eyes as she stared down at his bare chest.

Flat-out awe.

"You are..." She shook her head, clearly giving up on the words she was looking for. She used her hands instead, running them down over his chest, his abs, stopping just above the erection that was about to bust through his jeans. But then she quickly upped the ante by leaning over so that the tips of her silky hair were brushing over him at the same time that she was pressing soft, wet kisses to his skin.

He should have known that she would beat him at his own game, and that *she* would end up being the true master of distraction, because she had the zipper of his jeans more than halfway down before he even realized it. Suddenly, she had him in her hand, still covered by the cotton of his boxers, but as close to the edge of losing it as he'd ever been.

"Serena." He panted out her name, thrusting up against the flat of her palm even as he tried to keep from exploding. "I'm close. Too close." Hell, just looking at her got him too close.

But instead of giving him a few seconds to get any kind of grip at all, she smiled. And said, "Good," a beat before she slid her hand beneath his boxers and they finally came skin to skin.

The last of Sean's self-control snapped. He slid his hands into her hair and dragged her mouth back to his, their kiss spiraling off as fast, as hard, as he was now moving inside the tight clasp of her hand.

Everything but Serena disappeared. Everything but the sweet taste of her mouth. Everything but the tangle of her tongue against his. Everything but the scent of her skin and the silky slide of her hair between his fingertips. Everything but the sound of her gasps of excitement. Everything but the emotion that washed over him at the exact moment that pleasure shot through and out of him, over and over and over again.

"I knew it," she whispered against his mouth. "I knew I would *love* doing that with you."

Jesus, she wasn't the only one who had loved it. And after the way she'd just blown his entire world apart, it was nearly impossible to muster up the energy to clean both of them up and kick off the rest of his clothes. Fortunately, his reward was getting to wrap her in his arms and draw the covers over them. And as he mentally rewound the sexiest hour of his life, he was amazed to realize that being with Serena wasn't just about feeling good, just about getting off.

Love had changed everything—had taken every kiss, every touch, and magnified the impact a million times over. His mother had told him it would be like this, but he hadn't understood. Not until now. Not until Serena.

"She would have loved you."

It was an opening Serena could have taken if she'd wanted to push some more. But somehow she knew he still wasn't yet ready to tell her everything.

Instead, she simply whispered, "I would have loved her, too," then tucked her head against his chest.

Somehow, he thought as he pulled her even closer, *she knew*.

CHAPTER TWENTY-FOUR

At noon the following day, Sean's eighteen-year-old sister stood in her open front door and stared at Serena with big eyes. "Oh my God, I can't believe you're actually here. It's so amazing to meet you!" She threw her arms around Serena, instantly welcoming.

"Serena, this is my little sister, Madison."

"Maddie," his sister quickly corrected.

"I told them all you were coming and not to freak you out," he continued, "but you know how little sisters are."

Maddie shot Sean a frown when she finally let go of Serena. "We're awesome, that's how we are. It's not like I asked Serena to take a selfie with me, or anything." Maddie looked back at Serena and gave her a slightly crooked smile. "Sorry, it's just that I've seen you in like a million magazines and now here you are in my house."

"Not quite yet, Mads," Sean pointed out, "since you haven't actually let us in."

"Oh, sorry!" She jumped aside, and that was when she finally saw the box Serena was holding. The eggshell-blue box that could only have come from one store. "You didn't need to bring me a present." But from the way her eyes lit up, she was clearly glad that Serena had. Serena liked Sean's youngest sister immediately. She was as tiny as her brother was big, and also bright and fun.

Serena had agonized over what to wear to Maddie's party today. Her usual uniform of jeans and a baggy T-shirt would have been rude—plus she was feeling more and more ready to stop hiding who she really was—but she didn't want to be overdressed, either. Finally, Abi had suggested a pair of slim black jeans and a fitted white crocheted top with a matching white tank. Simple, but pretty.

"I hope you like it, Maddie."

She had handed the box to his sister just as Sean's father stepped into the entryway. She could easily see the family resemblance in all three of them, but it was especially strong between the two men. But even with a welcoming smile, Michael Morrison couldn't hide the grief in every line of his face, the too-deep hollows beneath his cheekbones and the lingering despair in his eyes.

"Mr. Morrison, thank you for including me today."

"Mike, please. And it's a pleasure to meet you, Serena. Come inside and let me get you a drink before you head into the backyard and meet everyone else."

"Sean mentioned that you were a pretty serious gardener, so I brought these for you." She reached into her bag and pulled out a bag of bulbs. "I've always loved the scent of freesias," she said when he simply stared at her gift.

"My wife did, too," he said softly, and Serena silently cursed herself for inadvertently causing him pain with her gift.

"I'm so sorry for your loss," she said, her throat tightening more on every word.

And then, from seemingly out of nowhere, Sean's other sister appeared, as if she had a radar for when her father was faltering and knew exactly when he needed her to save him. "Dad, I'm pretty sure Drew's about to break the gas grill by lighting charcoal on it." As their father headed out toward the backyard to deal with the situation, Olivia said, "You must be Serena."

Sean's arm around her waist tightened as she smiled said, "You're Olivia, aren't you? Sean has told me so many great things about you."

Serena held out her hand and made sure to keep her expression as easy as possible, as if she hadn't already picked up on all of the varied dynamics in their family. Because as far as she could see there was *a lot* going on, and she'd only met half of them so far...

Like any eighteen-year-old might have, Maddie looked caught between her older sibling's silent tug of war over Serena's presence and wanting to defuse the situation. "If you could point me toward something to drink," Serena said to her, "that would be great."

Maddie gave her a relieved smile. "Sure, come into the kitchen with me and I'll show you what we've got."

Leaving Sean and Olivia behind for a moment, Serena said, "Happy birthday," and then asked, "How's your senior year going?"

"Pretty good," Maddie said with a grin that looked so much like Sean's. "Although I'm pretty sure if I don't get into Stanford everyone is going to freak."

"Is that where you want to go?"

Maddie shrugged. "Six out of seven Morrisons either graduated from Stanford or are going to soon. It doesn't have a culinary program, but I figure I can major in business or something and then at least I'll know how to manage my finances when I open my own restaurant."

"You want to be a chef?"

"For as long as I can remember."

"Aren't there amazing cooking schools in San Francisco and Napa Valley?"

"There are, and I've done some of their summer programs. In fact, I made most of the food we're going to be eating today." She opened up the fridge. "Here's what we've got to drink. What looks good?"

Sensing Maddie wanted to move on from their talk about her future, Serena had just taken out a bottle of San Pellegrino when the side door into the kitchen opened and a man she hadn't yet met walked in.

"Want another one of these?" Maddie held up a beer bottle for him.

"Nope, water's good. I've got to head back to the office later." He held out his hand to Serena. "I'm Sean's brother Grant."

"Nice to meet you. I'm Serena."

Grant Morrison was a very good-looking man. Tall and ridiculously handsome like Sean, and yet, he wasn't having anywhere near the kind of effect on her that Sean had from the very first moment she'd met him. In fact, despite what she suspected was Grant's naturally high level of intensity, she actually felt quite comfortable with him. Immediately sensing what a serious and focused businessman he was, she thought about how she'd met many men like him over the years and had actually liked quite a few of them. At least, the ones who hadn't secretly hit on her when they thought her mother's attention was elsewhere.

Something told Serena that Grant would *never* hit on her in a million years. It was a very comforting thought.

"Serena," Maddie said, "come on outside and you can try the blue cheese bacon dip I made as a starter."

Smiling at Grant as she passed him, Serena nearly ran headfirst into Sean coming in through the kitchen door. Only...it wasn't Sean standing in front of her, but a really, really close copy of him.

"I'm Justin," he said, "and you must be the reason why my brother is finally happy again."

He said the words so easily that she might have missed the serious intent behind them if she wasn't already so attuned to Sean's happiness. What's more, Justin gave her a grin that was such a perfect replica of the way Sean looked at her that it should have set every cell in her body to tingling...only it didn't. Not at all.

But hadn't she always known that what was on the surface didn't make up the whole? She was more than her face. And so were Justin and Sean. Just because their outsides were so similar didn't mean they were the same inside. Although at the very least, she could tell from nothing more than Justin's smile that he was nice. Sizzling hot like his other brothers, certainly, and with a kindness that radiated even from the way he held the door open for her.

She almost second-guessed herself before replying, but decided that if she didn't have to be guarded with Sean, then she wouldn't be guarded with his family, either. "Sean is making me really happy, too."

"He always was the lucky one of the two of us," Justin said with the same easy grin that Sean and Maddie had. "Can I get you anything?"

"No, I was just heading outside to try Maddie's dip."

"Whatever you think of it," he said in a low voice, "tell her you love it."

"Isn't it good?"

"It's great," he said, but he'd clearly felt he had to warn Serena anyway, to make sure that no matter what happened his sister came away feeling good at the end of the day. Without siblings, Serena hadn't had a chance to see into a family dynamic like this. It was as fascinating—and fantastic—as she'd always thought it would be. At the same time, though, it was so much more complicated than she'd ever realized.

On the one hand, Maddie clearly felt pressured by her family's expectations, but on the other, she was obviously totally supported in her dreams. Grant was likely needed in his office this afternoon, but he'd chosen to take these hours off to celebrate his sister. Olivia was wary of Serena and wanted to protect Sean from being hurt because she loved him so much. And Justin...well, Serena didn't have a handle on Sean's twin yet, beyond sensing that he was really nice in addition to being ridiculously good looking.

She could only imagine how the Morrison house must have been overrun with phone calls and visits from all the people wanting to date them over the years. Surely, she thought, as she finally headed outside, Sean wasn't the only one dating someone. But when she looked around the backyard, there was only one other person she hadn't met.

Drew Morrison turned to her with the look of a man who knew *precisely* the kind of effect he had on women. And yet, though he had *BAD BOY* written all over him, from his black jeans to his spiky hair and tattoos, she was really happy to find that he didn't put her on edge the way so many other musicians did. Especially those creeps she'd filmed the video with.

"Great to finally meet you," he said as he came across the grass to say hello, even the way he moved rock-star sexy.

He wasn't putting on an act. Drew Morrison just *was*

a rock star. He owned it from the inside out and clearly had found his perfect career fit. Whereas Serena had never been doing more than pretending to be a supermodel.

"You, too." Again, though she felt more than a little shy, she didn't let it stop her from telling him, "I really like your music."

"Thanks. I appreciate that." And she got the sense that he really did.

A moment later, Sean's arms slid around her waist from behind. "Holding up okay? I don't have to beat Drew up for hitting on you, do I?"

She laughed as she shook her head, then smiled up at him. "You have a great family."

He smiled back at her even though she knew what he'd really been seeing since they walked in to Maddie's party was a family minus one very important person. She could see that same expression in all of the Morrisons' eyes in varying degrees. Some of them were probably just better at hiding, at bottling up, their grief. For now, at least.

Even though they were standing in front of his entire family, it was pure instinct to slide her arms around his neck. "When will everyone else be getting here?"

"We're all here."

"But...it's just your family and me."

"Maddie's going to blow it out with her friends later tonight in the city while Olivia drives her crazy by chaperoning. Today is for the family."

"But if it's just your family—"

Sean's mouth on hers stopped the rest of her protest. "I wanted you to be here today. We all do."

Just then, a small bundle of fur pushed against her legs and she looked down to see the cutest little black and white dog looking up at her with big brown eyes. "Oh my gosh, who are you?"

"Don't worry, buddy," Sean said as he scooped up the dog and handed it to her, "I was just about to introduce you. This is Bailey. And something tells me he's going to fall in love with you, too."

The way the cute dog started licking her made her think that maybe Sean was right. She couldn't stop laughing, even as she tried to dodge his tongue.

"Hey," Sean said in a gentle tone to the dog, "coming on too strong is no way to get a girl to love you back." He gave the furball a quick cuddle then put him down on the grass, where he scurried after a piece of food that had just fallen off the table.

"Sorry about that. He can be a little too friendly sometimes."

"Impossible," she said through her laughter as she watched Bailey stare greedily at the plates of food on the table. "No dog can ever be too friendly."

Sean took her hand and brought her over to the table set up in the middle of the lawn beneath the big magnolia tree. "Come sit down with me."

She knew everyone must be able to see that she was glowing from just being with Sean, and she really, really hoped Olivia was the only one who disapproved of her. It had never been so important for people to like her.

"So, Serena," Mike asked, "what year are you at Stanford?"

"It's my freshman year."

"Got your major picked out yet? Or are you still trying things out?"

Clearly, Sean's father didn't have much of a clue about what she'd done before attending college, and she was extremely glad. "I'm planning to major in English."

His eyes shuttered. "My wife was an English major. She ended up going on to teach third grade."

Oh God, how did she keep hurting Sean's father with every word that came out of her mouth? To make things worse, she felt Sean stiffen beside her, too. Each of his siblings also shifted slightly in their seats.

"Is teaching what you want to do, too?" Maddie asked.

Trying to answer as normally as possible, given the fact that she wanted to cry for every one of them, Serena said, "Maybe. Although at this point anything's possible, just as long as it involves books and libraries."

She was so incredibly glad when Sean smiled at her and said, "Serena's on a first-name basis with the entire Green Library staff. And actually, since I've started going so much to meet her there, I've started to think that someone should do some time-release photographs of the architecture and the way the light passes over it throughout the day. Somehow it manages to look different every hour."

"*You* should do it," Olivia said.

Serena held her breath along with the rest of them, but Sean only shrugged and said, "We'll see," before turning to Grant and asking, "How's the new product launch going?"

She was so amazed by Sean's response to Olivia that she was only able to listen with half an ear to Grant's response. Was he really thinking about doing photography again? It felt like such a big thing—and she knew from his siblings' expressions that she wasn't the only one who thought so.

Had she had something to do with the change? Or was it simply that the passage of time was finally starting to heal him?

Whatever the reason, knowing that Sean was coming alive again filled her with so much happiness, Serena wanted to dance around the yard. By the time she was able to pull her gaze from his gorgeous face, she realized that her plate was loaded up with some of the best-looking food she'd ever seen or smelled.

"You made all this?" she asked Maddie while Sean, Grant, and Mike talked business.

"I hope you like it."

"She will, Mads," Drew said from the far end of the table, ruffling his sister's hair so that she gave him a little mock growl of irritation.

"How many hearts have you broken on this tour?" his little sister asked him.

"Lost count in Miami," he teased her back.

"I'm glad you were able to come home for my birthday."

"Wouldn't have missed it," he said, "even if you're blowing me off to go hang with your friends tonight."

"You know they'd be thrilled if you came," Maddie said.

"Gonna have to take a pass on that one, thanks." His look of horror at hanging with a bunch of eighteen-year-old girls made Serena laugh. "Besides, I've got that meeting tonight with my professor about the student who wants to go on tour with me as part of her business major."

Olivia shook her head. "Do you really want to let some stranger on your tour bus?"

"My professor basically asked me to do it as a favor. Turns out she's his daughter and she really wants to get an insider's view of the music industry for some project she's working on."

"You can't be serious," Justin said, laughing. "This

professor wants to send his daughter on tour with you? Does he know *anything* about your track record with the ladies?"

"I wouldn't touch the guy's daughter," Drew said, as serious as he'd been so far. "Not in a million years."

Olivia abruptly shifted in her seat to face Serena. "Has it been difficult to fit your modeling and acting commitments around your classes?"

Trying not to act too surprised by the sudden question, or too flustered by the way everyone was now looking at her, Serena said, "I'm not modeling or acting anymore."

Olivia frowned. "But I read just this morning that you—"

"She's done with that," Sean said, cutting his sister off.

"Do you miss it?" Maddie asked.

"No." Serena didn't even have to think about it. "Not at all."

"That's cool," his youngest sister said. "I was just thinking it must be kind of weird to go to college and live in a dorm and go to classes after all the things you've probably seen and done."

"It was weird at first," she admitted. "At least until I met your brother." Knowing she couldn't pretend the tabloid story hadn't come out online with pictures of the two of them, or that there wouldn't be similar things coming in the future, she said, "I know it must have been strange for all of you when those pictures of the two of us came out."

"It wasn't a big deal," Sean immediately said.

Grant, however, was only a beat behind him with, "Actually, it *was* a surprise, but I don't imagine it's anything you can control, is it?"

"Unfortunately," she said with a little shake of her head, "it isn't."

She could feel Sean bristling beside her, not nearly as bad as he'd been when he'd caught his friends looking at her video the night before, but definitely not pleased with the way the conversation had gone. She wished she knew how to fix things, but before she could figure anything out, help came from the most unlikely quarter.

"Serena, do you want to come help me bring out Maddie's birthday cake?" Olivia asked.

Beyond grateful, Serena nodded and was sliding out of her seat when Sean slid his hand to the nape of her neck and kissed her, long and hard and in front of his entire family. Her head was spinning by the time he let her go, but she somehow managed to make it to her feet without tripping and into the kitchen, where his sister was waiting for her.

"When those pictures of the two of you came out," Olivia said, point-blank, "I told him to be careful."

Serena had barely closed the door behind her, and between the kiss and the roller coaster of a conversation during their meal, she didn't quite have her bearings. "You love your brother. Of course you would want him to be careful."

That was right when Olivia shocked her, yet again, by saying, "You love him, too, don't you?"

Whatever Serena could have imagined that she and Olivia would talk about in the kitchen, it wouldn't have been *love.* And yet, now that she'd met Sean's family and saw that love was the core of everything the Morrisons did, of everything they were, she realized it couldn't have been anything else.

"I do."

Olivia's smile flashed so quickly that Serena almost

missed it. Especially when she followed it up by saying, "Losing our mom...it was hard. So, so hard. But she and Sean had a really special connection." Serena badly wanted to reach out to her as she added, "He's finally starting to come back to life, and I hate the thought of him getting hurt."

"I won't hurt him," Serena promised.

"Now that I've met you," Olivia said, "I know you wouldn't do it on purpose. But what about when you leave to film that movie?"

Serena's chest clenched tight for a split second. "I'm not doing any movies."

"Didn't Smith Sullivan pick you to be in his new movie?"

"He did, but then the project was shelved this past summer."

Olivia stared at her, confused. "But I just read today that it's back on. And that you're in it."

Serena shook her head. "No, I haven't agreed to anything. It must just be old news that someone is circulating again. I'm going to stay at school, not leave to do a movie or model."

Sean came in through the door. "Everything good here?"

Olivia stared at Serena for another few seconds before she seemed to make up her mind and smiled. "Everything's great. I'm glad you came today, Serena."

Serena smiled back at his sister. "I am, too."

CHAPTER TWENTY-FIVE

"I had a great time with your family today."

Drew needed Sean's car for the evening to visit his professor, so Olivia had dropped them off in front of Serena's dorm, and this was the first chance they'd had to be alone since before the party.

"They all really liked you. Just like I knew they would. Even Olivia," he said with a grin, "couldn't help but join your team by the end."

"They're all amazing. And if at least one of them hadn't been just a little bit suspicious of me, well, I think that would have been the weird part."

In fact, the only truly weird thing about the afternoon was that no one had talked about his mom apart from an accidental comment here or there. It was as if they were all walking on eggshells around each other. Or, more specifically, Sean's father.

Was loving someone so deeply worth the pain of losing that love?

But she already knew the answer to that, didn't she? Because even if everything blew up between her and Sean, she didn't see how she could ever regret loving him.

Not, she reminded herself, that things were going to go wrong. Because for once in her life, she felt like she was exactly where she needed to be with exactly the person she needed to be with. And every time she thought about the way Sean seemed to be on the verge of wanting to take pictures again, it made her so happy for him that she knew nothing could possibly crush that joy.

Nothing at all.

As they walked inside and her dorm mates said hello, she could see all of them taking note of the fact that she and Sean were holding hands. She smiled, thinking that as far as she was concerned, every last one of them could take a picture and post it on the Internet.

And if her mother saw it? Well, she'd just have to accept that her daughter had finally grown up. Yes, she knew her mother's terrible track record with Serena's father meant that she would likely be extremely suspicious of Sean's motives, but surely Genevieve would soon realize that Sean was a good person and that he didn't mean Serena any harm, wouldn't she?

Still high on having spent the afternoon with Sean's family, Serena was more hopeful than ever that the two of them might one day be able to connect as mother and daughter, rather than as "momager" and client.

Because if Serena could meet a guy like Sean and fall in love, then surely anything was possible, wasn't it?

Soon. She'd tell her mother all about Sean really soon. Especially since she knew it would be better to tell Genevieve that they were dating *before* her mother read about it online and saw more pictures of them together.

Tomorrow morning, Serena assured herself, was soon enough. For the rest of today, all she wanted to do was focus on being with him.

"I like seeing you this happy," he said as he pulled

her close and nuzzled against her.

It was amazing how different—and magical—everything felt now compared to the first time she and Sean had walked across campus together, both of them prickly and unsure with each other.

"I like *being* this happy," she agreed. And she was hoping to feel even happier soon. Very soon, in fact.

The plan was to grab some of her books from her room so that they could study back at his place. But Serena knew the likelihood of getting much studying done tonight while alone with Sean was pretty much nil.

She'd finally made up her mind about the two of them. Even if he wasn't ready yet to share absolutely everything with her, she loved him enough to trust that he would one day...and she couldn't wait one more second to be his.

One hundred percent his and only his.

In fact, at this point, she wasn't sure she was going to have the willpower to make it all the way back across campus to his room. Maybe, she thought as she unlocked her door, she'd text her roommate to find out exactly how long Abi would be gone and whether they could have the room to themselves for a while.

The thought of finally making love with Sean made Serena giddy enough that she couldn't wait until they were inside to kiss him. When he put his hands on her hips and pulled her tightly against him in exactly the way she loved so much, it was clear that he couldn't wait another second, either.

By the time her door swung all the way open they were wrapped around each other. After a long afternoon where he'd constantly stroked her back, played with her hands under the table, and teased her with little kisses, she was ready for more.

Beyond ready.

Especially when she had all this joy, all this happiness, to share with him.

But then, in the exact moment that she realized he'd stopped kissing her back, she heard her name.

"Serena!"

She would instinctively have spun away from Sean if he hadn't been holding her so tightly.

"Mom?" She stared at her mother in shock. Genevieve was standing by the window, looking horrified at the sight of Serena in Sean's arms. "What are you doing here?"

Genevieve Britten was a very striking thirty-nine-year-old woman, and Serena was sure she must have turned plenty of heads walking through campus and into Serena's dorm today. People always said it was clear where Serena's looks had come from, though Genevieve's modeling look had always been crisp and angular, whereas Serena had never been able to shed her soft, slightly dreamy appearance.

"You lied to me," her mother said in a voice so sharp it could have carved a diamond. "You told me the tabloid pictures were setups. But here you two are, just like in the photos. *Worse.*"

As the first shock began to wear off, Serena realized her mother hadn't so much as looked at Sean. "Mom," she said in as steady a voice as she could manage, "this is Sean. Sean Morrison."

"I don't care what his name is. Do you think he loves you? Do you think he's going to stick around after he gets what he wants from you? After what you've probably *already* so stupidly given him?"

Maybe if she hadn't just come from spending the day with Sean's amazing family, this conversation wouldn't seem so surreal. And maybe if she hadn't been apart from Genevieve for so many weeks, she would still be numb to hearing her speak like this about men, about their unfaithfulness, their lies.

But today it all came in sharp contrast to the joy, and the faith in love, that she'd literally been embracing just moments before.

Still, though every word out of her mother's mouth felt like a knife cutting into her, Serena was torn. Torn between moving closer to Sean...and edging away from him in the hopes that it would cool her mother's ire and make her happy. Or rather, happier.

Sean, however, clearly wasn't wavering even a little bit as he kept a very protective arm around her. "Ms. Britten," he said in a low voice in which he was very carefully working to bank his fury, "I don't think you should talk to your daughter that way."

No one had ever stood up to her mother on her behalf before. Not her agent. Not any of the photographers or designers, not even the ones that Serena had thought were friends. She'd been too valuable a commodity for all of them to risk Genevieve forbidding them access to Serena.

"I can see why you fell for his lies," her mother said to Serena, still not directly acknowledging Sean. "He knows exactly how to get to you, doesn't he, by acting like all he wants is to take care of you. Well, let me tell you what he really wants. He wants to fuck you." She gestured toward the other dorm rooms. "All any of these college boys want to do is fuck you. They're going to say all the right things. They're going to make you believe they mean it when they say they love you. And you're going to make it so easy for them by being so desperate to hear their pretty little lies. But in the end all they're going to do is screw you, brag to their friends, then move on to the next stupid girl desperate enough to believe in love. *Forgotten*, Serena. You'll be forgotten. And I'll still be the only one who will ever love you. The only one who will still be here for you with open arms when the rest of the world turns its back on you. So if you're stupid enough to even *think* of giving up your career and this movie, I promise you that you will regret it for the rest of your life. Just the way I always regretted giving up mine."

"Serena."

Sean had moved in front of her and his hands were on her shoulders as if he could physically block her from the horrible things her mother was saying. Things Serena had heard her whole life, but hadn't wanted to be true.

"You don't have to stay here and listen to this. You know you don't."

When her mother's verbal assault hadn't let up, shock had automatically started to shift to that buzzing numbness that Serena had been familiar with for so long. But something pierced through. *Movie.* Her mother had mentioned the movie. Serena needed to ask what Genevieve was talking about. Needed to know exactly how her life was about to change. And yet, even the possibility that the Smith Sullivan movie really was back on wasn't the real reason Serena couldn't just turn and walk away.

"She's my mother," she told Sean in a soft voice.

Even though she'd left to go to college and Genevieve had been angry, Serena had never stopped hoping that the two of them would eventually find their way around to having a good relationship. The thought of letting that hope die nearly brought tears to her eyes, when even her mother's tirade hadn't.

And yet, just because Serena couldn't walk away from her mother, didn't mean that she could let Sean go, either. "Please," she whispered to him as she reached for one of his hands, "don't leave. Even if you don't agree with what I'm doing, stay here with me."

"I'm not going anywhere, Serena. You know I'm not."

Unfortunately, Serena wasn't at all certain that she could say the same about herself. Not when that same fear that had tickled her spine when Olivia had mentioned Smith Sullivan's movie was quickly taking over her entire body.

Though Sean still held tightly to her hand, Serena forced herself to step away from the protection of his body to face her mother again. "I'm sorry that you're so upset about my dating Sean. We were friends first and only just started to date, so that's why I hadn't told you yet. I was planning to call you tomorrow morning, actually, to share the exciting news. One day I hope that you'll realize what a great person he is."

"I don't care about your boyfriend, Serena." And by the way her mother said it, as if he was no more important than a fly buzzing around the room, she knew Genevieve meant it. "None of this nonsense matters now that Smith Sullivan's movie is back in production. I know how upset you were when Smith delayed his plans to shoot the movie. That's why I made a special trip to see you today. I simply couldn't share the amazing news over the phone that everything is back on and he still wants you to play the supporting actress role."

Just that quickly, her mother had flipped a switch, from utterly furious to perfectly reasonable now that they were talking business. Business she was positive was a slam dunk. Serena had seen it a hundred times—the way Genevieve could pull out a different mask and put it on without so much as a pause. If anyone should be the actress, it should be her mother. Especially since for all that she was claiming she hadn't wanted to share the news over the phone, it was obvious she'd already let it leak to the press before talking to her daughter about it.

So even though she'd previously vowed to disown Serena if she caught her with a guy at Stanford, she'd clearly decided that doing Smith Sullivan's movie was far more important. And that it would be exactly the thing to pull Serena back into the Hollywood life. Permanently.

"I wasn't actually too upset," she began, but her mother wouldn't let her finish.

"This movie—a role that is certain to win you an Oscar—is what we have worked for your entire life. We have so much to do to get ready for it."

Serena had only stood up to her mother once, when she'd been undeterred about going to college. But that had been when she thought the movie was permanently out of the picture. Now, more than ever before, she felt pulled in different directions. By what her mother wanted, had always wanted: for Serena to be an A-list star. By the promises she'd made to Sean to stay on campus with him.

And by her own dreams.

Maybe there was some way she could make everyone happy? Maybe after she made great grades this quarter and convinced the university to enroll her as a full-time student, she'd also be able to persuade them to let her take a short break to film the movie. And maybe Sean would forgive her for breaking her promise to stay on campus as long as she came back quickly.

"When is Smith planning to begin filming?"

"As soon as possible." Her mother looked around the dorm room with obvious distaste, clearly more than ready to get out of there. First class was barely good enough for Genevieve. Her shared bedroom, Serena knew, must seem little better than a slum. "Smith is expecting you in Seattle next week."

"But fall quarter won't be over by then. If I leave before I've finished one full quarter, they won't think I'm serious about being here and then I'm sure they won't turn my probationary acceptance into a permanent one."

"I know you think you're upset about having to leave, but we both know this life was never for you. It was never anything more than a little fantasy."

"Bullshit!" Sean had clearly done all he could to let Serena navigate the conversation on her own, but now he'd had enough. "Attending Stanford isn't a fantasy. Serena is one of the most serious, most motivated students I've ever met. If anyone belongs here, it's your daughter."

Finally, Genevieve turned her gaze to Sean. "She signed a contract with Smith, many months ago, in which she guaranteed him her participation in the film if and when it came to pass." Her mother finally smiled before focusing on Serena again. "Once you do this movie, your life will be changed *forever*."

Serena knew her mother was right about her life changing forever. Because she'd never be able to get away from photographers, would never have a chance to be even remotely normal...and she suddenly couldn't believe she'd been so stupidly, naïvely wrong to believe that nothing could come to crush her newfound joy.

"I gave up everything for you, Serena. You *owe* me this movie."

"Serena," Abi said as she barreled through the open door, "what's going on? People said they heard—" Her roommate broke off in midsentence when she belatedly realized she'd walked into the middle of a tense standoff. "I meant to tell you that I let your mom in earlier."

But Serena could barely hear what Abi was saying as

she watched Genevieve smooth a nonexistent wrinkle from her expensive designer dress and open a compact to make sure her makeup and hair were still perfect. "I'll email you your travel details." One air-kiss later, she was gone, leaving only her expensive scent behind.

"Serena?" Abi looked between her and Sean. "What just happened? Why are you so pale? You should sit down."

"I have to go." Serena's stomach was churning and she felt like she was going to be sick. "I can't stay."

Sean's hands were warm as he turned her face to make her look into his eyes. "You don't have to make any decisions yet." His mouth on hers was what finally pulled her all the way up and out of the thick fog. "Not tonight."

"But the contract..."

"Can be broken."

"If I'd known your mother was going to upset you so much, I wouldn't have let her in." Abi looked out the still-open door. "You guys go back to Sean's place, and I'll do damage control for whatever people heard." Her roommate hugged her. "Text me later to let me know you're okay?"

"I should have told you about my mom, Abi, about how things are between us—" But she'd been so afraid to trust anyone.

Just as scared as she'd been by the thought of having to one day return to her old life.

CHAPTER TWENTY-SIX

Sean didn't trust himself to say anything as they walked out of Serena's dorm and headed for his frat. Not only because he was so damned angry with her mother...but also because for everything Serena had ever said about wanting to stay at Stanford, he finally realized just how high the outside pressures on her were. Not only from her mom, but also from powerful movie stars like Smith Sullivan who wanted her to star in one of his films.

The truth was that when she'd brought up the movie the previous night, Sean hadn't asked for any extra details because he hadn't wanted to even think about the possibility that it might get put back on her schedule in the future. Instead, he'd stupidly wanted to bury his head in the sand and believe that nothing would ever pull her back to her old life. Exactly the way his sister had so wisely predicted it would, a handful of weeks ago.

Losing someone he loved again was his worst fear.

But how could he have stopped himself from loving Serena?

Especially when seeing her with his family today had changed something inside him, had taken the love he already felt for her and made it so much bigger. So much deeper. Even the small moments had mattered so much, like when his dog had licked her face and she'd been so carefree, so happy. He'd made a silent vow to do whatever he could to give her that happiness all the time. But the crazy thing was, it had taken her mom coming today to show him that facing the hard stuff tonight was probably the only way either of them could really get to that happiness.

Which was why, as soon as they were inside his room, he said, "Yesterday, when you found those pictures of my mom...I'm really sorry for what I said to you."

"You've already apologized. More than once. You don't have to apologize anymore, Sean."

"It just...whenever I think about what I said about you and your mom, how I refused to even try to understand why you hadn't spoken to her since you started school..." He regretted more than he could say every word that he'd flung at her about taking her mother for granted. "God, I'm an asshole, Serena."

"You're not an asshole, you just—"

"Made stupid assumptions. Really stupid ones. Because even without giving me the full picture, you gave me enough little pieces here and there that I should have put it together." He took her ice-cold hands in his to try to warm them. "My parents always completely supported me in doing whatever I wanted to do...and yet I *still* keep bowing to the pressures of playing baseball rather than spending time doing things I might end up liking better. I mean, I like baseball and going pro wouldn't suck. But sometimes I wonder what it would be like if I hadn't been good at it, if I might be more focused on photography by now. But you had no one to stick up for you, did you?"

When she replied with a soft no, he had to work like

hell to rein in his fury. "You are so damned brave, Serena. Do you even see it in yourself? How strong you are?"

She didn't respond for several long moments, and he knew she was going around and around and around inside her head over decisions about the future that she felt she needed to make right this second.

Finally, she asked, "What was that like? Having a mom who loved you just the way you are?"

He'd told her she could push him, that he *needed* her to push him when no one else would. But now that she was, and he knew it was finally time to let it all out...it wasn't easy. Not even close. Every muscle, every tendon in his well-tuned body was poised for flight. But he'd already admitted to her that he might want to take pictures more than he wanted to play baseball, which was something he'd never said to anyone. Hell, it was something he hadn't even wanted to admit to himself, not when it was easier just to keep moving in the direction everyone believed was his destiny. But what if he—and Serena—were actually meant for different destinies? Ones that veered from her beauty and his athletic prowess? Ones that had her poring over books in libraries and had him photographing sunrises in the mountains?

"I thought everyone had a mom like mine," he finally told her. "She was home with us until Maddie started kindergarten and then she went back to teaching third grade. We used to complain about having her at school with us, because it meant we couldn't get away with anything, but we all secretly loved knowing she was there. If you fell down or felt sick or just needed to ask her a question, she was just a few doors away. And always ready to listen."

"I'm sure it wasn't a secret to her how you really felt."

"It wasn't," he agreed, able to smile about those memories for the first time in what felt like forever. "There were a lot of us to wrangle, but our house was always open to our friends, too. The six of us would often turn into twice as many in the afternoons, and it was pretty crazy, but somehow everyone knew what was on the okay list and what wasn't."

"Was she strict?"

He nodded. "It probably came from having to keep classes of kids from rolling over her, but she was also really fair. Of course, even knowing the rules, we would still get into all kinds of trouble."

"Now that I've met your brothers and sisters," she said with a little smile that he was so damned happy to see, "I can only imagine the trouble all of you must have gotten into."

"I was eight years old and stupid as a brick when I broke my wrist. Justin stopped laughing when he broke his ankle. Drew had already been through it with two broken legs by then, though."

"Two?"

"We'd see him coming in the wheelchair going a hundred miles an hour and we'd all scatter trying to save ourselves. Even Olivia and Maddie broke fingers and toes. Only Grant skated through unscathed. The stories I could tell you..." He grinned, thinking back. "Most of the time, though, even when we got in trouble, as long as no one got really hurt, she'd tell us we were all grounded or doing extra chores for the next week. But then she'd also compliment us on our creativity and would tell us to keep thinking outside the box, just to be a little smarter about it in the future."

"She would actually encourage you guys to break the rules?"

"Amazingly, she did." He laughed. "And maybe it was because she trusted us not to screw up too badly that none of us really went too far." He laughed again. "Well, except for Drew."

"What did he do, beyond breaking both legs and terrorizing all of you with the wheelchair?"

"It's not my story to tell, unfortunately. But I'm sure you'll be able to get it out of him one day. There's nothing he likes more than bragging to a pretty girl about what a badass he is."

Serena smiled back, but he could see it was forced this time, and he knew why. He'd brought up their future together...one that suddenly seemed uncertain.

"My mom didn't tell us right away that she was sick. She'd had a cold for a while. At least, that's what she thought it was. My dad was the one who finally insisted on taking her to the doctor. She hated doctors and hospitals, ever since she was a kid and had ended up in a hospital with pneumonia. And since she was always really healthy, it didn't seem like a big deal that she didn't go much. The cancer...it was already pretty advanced by the time they checked her out. They said—" Oh man, he'd made it this far, but suddenly he didn't know if he could get all the way through it.

He heard Serena say his name and realized that she had put her arms around him and was holding him tight. "You don't have to keep talking about your mom. It's too hard."

But even though it *was* the hardest thing he'd ever done, he needed to get it off his chest. Finally, get it out there. "They said that if she'd just come in for her regular exams, they probably could have caught it in time." Anger rose up inside him. "In time to save her life."

"Oh, Sean. I'm so sorry."

"I was so mad at her. So damned mad." His throat had tightened up, and it was hard to get words out past the lump that had formed. "She left us all—she died—because she was afraid of getting poked at by some doctors a couple of times a year. Damn it..." The tears he hadn't let himself shed were finally falling, and he couldn't seem to stop them. "I'm still mad. I shouldn't be, but I don't know if I'll ever get over it."

* * *

There was such deep, powerful love in Sean's voice when he spoke about his mom. And such pain, too. Pain that broke Serena's heart into tiny little pieces. Especially now that she knew his grief was both for losing her...and because he'd been beating himself up over his anger at how it had all come to pass.

"You wouldn't be so angry," she finally said while his heart beat hard and fast against her own, "if you hadn't loved her so much. And I can see why you did. She sounds like the perfect mom I always used to dream of having."

"I thought she was perfect. But she wasn't."

"When I was modeling, I always hated the word *perfect* and the pressure that came with it," she admitted, "especially when I knew it wasn't possible to be perfect, that someone would always find some flaw, something about me that could have been better. I was expected to be prepared for absolutely every possibility, but I was just a kid trying to do my best and I think..." She swallowed hard as he drew back to look at her. She didn't have a clue if this was the right thing to say, but needed to risk saying it anyway. "I think your mom was doing her very best. And from everything you've told me, she was awesome and amazing and fun and loving. But she wasn't perfect.

None of us are."

As he continued to stare at her, she held her breath, praying she hadn't just upset him even more. Not when it was the very last thing she'd ever want to do. But then, when he finally reached out to cup her cheek, she knew it was safe to let her breath whoosh back out of her lungs.

"I thought it was going to be so hard to talk about her again." He leaned forward slightly so that his forehead was pressed to hers. "And it was, but you made it easier."

"Any time you want to talk about your mom, or anything else, I'll be there," she promised him. "No matter what else is going on——" Even if she ended up on a movie set far away from Stanford. "——I'll always drop anything to be there for you. So if you want to talk more tonight——"

But he was shaking his head, and she could feel the change in the way his fingers were stroking over her skin. From pure comfort...to the first stirrings of desire.

"I don't think we need to talk about my mom, or yours, anymore tonight." His other hand cupped the other side of her face. "Do you?"

There were a million more things they could have said to each other about the past and the future. But, suddenly, she realized he was right—they'd both gone through enough for one night. The hard decisions would still be there waiting for them in the morning.

But tonight, while they had each other, they should celebrate the one thing they both knew for sure: *They loved each other.*

"As the last remaining nineteen-year-old virgin on the planet," she said softly, "I used to wonder if I'd ever know for sure that I was ready, or if I'd just eventually end up having sex because I felt so behind the curve and needed to catch up." She couldn't believe she was actually smiling while speaking her most secret thoughts aloud, but that was the magic of being with Sean. Even the impossible no longer seemed out of reach. "But I've never been so sure about anyone or anything in my entire life. And I'm so glad you're my first, because I can't imagine trusting anyone else the way I trust you. I'm so glad I waited for you, that there hasn't been anyone else."

His mouth was almost over hers when he whispered, "I'm really glad there hasn't been anyone else for you, either."

And then he was kissing her, and it was their sweetest, sexiest, most incredible kiss yet. One that swam through her bloodstream like a drug she'd always crave more of.

And yet, in a night of revelations, when all she wanted to do was let herself drift away in sensation, she couldn't quite turn off her brain, couldn't stop herself from saying, "I wish—"

"Tell me, Serena. Tell me what you wish and I'll do whatever I can to make it come true."

She shook her head. "It can't happen, and anyway, it's not fair of me to ask for it."

"I'm pretty sure we've crossed a pretty big bridge tonight, one where we're not going to hold back with each other even if what we're saying isn't easy, right?" When she nodded, he said, "So, tell me."

"I can't help but wish I was your first, too."

He took her hand and put it over his heart. "You're right, I can't undo my past. But you have to know that you're the first person who has ever made my heart beat this hard. I want you around all the time. I want to bring you up in every single conversation. I thought letting myself feel again would mean feeling too much, but I couldn't resist falling in love with you. You've done more to open my eyes back up to the world I've tried to close myself off to than anyone else could have."

"You've opened me up, too," she told him. "You've helped me see and experience things I never would have trusted anyone else with."

"I've never loved anyone the way I love you, Serena. So in every way that counts, you *are* my first."

CHAPTER TWENTY-SEVEN

Oh so slowly, Sean stripped away her crocheted sweater. He seemed surprised—in a very good way—when her tank top came off with it and he realized she didn't have anything on beneath it.

"Beautiful." The word pulsed with sensuality as he tossed her top onto the floor and cupped her breasts in his large hands. "God, you're beautiful."

Serena loved how her curves, her height, every part of her, finally felt just right when she was in his arms. "So are you." It had been true when she'd said it to him the first night they'd met, but now she knew how beautiful he was on the inside, too.

"I want so badly to love you right, but—"

"No more waiting." She was panicked that he was going to pull back again, that he might think he was doing the right thing by not making love with her tonight.

"God, no," he agreed in a fervent voice that brought her immense relief. "Tonight should be romantic and special for you…but at this point I don't know if I'm going to be able to keep from ripping the rest of your clothes off and taking you right here on the floor."

"The floor works for me." She began to open the buttons on the front of his shirt to show him that she meant it.

Thankfully, that was all he seemed to need to get over the hump of feeling he ought to treat her like porcelain because she was a virgin, and a short—*very* short—while later, her jeans and panties were off. She tried to take his clothes off just as quickly, but her inexperience worked against her, so he had to help her pull everything off.

Soon they were both naked and his erection was big and hot and hard against her stomach. She wanted so badly to touch him, but just as she began to run her hands down his chest, he picked her up in his arms and brought her over to the bed.

"The floor—and you touching me like that—are both going to have to wait."

He kissed away any protests she would have made, his lips taking a breath-stealing path from her mouth down to her neck and shoulders and then her breasts. She could hear his soft laughter as he teased her by kissing everywhere except her tightly peaked nipples. She loved feeling the warmth and joy of his happiness against her skin as he made his way lower, over her rib cage to her belly, his tongue flicking out against her hip bones to tease her further still.

But when his mouth came down over her sex and she arched into his touch, she wasn't able to think at all anymore. Wasn't able to do anything but feel. And want more. And then *more* again until she needed him inside her *right that second.*

She gripped his hands and pulled him up her body. "Now," she said against his lips, tasting herself on them. "I need you now."

She was so desperate for him that she almost forgot about protection. Thankfully, he'd already taken care of it, so that the next thing she knew he was poised between her thighs. Hard. Big. Beautiful.

Hers.

Led by both her body and her heart, Serena lifted her hips up to him at the exact moment he moved inside her for the very first time.

"Serena?"

She'd stilled beneath him, but not because she was in pain. Coming together with him like this, letting go of her final barriers and her lingering fears that she'd never find anyone who truly loved her for who she really was, felt *so* good.

So amazingly, incredibly good, that she wanted to savor every second of it.

"I love you."

The words fell from her lips even as she lifted her hips higher to take him deeper. And all the while, as he finally made her his in the most incredible way possible, he also told her how much he loved her. How beautiful she was. How good she felt wrapped around him. How hot, how wet she was for him. She drank in every sweet and sexy word in the same way she soaked up the delicious friction between their bodies as, inch by inch, he thrust all the way inside her.

For a few moments, as he pulsed hot and huge and *perfect* inside of her, they simply stared at each other in wonder. Neither of them spoke, but they didn't need words, didn't need anything other than the warm press of her lips on his, the sweet caress of his hands over her bottom as he cupped her to fit them together even more deeply, and the instinctive rocking of their hips in perfect unison.

"Tell me. Tell me if it's good. Or if you need—"

"The best." She panted the word into his neck, licking at his salty skin. "I've never felt this good before. *Never.*"

"I've never felt this good before, either." His eyes were so dark and so full of heat as he moved his hands down her arms until his fingers were threaded through hers. "Hold on tight to me with your hands and your legs." He waited until she'd crossed her calves tightly behind his back. "Close your eyes." He waited until she'd done so to whisper against her lips. "Now let go."

She was amazed by how a few simple words and the rub of his palms against hers as he thrust deep, and then deeper still, could take her up so high, and so quickly. Because with her eyes closed and Sean holding her hands in his on either side of their bodies as he made love to her, every one of her senses leaped to brilliant life.

The ragged sound of their breathing.

The scent of their arousal, and the clean sweat on his tanned skin.

The heat of his body against hers, heat that rose with every roll of their hips, with every lash of his tongue over the hollow at the center of her throat and then the hungry tips of her breasts.

The taste of his skin beneath her own tongue where she kissed him just at the racing pulse point in his neck.

Every beautiful moment wound her tighter and tighter, especially since she knew what was waiting on the other side—a climax that was bound to be even more explosive than all the others Sean had given her simply because he would be a part of her this time when she came apart into a thousand pieces in his arms.

"I've got you," he said against her lips. "I've got you."

That was all it took—three simple words of reassurance that when she leaped he would be there to catch her—for everything that had wound so tightly within her to start unraveling from the center outward, one beautiful burst of pleasure after another that seemed to go on forever and ever.

And when Sean finally buried his face in her neck and groaned her name as he followed her over the edge, even though she'd only just said that nothing was perfect, she now knew that she'd been wrong.

Making love with Sean was *perfect*.

* * *

Sean was pretty sure his heart was going to pound all the way out of his chest as he gathered Serena into his arms and rolled over with her so that she was lying on top of him, rather than being crushed beneath him. After quickly removing the condom and tossing it into the garbage can, he brushed her damp hair back from her face so that she would be more comfortable. She was breathing as hard as he was and her full breasts were pressing in the best possible way against his chest.

She lifted her face from his shoulder, and he was amazed all over again not only by her beauty, but by *all* of her. He could never have predicted that she would come into his life, would never have expected to meet anyone like her on campus. She was warm, smart, loving. And his.

All his.

Only his.

He'd wanted to be careful with her for her first time, had tried to hold back and make sure that he was taking care of her needs. But when she'd begged for more, he was afraid that he'd forgotten everything but how much he wanted her, how much he needed her.

Silently, he vowed to take it even slower the next time, no matter what. Sean would never forgive himself if he selfishly moved too fast, or if he hurt her in any way.

Of course, the way she was smiling at him, at once innocent and yet powerfully sensual as she licked her lips and said—"*Again*"—already made it nearly impossible to stick to the vows he had just made.

Of everything he might have thought she'd say to him in that moment, there was no way he could have prepared himself for *again*. Even when there was nothing he wanted more than to take her again. And again. And again. Especially when he knew with perfect certainty that he'd never be able to get enough of her.

But damn it, he'd just vowed to be gentle. To slow down so that he didn't overwhelm her. "I want to make love to you again. Right this second. So damned badly." He shifted his groin against her hip so that she wouldn't be able to doubt him. "But I don't want to hurt you. I can't hurt you, Serena."

"I know you can't." She was still smiling at him, a sweet and sexy smile that made him grow even harder with every beat of his heart. The heart she owned completely. "You never could, not even that first night we met. You wouldn't have made me do anything I wasn't comfortable with." She shifted so that his erection was nestled against her lower belly. "But I've waited so long for you. I've waited *forever*." She wasn't just trying to persuade him with words, she was using her body, too, rocking into him with unquenched need. "I don't want to wait anymore." Her teeth nipped at his earlobe. "Not another second."

Over these past few weeks, he'd lulled himself into thinking that the two of them could work, that it would last. Tonight, her desperation to be with him again was echoed by his own. Because no matter how much he wanted to, he couldn't deny that she might be leaving soon...and that there might be nothing he could do to keep her from being ripped away from him. If she left to film the movie, their "normal" Friday night dates would quickly be overshadowed by the huge pressures that came with her being one of the world's most in-demand stars.

"No more waiting." He tugged her up over his hips so that she was straddling him. Looking up at the most beautiful woman in all creation, he could barely find his voice. "Anything you want. I'll give you anything, Serena."

"I like the sound of that." There was a sexy little smile on her lips as she slowly ran her hands over his chest. "And I like being able to do this, too." His muscles rippled beneath her fingertips as she explored his body with wonder in her eyes. "That first night when you held me, I couldn't believe how hard, how hot, you felt." She leaned over him, the tips of her breasts brushing him as she whispered, "Or how much I liked it."

He tangled his hands in her hair and brought her all the way in for a kiss. "I can never get enough," he said against her mouth between increasingly desperate tastes of her. "The more I have of you, the more I want."

"I want you, too." She rolled her hips over his erection and her breasts into his chest. *"Now."* She reached for the condoms he kept in the drawer beside his bed and pulled one out. "Can I put this on you?"

"Go for it." Each word was more strangled than the one before simply from the thought of having her hands on him. But it was the serious look on her face as she studied the instructions on the back of the wrapper that was the hottest thing of all, watching his beautiful, brilliant girl put as much focus and dedication into making love with him as she did with everything else.

Finally—*finally!*—she ripped open the package and, with her bottom lip held between her teeth, reached for him. "If I'm doing it wrong," she said as she began to roll it down over him so slowly that if he hadn't known better, he might have thought she was intentionally trying to tease him, "just tell me."

"You're doing it just right." His words were so hoarse it sounded as if he'd destroyed his voice by yelling for hours. And it took every last ounce of self-control not to lose it before she finished the job. As soon as she had, he took her hands in his and pulled her back up over him. "I need you now, beautiful. *Now.*" But she was already there, moving so perfectly over his shaft, her slick heat enveloping him.

"Slow," he urged her, keeping his hands firmly on her hips so that she couldn't go too fast their second time. And, Lord, the way she looked as she made love to him, like she'd never been so happy, or felt so good in all her life...

He couldn't keep from leaning up to take her nipples into his mouth, first one, then the other, repeating the pattern until he'd moved even deeper into her. So deep that she was gasping with pleasure and he had gone nearly crazy from her smell and taste and the feel of her all around him.

Needing to hold her close, he sat up and wrapped her legs around his waist so that they were heartbeat to heartbeat and face to face. She wound her arms around his neck and kissed him until neither of them could keep from giving in to what they both wanted so badly.

But even as he thrust up into her and she buried her face in his neck, holding on tight while her body started to come apart at the seams in the most beautiful way possible, Sean couldn't stop praying that tonight wasn't the beginning of good-bye.

CHAPTER TWENTY-EIGHT

Nothing, absolutely nothing, would ever be as good as waking up in Sean's arms. All night long he'd been wrapped around her, his chest to her back, her body fitting so perfectly into his that it was as though they'd been made only for each other. Serena wasn't usually a very sound sleeper, but she hadn't stirred once all night.

And yet, feeling so momentarily safe made the decisions waiting for her even harder to face. If only she could stay in his bed, in his arms, forever, and forget that she had any other life.

She wanted so badly to be strong, to continue making the choices that *she* wanted to make, rather than the ones she felt compelled to go along with to make her mother, Smith Sullivan, the investors in his movie, and her agent happy. But with Smith's movie thrown into the mix, it felt so much harder this time to say no and stand firm.

Maybe the way Genevieve had behaved should have made it easier, but Serena could still remember the times when her mother had been nice and kind and loving. And even if those times had more to do with Serena's performance in front of the cameras than anything else, she couldn't forget how good it had felt.

Serena's heart rate was already rising by the time she tried to get the panic to stop by telling herself that maybe it would all work out. Maybe she was freaking out for nothing. And maybe her mother was wrong and Smith didn't need her right away.

"Good morning."

Trying to hide her rising anxiety, Serena rolled over so that she and Sean were face to face on the pillow. He was gorgeous first thing in the morning. "I like this," she said as she reached up to brush her fingertips over his dark stubble.

He captured her hand in his and kissed her fingertips. "Good. Because you'll be seeing a lot more of it in the future."

Just like that, the tension that she'd only just managed to shove down burst open inside her. "Sean, I—" Just then she caught a glimpse of the clock on his bedside table. "Oh no, I didn't realize how late it is and how long we slept. I need to go. I have my presentation this afternoon and I need to get ready for it."

When he turned to look at the clock, he cursed, too. "I have to head out for fielding practice. And then I've got an Econ test." She was already dragging on her clothes from the day before, when he slid naked out of the bed and took one of her hands in his. "I'll text my coach to let him know I can't make it today, and I'll find a way to talk my professor into letting me make up the test later in the week."

"You don't need to do that." No matter how much she wanted him with her, she couldn't let him blow off the important things in his own life just so he could hold her hand all day and make sure she didn't lose it. She made herself—for the first time with him—put on one of the wide smiles she'd so often used in front of the cameras. "I'll be fine."

But she could see that he didn't buy it. Not for a second. "I know this might seem crazy," he told her, "but I keep thinking that if I let you go today, the next thing I know, you'll be calling me from an airplane or a film set."

"I won't." Because even if she *did* have to leave, she would never go without saying good-bye. "I know my mother made it seem like everything needed to change right away, but we don't know that for sure yet."

A muscle jumped in his jaw at the word *yet,* but he didn't press her on it. Instead, he was the one forcing a smile this time. "I'll come get you at the English Department after you ace your presentation. We can go celebrate with a slice of pizza."

"That sounds great," she said as she wrapped her arms around him.

They stood holding each other for as long as they could, but the clock was still ticking and they had to pull apart too soon.

* * *

Taking a scalding hot shower helped. So did putting on a little makeup for once so that she had some color in her face, then choosing one of the few dresses she'd brought to campus and slipping it on, along with some pretty flats. By the time she was dressed, Serena actually felt pretty normal. Or as close to normal as she could be, given the circumstances.

Okay, she told herself as she packed up her notes and books to head to the quiet of the library for a few hours to review her presentation, all she needed to do was keep everything in its own separate compartment. Right now she'd focus on her classwork. After her presentation, she'd focus on Sean. And after that, she'd finally deal with her career...and her mother.

When that thought had her heart rate picking up again, she forcefully pushed it away and steadied herself by looking at the book in her hand. *Jane Eyre*. Charlotte Brontë's beautiful words had always inspired her.

"Serena, you really need to start answering your phone!"

From the look on her roommate's face as she walked into their room, Serena's stomach sank even before Abi held out her own phone. "Katie just saw this and I didn't want you to be blindsided by it later."

Even the best self-control and all the pep talks in the world couldn't stop Serena from flinching when she looked at the picture of her and Sean walking together. It must have been taken last night after they'd left her dorm room because they looked tense. Upset. And anyone would think from looking at it that they'd been fighting. How would anyone ever guess that they'd both been shell-shocked by her mother's sneak-attack movie bomb? Especially when the headline that went along with the photo was *Serena Britten gets ready to leave Stanford to shoot a Smith Sullivan blockbuster: Will a long-distance relationship work? Vote now!*

She should have been used to this by now, to people voting online about a total stranger's life—a stranger who happened to be her. But after feeling like she might actually have started to pull away from that life during the past few weeks, dealing with the celebrity spotlight again felt worse than ever. Had it just been last night after Maddie's party that she'd told herself she didn't care about the paparazzi anymore? Had she actually been foolish enough to believe that they were tired of trying to get interesting shots of her?

Now she realized just how wrong she'd been. Photographers must have been lying in wait for her...or someone from her dorm had heard the commotion, taken the pictures, and decided to make some quick cash by selling them. But that wasn't all, because beneath the picture of the two of them were several more pictures of girls Sean was reputed to have dated before Serena. Pretty girls. Really pretty. And probably with normal lives that didn't go off like mines in a minefield from one second to the next.

"Stop thinking crazy thoughts," Abi said, clearly reading Serena's face. "He's not interested in any of those other girls."

"I know," Serena replied. Still, it wasn't easy to see photographic evidence of what a player he'd been, particularly on a day when it was getting harder and harder for her to pretend that she was going to be able to stick around. It wasn't that she didn't trust him—of course she did—it was more that she hated the thought of him holding himself back from fully living life because of her. Especially if her career spiraled off the way it always had before, from photo shoot to fashion show and now to movie set, and she couldn't come back to Stanford anytime soon...

"Last night with Sean," Serena said, needing to share the wonder of it with her friend, "was amazing."

Abi smiled at her the way she imagined a sister would. "Of course it was. Not just because of how hot your boyfriend is, but because he loves you." Abi took the phone out of her hand and threw it on the bed. "I know all of these pictures, these gossip stories, upset you. But they don't matter."

"I know they don't, but there's still the movie thing to deal with." Serena shook her head. "I know complaining about having a part in a Smith Sullivan movie is crazy."

"Pretty much every girl on the planet would sell her soul to get to be around Smith," Abi agreed. "But you can't beat yourself up if you dig libraries more than hot movie stars."

It felt good to laugh, even a little. It felt even better to be understood. "Speaking of libraries, I really need to get ready for my presentation."

"You want to run it by me?"

"You've already been so amazing," Serena said. "Dealing with having me as a roommate, answering endless questions about things anyone else would already know about by now, and then my mother yesterday. So even though I appreciate your offer to be bored to tears by my presentation, I think you've done more than enough for me already."

"It's what friends are for," Abi said with a little shrug that proved just how much she meant it. Clearly, none of the things she'd done for Serena had been a big deal for her. Because she was a nice person.

Wanting so badly to do something for Abi, too, Serena said, "I meant to tell you about meeting Sean's brothers."

"Oooh, tell me *everything.*"

"Justin looks like his carbon copy, but even though I think they're pretty different as people, it would be a little weird if you dated him. However," she said to quell Abi's disappointment, "his oldest brother Grant was there, although he might be a little on the serious side for you, too. But *Drew…*"

"Oh my God, Drew Morrison left his tour to come home for his sister's birthday party?"

Serena nodded. "He's a bit of a player, I think. More

than a bit. But I still really liked him." She smiled at her roommate. "And he's pretty darn sexy."

"I don't care if he's a player, and I already *know* how sexy he is." Abi licked her lips. "How long is he going to be in town?"

"Wait a sec, I'll see if I can find out." Serena quickly texted Sean, hoping she'd catch him before he started practice. She smiled when he texted right back. "Until tomorrow. Sean says he has a private gig in the city tonight." Serena sent him another note, hoping that she could at least give Abi this one small thing.

"What are you doing?"

She held up a finger as her phone buzzed again. "Hold on, he's checking with Drew."

"Checking? What's he checking?"

Thirty seconds later, the text she was hoping for came through. "Drew would love for you to be his special guest tonight for the private show. He'll come pick you up here at six if that will work."

"Of course it will work!" Abi threw herself at Serena and hugged her so tightly she almost lifted her off the floor. "Oh my God, what am I going to wear?" She looked at her watch. "I'm barely going to have enough time to go to the mall and get everything else done."

"Everything else?"

"You know, nails, makeup, hair."

"Abi." Serena wanted her roommate to have a good time, but she didn't want her to end up hurt. "It sounds like Drew is always on the road. I don't think he'd be good boyfriend material."

Fortunately, Abi just laughed. "Don't worry, I'm not in the market for a boyfriend. Even if the whole committed-and-in-love thing is totally working for you. But I'm definitely game for making out with a rock star."

She grabbed her purse and keys and blew Serena a kiss from the doorway. "Thanks again, you're the best! And don't worry about those stupid pictures, okay?" She poked her head back around the door frame. "Good luck with your presentation. I'm sure it will be amazing."

CHAPTER TWENTY-NINE

Ten minutes later, Serena was in her usual spot in the library, but she couldn't settle down. Not when everything around her reminded her of Sean. Surprising her the day those first pictures had come out. Showing her the photographs—and a deeply hidden part of himself—in the archives downstairs. Picking her up to take her to play Frisbee Golf. Surprising her with the bag full of Stanford Football clothes and face paint for one of their normal dates...and her surprising him right back by launching herself at him at the top of the stairs and kissing him. And then, on their most recent Friday night date, being surprised when he'd unzipped her bag and found tequila in it.

All the sweet and sexy moments blurred in her brain, making it nearly impossible for her to focus the way she needed to. But if she blew this presentation that made up fifty percent of her grade for the quarter, movie or not, her grade point average would be too low for the admissions department to change her probationary acceptance to permanent.

Pushing the hair out of her face, she stared down at

her notes and made herself carefully and deliberately go through them line by line, page by page. It took a little while, but finally, she started to sink back into the material the way she usually did. In fact, an hour later, when she finally thought to check her phone just in case Sean or Abi needed anything, she was surprised to see Smith Sullivan's name on the screen.

She hadn't heard her phone ring, but it looked like he'd left her a voice mail. Her heart rate immediately kicked into overdrive. And though she hated it when people used their cell phones in the library, she couldn't wait to get all the way outside before hearing what he had to say.

Holding it up to her ear, she pressed *play* and Smith's deep voice rumbled through. "Serena, I wanted to call to tell you how pleased I am that we will be working together on my film. I apologize again that it took this long for everything to be set in stone, and after worrying that we would lose you to other projects and commitments, I'm extremely glad to hear via your mother that you will definitely be able to make our first day of production next week." He said a few more things, but she could barely take them in and had to replay his message again to take down his full contact information just in case she needed to reach him between now and next week.

She shouldn't be shocked that her mother would have said Serena had "no other projects or commitments" that would interfere with his movie. And yet, even after the things Genevieve had said to her the day before, she was stunned. Stunned *and* heartbroken to know that what she wanted mattered so little to the person who had been the center of her world for nineteen years.

She dropped the phone into her bag and when she

turned back to her presentation notes, no matter how hard she tried to study them, she just couldn't stop thinking about Smith's call...and how if everything went the way her mother was hoping it would, Serena would be on set by this time next week. It would be as though her time here at Stanford—and Sean—had never happened at all, reduced to nothing more than a short little blip in her life.

* * *

Disaster.

Her presentation was a total disaster. It was so bad, in fact, that by the time she fumbled her way to the end no one in her class could even make eye contact with her.

"Serena," her professor said while the other students all shot out the door as fast as they could, "I'd appreciate it if you could stay behind for a few minutes."

She felt sick to her stomach. She didn't get the sense that Professor Fairworth paid much attention to pop culture, but it would just be her lucky day if he'd somehow seen the news reports that she was going to film Smith's movie. If he had, of course he would assume that she had intentionally wasted his time today with a ridiculously subpar presentation.

"Is everything all right?"

Considering how uncomfortable she'd been around him in those initial weeks, ever since he'd canceled their one-on-one meetings, she hadn't picked up on any weird vibes. Well, not too many weird vibes, anyway. Granted, she'd been too preoccupied with falling for Sean to notice much about anyone else.

"I'm so sorry about my presentation. I put so much time into preparing for it, but some personal things came up in the last couple of days."

She hated hearing the excuse come out of her mouth,

but for as fatalistic as all of this seemed, now that she'd actually blown the very thing she needed to get right, Serena was struck hard with a fierce need not to give up on everything that she'd had to fight so hard for in the first place. Maybe all of this was the universe telling her that she'd never belonged here anyway…but, darn it, that didn't change how badly she *wanted* to be here.

"I know it's no excuse and that you don't have to give me any special preference, but if there was any way that I might be able to have a second chance to prove to you that I take your class as seriously as I truly do—"

"Serena, it's okay."

Her professor put his hand on her arm to stop her mouth from running on. Perhaps she should have been more startled by the fact that he was touching her, and that he didn't immediately remove his hand from her bare skin, but she was so full of hope that he was going to give her another chance, the thought of pulling away didn't even cross her mind.

"It is?" Could this be the real sign that she was going to figure out a way to make it all work, after all? "I was so worried that you would think I'd flaked out, but I swear I haven't."

"Breathe," he said as he moved to draw her closer and began to stroke her back. "Just a few deep breaths will help. And then we can talk about our next step."

Finally—and with such suddenness that it stole her breath along with the relief she'd momentarily felt— wariness came. Along with a hit of fear as she realized that she'd just walked into her professor's arms.

Carefully, she took a small step back. "Thank you for agreeing to give me another shot at getting this presentation right. If I could have a couple of extra days to make a new plan for it, I know I could do a much better job."

"Absolutely, Serena, although I'm sure you agree that it would be best if you did your repeat performance outside of class. Otherwise, I expect your fellow students might wonder where their second chances are. We wouldn't want them to think you're getting any special treatment just because your picture is everywhere."

When he put it that way, it suddenly seemed like he *had* seen the story about her leaving school to film Smith's movie. Which mean he probably also thought she and Sean were breaking up. If Sean had been the reason her professor had backed off several weeks ago, did Fairworth now think she was fair game? Was that why he was suddenly behaving in such a way that he was giving her the major creeps again?

"Professor Fairworth, I really do feel terrible about my performance today," she began, but he raised his hand to stop her from saying anything else.

"We all have our off days. Perhaps before you redo your presentation, we should get together to discuss a few ways you might be able to improve your analysis. I have a full roster of classes tomorrow, but I could carve out some time for you in the evening."

All those vulnerable and icky feelings she'd had around him in those early weeks on campus were coming back stronger than ever now, strong enough that she couldn't quite force a response from her lips.

"This building will be shut by then," he continued as if her agreement was a given, "so why don't you come to my place?"

He dropped his gaze to her mouth before lowering it farther still and then slowly bringing his attention back to her face. And when he reached up to brush the backs of his knuckles across her cheek, she was so horrified that for a few seconds that seemed to stretch on forever she couldn't get any of her limbs to work.

"You're very special, Serena. Very beautiful, too." He let his utterly inappropriate words linger for a few seconds as he ran hungry eyes over her again. "I truly do believe that you have special talents, and I am very much looking forward to helping you rise to your full potential, one on one. I know you're upset about what happened today, but I promise I can make you feel good about everything again. So very good."

While working as a model, she'd come across more than one photographer who had a knack for spinning things around on the girls he worked with so that they actually thought they'd asked for what the creeps had made them do. But Serena had always been protected by her mother, with Genevieve making absolutely certain that no one got near her. In so many ways it had been a prison, but at least she'd never come out of a session hollow-eyed from the things she'd wished she'd never done with the photographer.

Today, there was no one to protect her from her predatory professor. No one, she suddenly realized, but herself.

She took a step away from him. A big enough one that he had to drop his hand. "Meeting at your house isn't going to work. I wouldn't want anyone to get the wrong idea about what I'm willing to do to improve my grade." *Especially you.* "I know I blew my presentation today," she said in a voice that grew stronger with every word she spoke, "but meeting in one of these classrooms would be best."

She could read her professor's frustration loud and clear from the way his face reddened and his eyes narrowed on her. "I know you're on academic probation until you can prove that you're a good enough student to be allowed to stay on for another quarter, Serena. I'm offering you a second chance. Are you really turning it down?"

She might be giving up her chance at recovering her grade, but it was so much better to live with that than letting her professor take advantage of her in exchange for it. "If the only option is to meet at your house—" She waited a moment to give him a chance to offer another alternative. She wasn't surprised when he didn't. "—then yes, I am absolutely turning down your offer." She was about to pick up her bag and walk out, when she had to also tell him, "And it is utterly and completely inappropriate for you or any other professor to comment on my looks or touch me like that. I was so excited when I heard that you were going to be one of my professors, but you're nothing like I'd hope you be." She let him see how disgusted she was by him. "You can will all the literary awards in the world, but that still won't make you a good man."

With that, she finally left the classroom. Even if she managed the miracle of getting out of the movie, by rejecting her professor's "offer" and telling him exactly what she thought of him, she was nailing the final piece of her college coffin in place. But at least she'd leave Stanford with her self-respect.

She had never been happier to see Sean coming down the hallway for her.

"Sorry I'm late," he said, his arms already open to pull her into them. "My professor was late so he gave us fifteen extra minutes for the test. I finished as quickly as I could."

Badly needing his arms around her, she reached for him. But before he could fold her against him, he stopped and looked carefully at her. "What's wrong?"

Her professor stepped out into the hall at that very moment. Smith Sullivan might have cast her for a major role in his movie, but her acting wasn't nearly good enough to hide the revulsion that crossed her face.

"Serena?" Sean's voice was a low growl. "What did he do?"

She shook her head. "He tried to get me to come to his house for a 'one-on-one' session tomorrow night, but I've already—" Before she could finish her sentence, Sean was moving toward her professor, fury in his eyes. "Sean, you don't have to—"

"Does it make you feel powerful, preying on your students?" Sean was big enough and broad enough to stop her professor in midstride.

"Get out of my way."

"Not a chance, asshole."

Her professor raised an eyebrow. "I'm not going to ask you again. Get out of my way."

Sean's fists bunched up, just seconds from throwing a punch. Serena couldn't deny that it was amazing to have him stick up for her like this, but at the same time, if news of a fight between the two of them over her got out—which it would, no question about it—and especially if her professor played innocent and the faculty believed him, Sean might get kicked out of school. She'd already accepted that she was done here. But she'd never forgive herself if he lost his spot at Stanford, too, because of her.

"Stop." She managed to slip between the two men, facing Sean. "Please, stop. He isn't worth it." She could see Sean warring with himself, knew he was so angry over what might have happened to her that he wanted to tear the guy apart with his bare hands. "I've already made things just as clear to him as he did to me."

For a few moments, she wasn't sure that Sean had even heard what she said. Not until he finally told her professor, "Don't you dare ask Serena, or any other of your female students, to be alone with you again. If I find out you have, I won't stop next time. Not just ripping your sorry ass to pieces, but exposing you to the faculty."

"You can't touch me."

"Want to bet? I have more Stanford connections than you can imagine, including one of the biggest donors to the university."

She shouldn't have gotten such pleasure from seeing the other man's face turn white. But he'd played the all-powerful role with her for so long that it was really nice to see that shift. And so suddenly, too.

With that, Sean turned his back on her professor and took Serena's hand in his. "Ready to get that pizza?"

Somehow, even when everything was a mess, he always knew how to make her smile. And to forget everything but him, even the really bad stuff. "Let's go."

CHAPTER THIRTY

Hand in hand, they walked nearly the entire length of Palm Drive into downtown Palo Alto in silence. It was the same route they'd taken the day the photographer had snapped the shots of them just starting to get to know—and fall for—one another. But Sean wasn't thinking about paparazzi now. Frankly, he didn't give a shit about any of that anymore.

All that mattered was Serena.

"I should have been there with you."

The second he'd seen her face, he'd known something bad must have happened in class. She hadn't been crumbling—on the contrary, she'd looked determined and disgusted—but he'd learned to read her expressions so well that he'd been afraid every bad feeling he had about her professor had come true.

"I'm not going to lie and say that I didn't wish you were there, too, but—" She surprised him with a smile. One that made his heart race the way it had from the very first time she'd ever smiled at him. "I stood up to him, Sean. And even though it means he's going to flunk me and I'll be done here, I couldn't have done anything else."

She squared her shoulders, "It felt good to tell him that I knew what he was trying to do and that I wasn't going to let him do it. I honestly wasn't totally sure that I had it in me."

"I knew you did."

Serena reminded him of his mother in the way her inner core of strength lay just beneath the surface of her beauty. His sisters had not only inherited that quality from their mom, but they'd also been taught to respect themselves and their inner strength. Whereas Serena...well, he wasn't exactly sure what Genevieve Britten had thought she was teaching her daughter.

All he knew was that Serena continually blew his mind.

"If that douche bag even thinks of flunking you, I'll rain hell down on him so hard—"

"My presentation was really bad, Sean. I mean, I know he probably would have wanted to give me a bad grade for not sleeping with him, but in this case, the grade is going to be warranted. It was when I asked if there was a chance that I could redo it that he made me an offer I *had* to refuse."

"I don't get it. You were ready to ace this presentation." He stopped them in the middle of the sidewalk. They were almost at Pizza My Heart, but he needed to know, "What happened between my leaving you at your room and your class?"

"Smith Sullivan called."

Her blue eyes were so bright, so striking as she looked at him, her emotion so pure and beautiful on her face, that Sean understood exactly why every photographer—and now the biggest movie star in the world—wanted her in front of the camera. If it had been what Serena also wanted, he would have supported her in any way he could, even if it meant changing his own life to fit with hers.

But she didn't want that career, or that life. No, what Serena wanted most of all was to be holed up in a big library with her books, surrounded by people who loved them just as much as she did.

Somehow, some way, he needed to figure out how to help her get that.

"What did Smith say?" He couldn't keep the undertone of anger out of his voice.

"Don't blame Smith. It's not his fault that he thinks my schedule is free and clear so that I can start filming in Seattle next week."

"How could he think that when you're right in the middle of the quarter?"

She lowered her gaze to the sidewalk and said softly, "You know how."

Sean fought to hold back his rising fury. Regardless of how he felt about Genevieve Britten, she was still Serena's mother. They might have a supremely screwed-up relationship, but he'd seen for himself the day before just how strong a hold her mother had over her. Simply because Serena wanted so badly to be loved.

More than ever, he wished his mother were still alive so that she could meet Serena. Lisa Morrison would have known exactly what to say. She would have known what to do. She would have known how to make everything better.

Of course, Serena saw right through him, could always see everything he tried to keep hidden as she went up onto her tippy-toes to press a soft kiss against his lips. "Let's try to stop worrying about everything for a few minutes and go have the best pizza in the world."

This time she was the one leading them inside and

ordering slices with everything. And by the time she'd handed him a bottle of Coke and they sat down at what he now thought of as their table by the window, he knew what he needed to do.

His mother might be gone, but before she passed away, she'd left each of her children a special note just for them. She'd promised that she would always be there watching over all of them and, finally, he realized that it was true. Because her final note hadn't just been meant for him.

It had been meant for Serena, too.

* * *

Ever since Genevieve had surprised them by showing up in Serena's dorm room the day before, Sean had been vibrating with emotion. Anger at her mother. Frustration at the way the pressures of Serena's career had leaped back to the forefront. And then love—*so much love*—for her. Love he'd shown her last night in the sweetest, sexiest way possible. Only to be slammed by fear when he'd thought her professor had hurt her this afternoon.

Serena wanted to soothe him, wanted to see him smile again, wanted to tell him that everything was going to be okay. Only, how could she when she was still so confused? Not about being in love with Sean, or about standing up to her predatory professor, but about how to deal with the rest of the mess of her life.

What, she desperately wanted to know, *was the right choice to make?*

Sean had been quiet for most of their walk from her classroom to the restaurant, and she'd been glad for the space and the chance to process her thoughts a little before she brought him up to speed on everything that had happened since that morning. But now as they ate their slices in silence, he looked serious, and a little sad. But also like he'd made an important decision. A big one.

"I've never shown this to anyone else," he said when their plates were empty. "I never thought I would." He reached for his wallet and pulled out a folded piece of paper, quickly scanning it in a way that told her he already had every word memorized. "My mother wrote a special letter for each of us."

She couldn't stop her hands from shaking as she took it from him. "Are you sure you want me to read this?"

"If she were still here, I'm positive this is what she'd say to you. To both of us—since I don't think I ever really took it in all the way until today."

My darling Sean, I remember the day you were born, how bold and strong and sweet you were from your very first breath. You smiled at me, and even though all the books say babies can't do that on their first day, I knew they were wrong. Because you've always been special. You've always been such a joy. And even when you were naughty, it was all I could do not to laugh right along with you every single time. I've loved every second of being your mother.

Serena looked up from the letter, unable to stop her tears. "Sean," she asked again, "are you sure—"

He nodded. "Keep reading."

I've been writing this letter to you in my head for a long time, since before I got sick. Ever since I realized just how good you are at everything. School. Sports. Photography. Girls.

That made Serena laugh through her tears before she

realized it was bubbling out.

"I know," he said, a small smile also playing on his lips despite his otherwise extremely serious expression. "She got me with that, too. On purpose, I'm sure of it."

Life is full of choices, always and endlessly. It is, I promise you, one of the joys of being alive, even if it doesn't always seem like it when you're frustrated and overwhelmed and being pulled in different directions. But through it all, here's what I hope you will know, and remember, no matter what: It doesn't matter what anyone else thinks you are, Sean. It doesn't matter what anyone else thinks you should be, or what the right path is for you. All that matters is what you think, and what you feel. Because all the answers are right there inside your head, your body, your heart.

It's perfectly normal to be led off course and away from the answers that are right for you. We all are, for both good and bad reasons, by both good and bad people. But no matter how dim, how dark, how numb or static things may sometimes feel, the true answers are always within you, and have been from that very first moment when you looked into my eyes and smiled at me.

The page was blurring so badly that Serena had to stop to brush away her tears—carefully, so that they wouldn't fall on the letter. She needed to pause for a moment, too, so that she could settle her heart down and make sure she took in every beautiful word Sean's mother had written for him.

The answers are in your dreams. The answers are in the things you're passionate about. The answers are in what brings you joy. You can follow the path that everyone assumes you should follow. Or you can do what really matters most to you.

And when you do, I promise that you will always be supported by the people who love you exactly as you are: Strong. Smart. Talented. Uniquely, perfectly you, with a heart as big and boundless as the sky.

I love you, sweetie, not just from your first breath to my last, but until forever.

Serena's tears continued to fall as she read and reread the letter until she'd committed it to memory. "Thank you." Each word was drenched with tears. "It's the most beautiful thing I've ever read." Or that she ever would.

Sean carefully folded it and put it back into his wallet. He kept it with him all the time. She would have, too.

They had walked out of the restaurant and were heading back to campus by the time she felt composed enough to say, "Everything your mom wrote...I know she wrote it only for you, but it feels like—"

"She wrote it for you, too. Somehow she must have known you'd show up right when I needed you most."

"Just like you showed up for me." Serena wiped away the last of her tears and knew the power of his mother's letter had seeped into her veins. All the way. "I need to make a call. A couple of calls, actually."

"Okay, but I want to go with you when you see Smith and your mom."

She should have been amazed at how perfectly he could read her mind, but their connection had been like that from the start. "I want you to go with me, of course I do, just like I wanted you there with me in class today. But I have to prove to myself that I'm strong enough to deal with it by myself."

"You've already proven that, Serena, over and over." He reached for her hand. "You're not alone anymore. You have me. And you should know that from all the texts and emails I've been sent since the birthday party, my entire family has adopted you, too."

She had to kiss him. Had to tell him in the most basic of ways just how much he meant to her.

He reached into her bag and pulled out her phone. "You'll feel better after you've called. It won't be hanging over you anymore."

Knowing he was right, she dialed Smith's number. "Smith, hi, it's Serena Britten." It sounded like he was at a big, loud party. "Is there any way we could meet before next week? I can come to Seattle any time that will work for you." She shot Sean a surprised look at Smith's response, then said, "That would be great. See you soon."

She hung up, then told Sean, "Smith is currently in San Francisco, but he's heading out for Seattle tomorrow morning, so he told me to come up to his house tonight. Now, if at all possible." For all that she was determined, just thinking about what she needed to do next had her belly fluttering. "Guess I should let my mother know about the impromptu meeting, shouldn't I?"

Sean took her face in his hands and kissed her until her brain melted out her ears. It was, she had to admit, the perfect way to make her belly flutter for entirely *different* reasons.

"Okay," he said while she was still trying to get her synapses to fire again, "now you can call her."

Even in the wake of his mind-melting kiss, it was tempting to wait until the very last second, but Serena was determined not to hide anymore. Not even from the one thing that had always scared her most...disappointing her mother.

When Genevieve picked up immediately, though Serena's belly fluttered again at the thought of facing her tomorrow at Smith's house, she didn't let it frighten her away. "Smith and I are going to be meeting at his house tonight in an hour. I was hoping you could be there, too, if you're still in town."

When her mother enthusiastically replied that she had stayed in San Francisco to shop and wouldn't dream of missing the meeting, Serena could no longer get out the rest of what she'd planned to say. She didn't want to blindside her mother during the meeting with Smith, but now that she'd learned Genevieve had spent the day *shopping* after turning Serena's entire world upside down, all she could manage was, "I'll see you there, Mom."

Sean didn't say anything after she hung up, just pulled her into his arms and held her.

Exactly the way she needed him to.

CHAPTER THIRTY-ONE

Perfectly attuned to her every emotion though she hadn't said much since they'd left the pizza place, Sean hadn't let go of her hand even once during the drive from campus to Smith's house. Now, as they stood on the front steps, he gently brushed a lock of hair away from her cheek and smiled reassuringly at her. "Ready?"

She'd expected to be nervous. Scared. Sick to her stomach. But, amazingly, she *was* ready.

It had taken her nineteen years to get to the point where she could finally stop second-guessing herself. At least for now, she thought with a small smile. Because Sean's mother was right—difficult choices wouldn't stop coming after this. After tonight, however, at least she'd know for certain that she was strong enough to brave each and every one of them.

"I'm ready." She rang the doorbell. and the door opened only a few seconds later.

"Serena, hello! It's great to see you again. Come on in, you two."

Serena always thought that pictures of Smith's wife Valentina didn't come close to doing her justice. On top of being beautiful, she was smart and nice, too.

"It's nice to see you again, too. This is my boyfriend, Sean."

"Lovely to meet you, Sean." Valentina, thankfully, didn't look the least bit put out that Serena had brought him to the meeting. "Sorry the place is a mess—we're getting ready to head back to Seattle tomorrow morning, but we couldn't leave without having a big Sullivan family get-together first."

"I hope you didn't break up the party because of me."

"Not at all. All the babies needed to go to bed anyway. Although if you ask me," Valentina said with a laugh, "it's their parents who looked like they were going to fall asleep at any moment."

Smith called down from the top of the stairs, "Serena, it's great to see you again."

He looked every inch the movie star even in jeans and T-shirt. After going to enough Hollywood parties over the years, Serena had eventually stopped being starstruck. But Smith was different somehow, and not just because he was a thousand times better looking than any other actor she'd ever met.

"Smith, this is my boyfriend, Sean Morrison."

Smith shook his hand, studying his face for a few seconds before saying, "Any chance you're related to Drew Morrison?"

Sean grinned. "Guilty as charged."

"In that case, maybe you can put in a good word for us for this soundtrack."

"Sure, I'd be happy to," Sean said, before turning to give Serena another reassuring smile. Clearly, he'd guessed that she might be a little freaked out by whatever additional complications this new twist might add to the whole situation.

Just then, the doorbell rang and Serena suddenly didn't know what to do with herself—whether to sit or stand. Or run.

"Why don't you two have a seat and relax while I go greet your mother?" Smith suggested as Valentina brought over bottles of sparkling water for them.

Serena didn't know what magic dust Smith sprinkled over her mother between the front door and the living room, but Genevieve was positively glowing by the time she glided in on her five-inch heels. At least, until she spotted Sean sitting next to Serena.

Like a gentleman, he stood when she entered the room. "Genevieve, it's nice to see you again."

Serena could read each of the not-so-happy thoughts as they crossed her mother's face before she finally settled on, "What a surprise to see you, Sean." She was bristling as she gave Serena an air kiss on either cheek, but was smiling again by the time she turned back to Smith and Valentina. "It's been far too long." Genevieve's voice was pure syrup. "Serena and I are just so glad the movie is off and running. Aren't we?"

It was too late for Serena to turn back. Too late to pretend she was someone she wasn't. And too late to play by the rules of anyone else's game but her own. It had been scary to trust her instincts with Sean and leap into the unknown, but if she hadn't, she never would have found love.

And as he slid his hand onto hers, warm and steady and there for her in a way she could still hardly wrap her head around, she knew it was time to trust her instincts again. "Actually, that's why I asked if we could all meet tonight."

Her mother was just about to sit down when she abruptly came back to her feet. "*You* called this meeting,

Serena?"

Gone was the syrup. In its place was a warning behind every word. One that Serena had always obeyed before.

"Yes, I needed to speak with Smith and Valentina," she replied in a voice that she was working really hard to keep steady. "And you, Mom. I needed to speak with you, too."

"Serena, there's no need to be so dramatic—"

"Genevieve." Smith stopped her mother before she could say anything more. "I'd like to hear what Serena has to say."

With that, he turned to smile at Serena. His smile reminded her of the one Sean gave her when he wanted her to know that it was okay to say anything she needed to say, anything at all. Amazingly, she found herself smiling back at the larger-than-life movie star.

"Smith, Valentina, you've been so kind to me every step of the way," she began. "I can't tell you what an honor it was to even be asked to audition for your movie, let alone be given a part in it. But—"

"It is so much more than an honor," Genevieve exclaimed. "Working on your movie is everything she's ever dreamed of!"

But Smith never looked away from Serena. "Is it really, Serena?"

She swallowed hard. "No." Sean ran a thumb lightly across her palm, and his touch helped keep her grounded. "I love books. I love to read them, and maybe one day I'll write them, or teach about them, or help people find information in them. I don't know exactly how I'm going to make a career out of books yet, but I'm hoping to find out. That's why I enrolled in Stanford this year, which I love. And even though I don't know if they're going to agree to let me go beyond this first probationary quarter to make me a permanent student, I can't leave in the middle of the quarter." But that wasn't the full truth. "I don't *want* to leave school, not now, or after the quarter ends. I'm so sorry—I know this will probably cause all sorts of problems for you both and it's why I was going to do the movie anyway, because I don't want to disappoint you. But I don't want to be an actress."

"Of course you do!" Genevieve exploded. "This is what you've been working for your entire life!"

Serena knew she needed to say no again, but if it had been hard to bail on Smith Sullivan's movie, it was a thousand times harder to finally make it clear to her mother that she was never, ever going back to modeling or acting. In an instant, her palms were sweating, her heart was racing, and her breath was coming way too fast.

"Serena."

Sean's voice was soft, but firm enough that she had to snap out of her growing panic at least long enough to turn to face him. When she looked into his eyes, she saw not only love, but a reminder of the love he'd come from. *"All of the answers are there inside your head, your body, your heart,"* his mother had written to him. *"And I promise you that your choices will always be supported by the people who love you exactly as you are: Strong. Smart. Talented. Uniquely, perfectly you."*

"You're right," she finally said to her mother. "Up until two months ago, this was exactly what I'd worked toward. But I was wrong to keep going when I knew it wasn't what I really wanted. I don't want to act or model. Not ever again."

Valentina and Smith both stood up. "We'll leave the three of you alone for a few minutes," Smith said. As they walked past Serena, Valentina mouthed, "You're doing great," and gave her a thumbs-up.

Serena already knew the Sullivans were nice people, but after pulling out of their movie at the last minute, *anyone* would have been mad. Instead, they were being completely supportive of her in ways she'd never expected anyone to be. At least, not until Sean and Abi had shown her what true friendship, and love, was all about.

"Look at what you've done! Do you know how hard it's going to be to get them to sign you on again once you come to your senses?"

Finally, Serena snapped. "I *have* come to my senses!" God, she didn't want it to be like this, didn't want to stand here yelling at her mother in a movie star's living room. But before she could get a grip and somehow try to fix everything that was breaking more by the second, Genevieve turned on Sean.

"This is all *your* fault!" Her mother was practically breathing fire. "She was never headstrong like this, never would have dared yell at me until you appeared."

"If Serena wanted to go back to modeling, I'd support her." Sean held her close with an arm around her waist, his voice raw with emotion he wasn't trying to hold back. "If she wanted to be an actress, I'd support her. But if you'd listen to what she's been saying to you, you'd know that she doesn't want either of those things."

"How dare you speak to me about my daughter as if you know her better than I do!"

Serena knew how hard Sean had been working to let her speak for herself when he wanted so badly to protect her. So now, even though she knew he wouldn't be able to get through to her mother, she let him say what he needed to say.

"I love your daughter exactly as she is," Sean said.

"And so should you."

It was the most beautiful thing she'd ever heard anyone say. So beautiful that it gave her the final strength she needed to finish what *she* needed to say, too.

"I know you've only ever wanted the best for me." She made herself look her mother in the eye, made herself stand strong and steady. "And I know you think that teaching me your beliefs about men and love was a way to protect me from getting hurt. But I'm not a little girl anymore." When her mother didn't leap straight down her throat, Serena hoped—prayed—that she was finally getting through. "Mom, please can't we—"

"You did this on purpose, didn't you? Brought me here to shame me in front of Smith Sullivan to try to teach me a lesson."

"I would never do that to you." She instinctively reached out for her mother, but Genevieve pulled back.

"Some day," Serena said in a choked voice, "I hope you'll forgive me. Not just for walking away from this movie and my modeling career...but for having to give up your own dreams for me. I tried so long to give them back to you any way I could. But now it's time for me to live my own dreams." Sean's arms surrounded her as though he was trying to take away her pain. "I love you, Mom. I always have and always will, and one day I hope you'll believe it's true."

Her mother was staring at her in a way that Serena had never seen before. A way that scared her. *It was over.* Her mother hated her...and Serena was going to break into a million pieces, right here in the middle of the living room. She buried her face in Sean's chest, felt his hand stroke her hair.

"I don't understand."

The ringing in her ears was so loud that Serena

thought it had to be her stupidly boundless well of hope that was making her hear things. But then she heard it again.

"I don't understand."

As if in slow motion, Serena lifted her face from Sean's chest and turned to look at her mother. "Mom?" The short word broke in her tear-clogged throat, one syllable becoming two.

Her mother was crying, too, now. And saying, "I don't understand," again and again until the words all ran together.

IdontunderstandIdontunderstandIdontunderstand.

Serena had to go to her. And when she did, she realized Sean was right beside her, helping her mother sit down. Finding a box of tissues. Being Serena's rock through absolutely everything.

"I wanted you to have everything. To be everything. To never wonder *what if* like I did."

"That's why I had to go to college." Serena felt as though her heart was finally starting to beat again. "Because if I didn't, I'd never stop wondering what I had missed."

Her mother finally looked at her. Really, truly *looked.* Mascara was running in black streaks down Genevieve's cheeks, but for the first time in Serena's memory, she didn't try to fix it.

"I don't understand," her mother said again, but it sounded a little different now. "I never wanted to go to college. I never liked books, wanted to run screaming from the library. But you...even when you were a little girl, you had to have a book with you all the time." Genevieve shook her head. "I thought that would change. That you would change. That you'd become more like me." She brushed the back of her hand over her cheeks, smearing red lipstick into her running mascara. "But why would you want that when I was never anything? Never anything that mattered to anyone."

"Yes, you were. You *are*."

"What?" Her mom had never looked so lost. Or so afraid. "What am I?"

"You're my mom. And you matter to me. So, so much."

And this time, when she reached for her, Genevieve leaned all the way into Serena's arms.

* * *

Thank God, thought Sean as they got out of his car behind his frat house a couple of hours later, Serena was smiling again. Ever since they'd left Smith's house, she'd practically been floating.

"I feel so free," she told him. "For the very first time in my life, I feel like I can do anything. Anything at all. And wasn't it amazing when Smith offered to introduce me to his sister Sophie? She's a librarian in San Francisco and also went to Stanford. How cool is that?"

Standing in the middle of the parking lot, Serena fit into his arms so perfectly and her lips tasted so sweet as she kissed him that he could hardly remember what his life had been like before he'd met her. Parts had been great, parts had been terrible, but none of it had ever been this real. This powerful. Or, he thought as she pressed the full length of her curves against him and made a little sound of pleasure into his mouth, this *hot*. It wasn't until when one of his frat brothers whistled that they finally remembered they were in public and headed for his room hand in hand.

In the wake of tonight's events, Sean was happy, too. Happier, at least, knowing that Serena definitely wasn't going to be leaving to film the movie. Unfortunately, her academic status on campus was still in question, and he'd been racking his brain all night trying to think of the best way to deal with her lecherous professor. Plus, he couldn't help but worry about Serena's mother. Because even though Genevieve had taken a giant step forward tonight, what if Serena put all her hopes into having a great new relationship with her mother...and then was disappointed if another big breakthrough never came?

In the end, though, Sean knew he couldn't protect her from everything, even if he wanted to. Besides, Serena had proved that she was more than capable of taking care of herself. Still, he silently vowed to always be there as backup.

He'd planned on picking up where their kiss had left off once they were in his room, but once they were inside and the door was closed, the box of photos was suddenly all he could see.

Serena had finally faced down her biggest fear of disappointing—and losing—her mother. But he still hadn't dealt with the reality of losing his.

"The last day with my mom, I took pictures of her. Pictures I've never developed." He'd smashed his camera on the pavement outside the hospital, but he hadn't been able to walk away without picking up the film. "There's a darkroom on campus."

Serena lifted his hand to her lips and pressed a kiss to it. "Let's go."

* * *

As soon as the two of them got to the darkroom, Sean realized his family needed to be there, too, when he developed the pictures, so he sent a group text to them. Grant arrived a few minutes later still wearing his suit.

Olivia had glasses on and her hair pulled back into a ponytail. Justin came straight from the lab. Only Drew couldn't make it because he was playing a private show in the city, but Sean knew he'd definitely come see the pictures before he headed back out on tour the following day.

Maddie was the last to get there, her eyes red as though she'd already been crying. "Dad wanted to come, I know he did, but he..."

When her tears came again, Grant put an arm around her and pressed a kiss to the top of her head. "He'll look at the pictures when he's ready."

"All of us should be able to cram inside," Sean said, not letting go of Serena's hand so that she knew he needed her there, too.

No one spoke as he worked carefully to make the prints. He'd taken pictures of each of his siblings and his father with his mother that day, and Drew had used Sean's camera to take a picture of him with her, as well.

Sean had expected developing these pictures to bring back all his grief, and for a little while, it did. But then, slowly, that sadness began to shift. And when he was finally done developing the entire roll and made himself take a close look at each of the pictures, he realized why.

Lisa Morrison had been such an amazing mother to each and every one of them that, in the end, all that was left for Sean to see wasn't how sick she was, or how frail she'd become.

All he saw, and all he felt in the darkroom surrounded by his brothers and sisters and girlfriend, was love.

CHAPTER THIRTY-TWO

"Serena, this is Barbara Canfield from the English Department. Would you be able to come by the main office today?"

Barely fifteen minutes ago, Serena had decided that she had to tell the department chair what had happened with Professor Fairworth. There was a pretty good chance that they wouldn't believe her. After all, she was famous for being photographed in skimpy lingerie and barely-there bathing suits, so if he wanted to make the case that she'd come on to him, it wouldn't seem all that farfetched. But she couldn't live with the idea that he might try it again on another student who wouldn't be able to say no.

Only, she hadn't sent an email or called them yet to set up an appointment. In fact, she'd just been typing in a text to Sean to let him know her plan when her phone had rung. Why were they calling her? Had Fairworth preemptively tried to make a claim about *her* or the threats Sean had made outside class the day before?

"Absolutely," she finally replied. "I'm at the library and can come now if that will work."

Ten minutes later, when Serena walked into the English building, the woman from the phone gave her a warm smile. "Serena, we really appreciate you coming in this quickly. If you could follow me, I'd like to introduce you to Professor Cynthia Adams."

Standing in an office doorway, an attractive middle-aged woman in a well-tailored black suit held out a hand. "Serena, it's lovely to meet you."

"It's nice to meet you, too," she replied, though she still had no idea what was going on.

"I apologize," Professor Adams said as the receptionist left the room and closed the door behind her with a soft click. "I should have asked them to let you know before you walked in that I have taken over your *History and Theory of the Novel* class."

As a model, Serena had been trained to control her expressions under every possible circumstance. But even that didn't mean she could contain her surprise today. "But what about Professor Fairworth?"

The woman's expression twisted into one of pure revulsion. "I believe he has decided to take a sabbatical."

"He has?" Serena knew she must be making a terrible first impression, but she was so shocked that she couldn't pull herself together.

"He has." Her new professor looked more than a little angry as she said, "He admitted to what he tried to get you to agree to, Serena, and for the way he inappropriately spoke to you and touched you. I'm very sorry you had to go through that."

"I was just about to come here to tell the dean of the department what happened."

"I'm glad to hear that, because they will likely need to interview you about the incident, or incidents as the case may be, to make sure they have everything well documented. But for now, I thought you might like to know that it is *extremely* unlikely that he will return to teaching at the end of his break. Here or anywhere else."

Now that she'd had a few seconds for it to sink in, relief—and pure joy—broke through. "Thank you for telling me all of this." She couldn't stop smiling and couldn't wait to tell Sean the amazing news.

"Now," Professor Adams said as she opened up a file that had Serena's name on the tab, "I know you recently gave your midterm presentation on the Brontë sisters. However, because I haven't yet had the pleasure of working with you, I'd appreciate it if you'd be willing to repeat it for me. Early next week, perhaps, so that I have some time to settle in with the class first?"

"That would be great." Serena could hardly believe her good luck. Everything that had gone so wrong had completely turned around to be even better than she could have imagined. "Thank you so much."

"I must warn you, however, that I am going to have very high expectations." She pulled out a set of papers. "I read the paper you wrote a couple of weeks ago on the same subject. My specialty is Jane Austen, but I know enough about the Brontës to be very impressed with your initial analysis of their impact on the modern novel."

Serena was so bowled over by the unexpected praise—Professor Fairworth had told her that her paper had only skimmed the surface—that she almost didn't realize why the woman's name was so familiar. "You're the leading academic in the field of Early Romantic literature. Your book last year on Jane Austen was pure genius!"

Professor Adams grinned. "I'm sure there are several people who might like to lay claim to *leading,* and who might argue with *genius,* but just between you and me, I'll take them both.*"*

A handful of minutes later, after Serena had admitted to being a total fangirl who had read everything the professor had ever written, she all but skipped out of the English Department.

* * *

"Thank you." Serena got to the stadium just as Sean was walking out of the locker room. She threw herself into his arms and kissed him, loving the way he smelled of soap and totally yummy *him.*

"You're welcome." He kissed her again, before he drew back enough to ask, "What great thing did I do now?"

She laughed. "You know what you did. And even if his career is ruined, the truth is he brought it on himself."

"Wait a minute, did something happen with your professor? I didn't think you had class with him today. You know I wanted to go with you the next time."

"It wasn't class. The English Department called me in for a meeting. The thing is, I was already going to see them. I decided they needed to know what happened."

"There's nothing you won't face down, is there? But if you're the one who got him fired, then why are you thanking me?"

Finally, she realized he'd meant it when he said he didn't know what was going on. "Fairworth is already gone. I didn't even have to say anything, because they already knew! And now I have a new professor. A really, really nice woman, who happens to have written the definitive book on Jane Austen and is a legend. And on top of all of that amazingness, she told me she was impressed with my paper on the Brontë sisters. *Very* impressed!"

"Seriously, do you have any idea how hot it is when you start talking about books?" He pulled her closer. "Tell me more about these Brontë sisters."

He always made her laugh—and burn so hot, too. She loved it, but she also needed to know, "What do you think happened?"

"I don't know for sure yet. Although—" He pulled out his phone. "—Drew sent me this text earlier. Now I'm wondering if this is what he was talking about." He showed it to her.

SMITH TOOK CARE OF IT

At her confused expression, he said, "I was talking to Drew about how Smith wants his songs on the soundtrack to his new movie, and of course my brother asked about you. I mentioned that you'd had trouble with a professor. We talked about a few possible plans to deal with the guy that I was going to run by you, but I'm guessing he said something to Smith before that. And now the guy is history."

Amazing. She didn't just have the Morrisons behind her. She had the Sullivans, too. Not to mention Abi, who had offered at least a dozen times to ambush Fairworth and kick him in the balls hard enough that he wouldn't have any reason to hit on a student ever again. That is, when Abi wasn't *raving* about how gorgeous and perfect and sexy Drew Morrison was.

Serena had been glad to hear that nothing had happened between the two of them—apart from Drew making Abi feel like the prettiest, most important girl in the world for one special night. Maybe Sean's rock-star brother was a player, but something told Serena that one day, when he found the right girl, his life would change in the best possible way.

Just like hers had.

* * *

The sun was just setting in front of the library when Serena said, "Are you ready?"

Sean was holding the classic 35mm Canon film camera he'd been lucky enough to find online, and feeling a hell of a lot shakier than he liked. "Sure."

"You don't have to do this today."

But he did. And he was going to completely lose the light if he kept stalling.

Clearly, she saw that he'd made his final decision, because she said, "Tell me what you need me to do."

"You're already doing it." And it was with Serena standing right beside him that he finally lifted his camera, framed a shot of the setting sun illuminating the library's pillars, and took his first picture in months. At first he was unsteady, and it was frustrating to feel like he was starting all over again. Soon, though, he found his groove.

He didn't know how long he'd been taking pictures when a couple of students walked up to Serena. She was no longer hiding in baggy jeans, sweatshirts, and baseball caps, and he'd noticed more than one person do a double take today. He assumed they wanted an autograph, but all the students wanted to know was how to get to the Engineering building.

The moment he heard Serena laughingly confess her utter lack of directional skills, it was pure instinct to turn his camera so that he could see her through its viewfinder. She was pointing, then laughing again when she realized she was pointing in the wrong direction. By the time she turned back to him, he'd already taken a dozen pictures of her. Each one, he already knew, would be beautiful.

Especially the one he took when she looked straight into the lens and smiled the biggest, happiest smile he'd ever seen.

* * *

A little while later, Serena and Sean had just made it up the steps to her floor when his large, warm hand curled around her waist. He turned her to face him in the deserted stairwell, then drew her against him so that she was looking up into his incredible green eyes.

When he touched her, she lost not only her breath, but most of her brain cells. Which meant the best she could manage was, "Hi."

He smiled down at her. "Hi." Once upon a time when he'd smiled at her, it hadn't reached his eyes. Now, it did.

"Have I mentioned in the past five minutes," he said in that deep voice that always made her insides all melty, "how much I love you?"

"It might have been six minutes ago," she teased.

He framed her face with his hands. "I love you."

"I love you, too," she said, and then, "Have I mentioned in the past five minutes how happy I am that you're taking pictures again?"

He answered her with a kiss, and by stroking her with deliciously demanding caresses. He ran his hands down over her back and waist and hips until he was grasping her bottom and dragging her tightly against him. *This* was the unquenchable passion, the never-ending glow, the endless desire she'd been waiting all her life to feel.

Wanting even more, she threaded her fingers into his hair and pulled his mouth down harder against hers. On a groan, he complied with her silent request and took the kiss deeper.

In the tiny space he gave her between kisses, she

whispered, "My room," deliberately bringing them back to the first night they'd met.

The next thing she knew, he had her hand in his and they were hurrying down the hall to her room. The second the door was closed and locked behind him, he said, "What about Abi?"

"She's not coming back until late tonight."

"Thank God." His hands tangled in her hair as he kissed her hungrily, his mouth roaming from hers down to the pulse point at the side of her neck. "I love it when I can feel your heart beating this fast."

He licked against her skin, then followed it up with a light scrape of his teeth that had her moaning. She wasn't thinking—*couldn't* think at all when he was slicking his tongue across hers—but it was okay. She didn't need to be in control all the time anymore. Especially not when *losing* control with Sean was so much fun.

"I love how hot your skin gets when I touch you." He rubbed his five o'clock shadow across her skin, and she arched into him, desperate to get closer. "I love hearing the sounds you make when you come apart for me." He moved his hands so that he was cupping her hips and dragging them against his, nearly taking her over the edge with nothing more than that. "And I love how bad you need me," he said as he gripped the bottom of her shirt and had it off over her head before she could take her next breath. "Just as much as I need you."

She didn't know what was hotter, his tongue licking a wet path over the upper swell of her breasts...or the way he was talking to her, telling her everything he loved about being with her. Showing her that he noticed *everything*.

"But do you know what I love most of all?" He brought his mouth back to hers. "I love it when you kiss me like this."

Kissing Sean was like having the most amazing dream, one that she never wanted to wake up from, an erotic and sweet seduction that sent wave after wave of helpless pleasure through her.

"Please."

He was so eloquent, so good at telling her everything he was feeling, but all she could do was beg...and tug at his clothes, even as he stripped the rest of hers away. Thank God they were soon completely naked. He quickly took care of protection, and then she was lying beneath him in the bed, wanting him so bad she thought she actually might burst if he didn't take her soon.

As if he could read her mind, he threaded his fingers through hers and held her as he slid into her, so slowly, so perfectly. His kiss was as sweet and sinful as the movement of his body inside hers, and she gripped his hands tightly, crossing her ankles behind his hips as she rocked with him, getting closer and closer to a peak that was higher than anything she could ever have imagined.

She'd given him all of her trust, had surrendered all of her defenses. And he'd done the same for her.

As sweet turned to wild, Serena whispered against his lips, "Kiss me again, Sean." And even after they'd tumbled into ecstasy together, they didn't stop kissing for a long, long time.

EPILOGUE

As the stage lights went dark, Drew Morrison took a few seconds to ground himself before stepping away from the mic. He'd started recording and doing shows so that he could play the music that had always been in his head...and it had quickly turned into something bigger than he ever could have expected.

Press. Parties. Groupies.

He could have anything he wanted, but every night as he stood onstage after a show, he thought about what his mom had written in her final letter to him: *"When nothing else makes the pain go away, all I have to do is put on one of your songs and it works every time. Every single time."*

Music. That was why he was here.

"Great show tonight, man."

The crowds had gotten so big—and hungry for a piece of Drew—during the past several months that the label had hired a security team to keep away the crazies. James was well over six feet and nearly three hundred pounds. He was also one hell of a nice guy.

"Thanks, James."

Drew and his backup players had been working out

the kinks on a couple of new songs and tonight everything had finally gelled. He was planning to lock himself into the portable studio he'd set up in the back of the tour bus tonight and get it all down while it was still fresh.

"They ready for me in the meet-and-greet room?"

James nodded. "I'll take you back."

It didn't matter how drained Drew felt after a show. He always took the time to meet with his fans, especially the ones who needed the music like his mother had. Sick kids and adults got priority over everyone else for the VIP post-show tickets, and they didn't have to pay for them, either.

An hour later, he'd signed dozens of autographs and taken even more selfies with his fans, big and small, young and old. He was just about to head back to his tour bus when a woman stepped out of the shadows in the corner.

She should have just blended into the background in her conservative dark pants and top, with no makeup on and her hair pulled back from her face.

And yet, she was still the most beautiful woman he'd ever seen in his life. By miles.

How the hell could he have missed seeing her backstage until now?

"Your show tonight was really great."

"Thanks." He grinned to try to put her at ease. "I'm glad you came. What's your name?"

"Ashley Emmits." Something jogged in his brain, but her hand felt so soft and warm in his and her hair and skin smelled so good that he couldn't quite nail it down before she added, "I know you've got to be exhausted after your show, but I just wanted to tell you that I really appreciate the opportunity you're giving me to go on the road with you for my research."

Belatedly putting two-and-two together, Drew asked, "You're Professor Emmits' daughter?"

She nodded. "He told me you were expecting my call about setting up all the details, but I thought it would be better to meet in person the first time we spoke."

"But—" Drew still couldn't get his brain to work right. "The picture he had of you on his desk—"

"Is really old." She wrinkled her nose. "I think he likes pretending I'm still his little girl."

In the picture she'd been wearing huge glasses, so big and thick that Drew had barely been able to make out any of her features. All he'd known was that he was going to be totally safe taking her out on the road with him since he could *never* touch his professor's daughter in a million years.

"Drew?"

Oh man, she wasn't only drop-dead gorgeous, her voice had that husky edge to it that he always loved to hear after he'd made a girl come apart beneath him over and over again.

How the hell was he going to keep his hands off her while they traveled the country together in his tour bus? Especially when he was already *this* tempted by her...

~ THE END ~

Watch for Drew Morrison's story, TEMPT ME LIKE THIS, coming early 2015!

* * *

And don't miss Bella's *New York Times* & *USA Today* bestselling series about The Sullivans! Please also enjoy the following excerpt from THE LOOK OF LOVE (The Sullivans, Book 1)

Chloe Peterson is having a bad night. A really bad night. The large bruise on her cheek can attest to that. And when her car skids off the side of a wet country road straight into a ditch, she's convinced even the gorgeous guy who rescues her in the middle of the rain storm must be too good to be true. Or is he?

As a successful photographer who frequently travels around the world, Chase Sullivan has his pick of beautiful women, and whenever he's home in San Francisco, one of his seven siblings is usually up for causing a little fun trouble. Chase thinks his life is great just as it is—until the night he finds Chloe and her totaled car on the side of the road in Napa Valley. Not only has Chase never met anyone so lovely, both inside and out, but he quickly realizes Chloe has much bigger problems than her damaged car. Soon, Chase is willing to move mountains to love—and protect—her, but will Chloe let him?

Enjoy the following excerpt from THE LOOK OF LOVE...

Chase almost missed the flickering light off on the right side of the two-lane country road. In the past thirty minutes, he hadn't passed a single car, because on a night like this, most sane Californians—who didn't know the first thing about driving safely in inclement weather—stayed home.

Knowing better than to slam on the brakes—he wouldn't be able to help whomever was stranded on the side of the road if he ended up stuck in the muddy ditch right next to them—Chase slowed down enough to see that there was definitely a vehicle stuck in the ditch.

He turned his brights on to see better in the pouring

rain and realized there was a person walking along the edge of the road about a hundred yards up ahead. Obviously hearing his car approach, she turned to face him and he could see her long wet hair whipping around her shoulders in his headlights.

Wondering why she wasn't just sitting in her car, dry and warm, calling Triple A and waiting for them to come save her, he pulled over to the edge of his lane and got out to try and help her. She was shivering as she watched him approach.

"Are you hurt?"

She covered her cheek with one hand, but shook her head. "No."

He had to move closer to hear her over the sound of the water hitting the pavement in what were rapidly becoming hailstones. Even though he'd turned his headlights off, as his eyes quickly adjusted to the darkness, he was able to get a better look at her face.

Something inside of Chase's chest clenched tight.

Despite the long, dark hair plastered to her head and chest, regardless of the fact that *looking like a drowned rat* wasn't too far off the descriptive mark, her beauty stunned him.

In an instant, his photographer's eye cataloged her features. Her mouth was a little too big, her eyes a little too wide-set on her face. She wasn't even close to model thin, but given the way her T-shirt and jeans stuck to her skin, he could see that she wore her lush curves well. In the dark he couldn't judge the exact color of her hair, but it looked like silk, perfectly smooth and straight where it lay over her breasts.

It wasn't until Chase heard her say, "My car is definitely hurt, though," that he realized he had completely lost the thread of what he'd come out here to do.

Knowing he'd been drinking her in like he was dying of thirst, he worked to recover his balance. He could already see he'd been right about her car. It didn't take a mechanic like his brother, Zach, who owned an auto shop—more like forty, but Chase had stopped counting years ago—to see that her shitty hatchback was borderline totaled. Even if the front bumper wasn't half smashed to pieces by the white farm fence she'd slid into, her bald tires weren't going to get any traction on the mud. Not tonight, anyway.

If her car had been in a less precarious situation, he probably would have sent her to hang out in her car while he took care of getting it unstuck. But one of her back tires was hanging precariously over the edge of the ditch.

He jerked his thumb over his shoulder. "Get in my car. We can wait there for a tow truck." He was vaguely aware of his words coming out like an order, but the hail was starting to sting, damn it. Both of them needed to get out of the rain before they froze.

But the woman didn't move. Instead, she gave him a look that said he was a complete and utter nut-job.

"I'm not getting into your car."

Realizing just how frightening it must be for a lone woman to end up stuck and alone in the middle of a dark road, Chase took a step back from her. He had to speak loudly enough for her to hear him over the hail.

"I'm not going to attack you. I swear I won't do anything to hurt you."

She all but flinched at the word *attack* and Chase's radar started buzzing. He'd never been a magnet for troubled women, wasn't the kind of guy who thrived on fixing wounded birds. But living with two sisters for so many years meant he could always tell when something was up.

And something was definitely up with this woman, beyond the fact that her car was half-stuck in a muddy ditch.

Wanting to make her feel safe, he held his hands up. "I swear on my father's grave, I'm not going to hurt you. It's okay to get into my car." When she didn't immediately say no again, he pressed his advantage with, "I just want to help you." And he did. More than it made sense to want to help a stranger. "Please," he said. "Let me help you."

She stared at him for a long moment, hail hammering between them, around them, onto them. Chase found himself holding his breath, waiting for her decision. It shouldn't matter to him what she decided.

But, for some strange reason, it did.

...Sample chapter from THE LOOK OF LOVE by Bella Andre © 2013.

Please visit www.bellaandre.com to sign up for Bella's newsletter and to stay up to date on all the latest books now available.

BOOKLIST

The Morrison Family series
Kiss Me Like This
Tempt Me Like This (Drew Morrison's story, coming early 2015)

The Sullivan Family series
The Look of Love
From This Moment On
Can't Help Falling In Love
I Only Have Eyes For You
If You Were Mine
Let Me Be The One
Come A Little Bit Closer
Always On My Mind
Kissing Under The Mistletoe
One Perfect Night
The Way You Look Tonight
It Must Be Your Love
Just To Be With You

Game For Love series
Game For Love

Take Me series
Take Me
Love Me

Stand-alone Novels
Candy Store
Ecstasy
Red Hot Reunion
Tempt Me, Taste Me, Touch Me

Hotshot Firefighter series
Wild Heat
Hot As Sin
Never Too Hot

Bad Boys of Football series
Game For Anything
Game For Seduction

ABOUT THE AUTHOR

Having sold more than 3 million books, *New York Times* and *USA Today* bestselling author Bella Andre's novels have been #1 bestsellers around the world. Known for "sensual, empowered stories enveloped in heady romance" (Publishers Weekly), her books have been Cosmopolitan Magazine "Red Hot Reads" twice, have been translated into ten languages. Winner of the Award of Excellence, The Washington Post has called her "One of the top digital writers in America" and she has been featured by NPR, USA Today, Forbes, The Wall Street Journal, and most recently in TIME Magazine. She has given keynote speeches at publishing conferences from Copenhagen to Berlin to San Francisco, including a standing-room-only keynote at Book Expo America on her publishing success. Harlequin MIRA is releasing her bestselling Sullivan series in print in the US, UK, Canada, Australia and New Zealand.

If not behind her computer, you can find her reading her favorite authors, hiking, swimming or laughing. Married with two children, Bella splits her time between the Northern California wine country and a 100 year old log cabin in the Adirondacks.

For a complete listing of books, as well as excerpts and contests, and to connect with Bella:

Visit Bella's website at: www.BellaAndre.com
Follow Bella on twitter at:
http://www.twitter.com/bellaandre
Join Bella on Facebook at:
http://www.facebook.com/bellaandrefans
Sign up for Bella's newsletter at: http://eepurl.com/eXj22

Made in the USA
Middletown, DE
23 January 2018